# THE RUNE STONE CURSE

## A CRYPTID MYSTERY

## DEBRA OAS

KDP

# ACKNOWLEDGEMENTS

*Much Love and thanks to all of my family, just because.*

**Special thanks to:**
*Carrie the Rune Reader*
*Jordan, for giving me this great idea*
*Joe for all your input*
*Cover art: getcovers.com*
*Wayne Luman Photography for silo photo*

# PROLOGUE

*The sound of fat raindrops striking the metal roof was soothing. It was difficult sleeping in this musty old house, especially with all the outside disruptions night after night. The sound of the rain allowed him to rest. A thunderstorm was approaching. He could hear the wind building strength, howling like a ghost around the old windows, whoooo!*

*He lumbered out of his warm bed to peek outside and saw a few scrubby trees bent and swaying, their branches whipping around wildly. His nostrils were filled with the smell of wet dirt. A storm would be a good thing.*

*What he could see of the sky was gray, quickly turning darker and more ominous as the minutes passed and clouds gathered. Branches, leaves and other debris formed little whirlwinds that twisted around the farmhouse.*

*Finally the lightning appeared, flashing quickly, one streak after another. The lightning was close enough to illuminate the empty, bare fields. It was a strobing light show that normally would be unwelcome, but not tonight.*

*He sat down heavily and breathed a sigh of relief. Thank goodness for the lightning - it was the only break he would get this night. It was afraid of lightning, at least that's what he'd been told.*

*It was technically his own fault that it was stalking him. How was he to know that reading those runes aloud would cause trouble? You would think it would be grateful, but it was pure evil.*

*He peered out the window again. The lightning continued its show, streaking across the sky over and over again. In the bright flashes he saw something run away quickly, a shadow moving around outside. He recognized it immediately and was again glad of the lightning. He would have reached for a gun or some sort of weapon, to use against it, but knew a gun, or any other weapon for that matter, would be pointless against the thing that ran from the lightning.*

# CHAPTER 1: PETE

A mere two months ago, Pete Magnusson had considered himself one lucky bastard. His uncle Fritz on his mother's side, had passed away at the ripe old age of 86. Pete never cared much for his uncle, he was a crabby old curmudgeon that was mean to everyone most of the time. Fortunately for Pete, he was the closest living relative (that still spoke to Uncle Fritz) so he inherited his farm when the old fossil passed.

The farm was old, probably older than Fritz. It was located in the Northwestern area of Minnesota, about an hour or so south of Lake Superior. Pete had visited his uncle a few times over the years, purely out of family obligation. Uncle Fritz was his mother's brother after all, and nobody else bothered to visit him. No surprise there, Uncle Fritz was not liked by many people (or any people that Pete knew of).

When Pete was a youngster, his father used to enjoy telling stories about Uncle Fritz, which was always entertaining. Whenever Pete and his brother Viktor would misbehave at the dinner table, he would regale them with Uncle Fritz tales. "He's crazy you know," Pete's dad would whisper to them. "That Fritz Kolbeck is a crazy Norwegian that likes to sing at the dinner table. Don't you boys be acting like your Uncle Fritz." Pete's mother would smile and shake her head at the stories, making Pete and his brother wonder if Uncle Fritz actually did sing at the dinner table.

"Fritz isn't so bad," Pete's mother would say. "He can be a very nice person when he wants to be. He's always been good to me."

"Yeah, but the key word there is 'nice when he wants to be," said Pete's dad. When you visited Fritz, you never knew which one would show up. The nice one or the crabby one. More often than not, it would be the crabby one.

Again, Pete's mother shook her head and smiled. She couldn't argue with that logic, because it was true. Sometimes Uncle Fritz could be very personable. You just weren't sure when that was going to be, and it wasn't often.

Pete remembered back when his uncle's farm was still a working farm. His uncle grew corn and he always wanted Pete and Viktor to help "tassle" the corn when they visited. Pete remembered the cuts on his hands and the sweaty, hot work in the humid, Minnesota summer sun. When that chore was done, there were always the rocks. Pete and Viktor spent endless hours picking rocks up out of the field, loading them into a wheelbarrow and hauling them to the rock pile. That rock pile grew every year, representing hours and hours of back-breaking work.

Pete's memories of the farm were not good ones, but he did it for his mother, who tried her best to maintain a civil relationship with her brother. After a particularly hot, humid summer, Viktor announced he was going to college and wouldn't come back to Uncle Fritz's farm (ever). He actually kept that vow and never returned to the farm. Viktor claimed that Uncle Fritz was losing his mind.

"Hey Pete, have you noticed Uncle Fritz has started talking to himself? Just like dad used to tell us, the guy is crazy. Yesterday he started singing "Bad Moon Rising," (you know, the Creedence Clearwater Revival song,) at the table. I left the kitchen and when I went back in he was whispering to himself, "He's coming after me when the bad moon rises.""

"Yep, dad was right, old Fritz Kolbeck is a crazy Norwegian," Viktor continued. "I am out of here, and you should be too Pete." As far as Pete knew, that was the last time Viktor set foot on the farm.

Pete shook off the memories and looked around at his inheritance. The farmhouse and barn had appeared old and rickety when Pete was a kid, many, many hot summers ago. Uncle Fritz hadn't changed a thing. There were still evil looking farm implements stored in the barn. Scythes, shovels, sickles, pitchforks (for what purpose? he wondered,) and numerous other rusty, sharp tools that invited tetanus. The huge rock pile was still there too.

"I wonder how long it will take me to sell this place," thought Pete. He was a little leery of any person who would actually want to buy this old wreck of a farm. The acreage was certainly worth something, and with lots of fixing up, the farmhouse could be liveable. The barn and silo, well sir, Pete was no farmer, but they looked as if they'd seen better days, and probably would be better off torn down.

When he first arrived, after he was informed of his inheritance, Pete planned to spend most of his time searching the yard behind the farmhouse for buried coffee cans. Uncle Fritz didn't trust banks, so he would bury old coffee cans filled with cash in his backyard, rather than using a bank account. Once Pete had unearthed all the cans, he would put the old place up for sale and take whatever he could get for it. He didn't particularly like staying here, but cans full of cash... worth it.

The way Pete found out about the buried cans was purely by accident. He was roped into yet another season of what his uncle called tasseling the corn and picking up rocks. Pete actually corrected him one day and said it was actually detasseling (removing the tassel at the very top of the corn plant). Uncle Fritz called him "know it all", told him to get back to work, and stomped back to the farmhouse. Pete started to follow Uncle Fritz, intending to tell him off and leave the farm for good, when he saw the old guy carry a shovel from the barn to his backyard.

Since he was in no rush to get back to the corn, Pete hurried up to his room, a space his uncle converted in the attic for sleeping. The attic window overlooked the section of the backyard located alongside the old silo. An unobstructed view. Pete grabbed his binoculars to see what his uncle was up to.

Uncle Fritz left the shovel in the yard and went into the house. A few minutes later he came out carrying an old tin coffee can. Pete watched as his uncle removed the top of the can, and took a wad of cash out of his pants pocket. He put the cash in a plastic bag and dropped it into the can, then paused to glance at what appeared to be a compass. He then paced off several steps, stopped, looked around and proceeded to dig a hole in the yard and bury the can.

Pete couldn't believe what he was seeing. The old geezer was actually burying cans of money in his yard. Occasionally his uncle would holler about banks and how they were all crooked, but to actually bury money instead of banking it? What a stubborn old idiot. He later told his mother about what he had witnessed and she wasn't a bit surprised.

"He's too cheap to hire help for the farm, and buries cash in his yard," said Pete. "Why am I even coming here to help out?" he asked his mother.

"Because he's family," was her answer. She tried her best to keep some sort of connection with her brother Fritz when she was alive. That was the last summer Pete worked at the farm. The next year he got a summer job helping out on a fishing boat, which was much more to his taste and abilities. He heard that Uncle Fritz finally had to hire a farm hand to help with the chores.

Years later, after his mother passed, Pete continued to visit his uncle now and then, purely for her sake. His uncle remained an unpleasant person most of the time, and that didn't improve with age. He kept ties with his uncle because that's what his mother would have wanted. Pete didn't like farming or even anything to do with gardening. He bought his food from the grocery store, roadside stand or a farmer's market. His passion was always fishing, which his uncle didn't appreciate.

"Why do you spend all your time floating around a lake?" Uncle Fritz asked.

"Because I love it," Pete would answer. "Besides that, I do have a good supply of fish in my freezer, some of which I brought to you."

"No argument there, Petey," said Uncle Fritz. "Those are some good tasting fish. You know, Petey, you're the only one that visits me now. I guess you'll be the one to get my treasure."

"Treasure?" thought Pete. His uncle's farm was no treasure, but he had to admit it was a nice gesture on Fritz's part to leave him the farm.

"Petey," his uncle whispered, leaning in close. "Remember this: trust no one."

That was the last time Pete saw his uncle before he passed away. The cause of death was determined to be "old age." There was no funeral, per his uncle's wishes. His ashes were sprinkled on the farm by someone, Pete wasn't sure who actually did that. Shortly afterward, Pete received notice that he was his uncle's sole heir. The old farm now belonged to Pete. Little did he know that there was something else waiting for him at the farm.

## CHAPTER 2: SETTLING IN

When he arrived in Minnesota, Pete was already feeling homesick. He missed his beloved Lake Superior. His first stop was at an attorney's office in Fergus Falls, about ten miles from where his uncle's farm was located. He had no problem locating the office, an ostentatious building downtown with a large sign indicating, "Korhonen and Associates, Attorneys at Law."

Pete had a brief visit at the office of his uncle's attorney. A tall, slim, pointy-nosed fellow with a full head of thick, white hair by the name of Isaac Korhonen, presented himself as the managing partner. Korhonen introduced his law partner, Ollie Nilsen, as the attorney in charge of Fritz Kolbeck's affairs. Nilsen was a smaller dark haired fellow with a wiry build and ice blue eyes. Pete shook hands with them both and proceeded to sign the necessary mounds of paperwork after the explanation of his uncle's will.

Pete glanced briefly at the document, which was fairly straightforward. Everything Uncle Fritz owned would go to Pete, he was the sole heir.

"We're so sorry about your uncle. He will be greatly missed," said Korhonen.

"Yeah, by who?" asked Pete with a chuckle. "Uncle Fritz was an asshat to most everyone he met."

"Ahem, are you planning to keep the farm?" Nilsen asked him, clearly at a loss for words at the brutal honesty as he handed Pete house keys, and copies of the final paperwork.

"Nope, just gonna visit for a while, then put it up for sale," Pete answered.

"Are you staying out there?" the attorney questioned. Pardon my saying so, but the place is somewhat rundown."

"Nope, I'm not staying there just yet. I got a hotel room here in town. You ain't wrong about the farm being rundown. I'm having the house cleaned up first. I contacted the local real estate agency and an agent there told me she would arrange it. My uncle wasn't a good housekeeper and I like things clean."

"Probably Talia," Nilsen mumbled.

"I can recommend someone to help with any outdoor work you may need done," Korhonen quickly offered.

"Nope, I'll take care of that myself. Thanks anyway," said Pete and he bid them goodbye, tossing the house keys around in his hand. He drove out to the farm and the house was about as he expected it to be. It smelled of bacon grease, mildew and old man. After taking a quick look around for anything important, he left and locked up.

Pete drove back into town and dropped the keys off with the realty office he had contacted. A fiftyish, smartly dressed real estate agent with perfectly styled honey blonde hair, by the name of Talia Hovlund greeted him. She introduced herself and said she was the one that had arranged for a cleaning company to take care of tidying up the farmhouse.

"Thank you for taking care of that, Ms. Hovlund," said Pete.

"You are quite welcome Mr. Magnusson, and please call me Talia."

Talia took in Pete's appearance and was fairly certain she was going to get him to sell off that farm in no time. The grease-stained jacket and matching cap (worn a bit askew) smelled a bit like fish. She knew, from a bit of research, that he was a fisherman and wouldn't be interested in that old farm. She started asking him about listing the farm for sale, and Pete put her off.

"I want to look around a bit first, then I'll get in touch," he told her, rubbing a hand over his whiskers. She smiled and gently placed her business card in his meaty hand and said "call me." He assured her that he would contact her soon about listing the farm and quickly exited. He was not ready to schedule showings and whatnot, he had just barely arrived.

Pete knew he would never keep the farm. He was not one for farming or farm country, he enjoyed living near the water. He hailed from a small town in the Upper Peninsula on the southern shore of Lake Superior, and as an adult moved to an even smaller community. His small, efficient, comfortable house with a million dollar view of the big lake, was located in the village of Trygghaven Bay (taken from the Norwegian 'Trygg Havn', which translated means Safe Harbor). The village had a few year-round residents, and in the past few years, had grown to a bigger number. The advent of the internet made it possible for people who preferred to live in a somewhat isolated area the ability to work remotely.

Fortunately for Pete, he was able to live and work where he wanted to. He loved to fish more than anything, so he designed fishing lures and was quite good at it. His specialty deep sea fishing lures were sold at various sporting goods stores, boat and sport shows and recently via the internet. He had a specially designed spoon that the Lake Superior fishermen agreed worked very well. Garvin's Merchandise carried the lures, and they sold like hotcakes.

When he was younger, Pete had been trained as a machinist. He worked a few years at it and then designed a downrigger, which he sold the patent for, along with his lures and made a very good living. He was able to semi-retire and fish to his heart's content. His boat was like a second home to him.

Trygghaven Bay was a close-knit community, and Pete knew everyone that lived there, year-round residents, summer folks and visiting tourists. He was a gruff, but personable man with a sharp wit and wicked sense of humor. As he got older, a bad hip gave him a "rolling gait", or as his buddy Bill termed, a "tippy walk." Pete was a large man with stubbly whiskers and a few extra pounds around the middle. Probably due to his taste for cinnamon rolls made by Ginny Garvin at her lunch counter. Pete spent many hours at Garvin's General Merchandise, parked on a stool at the counter shooting the breeze with other locals while polishing off those incredible rolls with his coffee.

It had been many years since Pete had traveled anywhere, so when he awoke in a strange bed, it took him a moment to realize he was not at home, but in Minnesota. None of Ginny's sweet rolls for him today.

The morning started warm and humid, just as he would have expected in Minnesota. No cool Lake Superior breeze here. Pete had risen early and was restless in the hotel room, so after a shower he went out for a big breakfast. There was a nice little restaurant nearby, and he ordered eggs, bacon, pancakes and sourdough toast, as well as coffee and orange juice.

"Are you vacationing here, darlin'?" asked his server as she set down his coffee and juice. She was a middle aged, chunky woman with puffy dark hair, black eyeliner and a friendly smile. Her name tag read Patti.

"Nope, not really Patti. I'm here to settle my uncle's estate."

"If you don't mind my asking, who is your uncle?"

"Naw, I don't mind. Fritz Kolbeck was my uncle."

"Oh yeah, I know him. He was an old Norwegian fellah that came in about once a week for lunch. He always ordered soup and pie. I'm sorry for your loss."

"Thanks, but we weren't exactly close."

"Ah...okay then, I'll be back with your order, shortly hon," she added and walked away.

After polishing off his lumberjack breakfast, Pete checked out of his hotel and wandered a bit around town. Fergus Falls was a nice, small community, but what to do all day? He found a library and settled in to look over the real estate market on one of their computers. He was surprised at the decent prices on farmland, and hoped his realtor would have good news for him.

Lost in thought on the internet, Pete was startled when his phone buzzed. It was the realtor, Talia Hovlund, telling him the cleaning job had been completed and the house keys had been left where he requested. He thanked her and asked if she would stop by sometime in the next few days to discuss the sale of the farm.

"I can come out tomorrow," she said anxiously.

"No, thank you, that's a bit soon. Give me a couple of days to settle in. I'll call you."

Pete drove to a nearby grocery store and picked up a few essentials, then to a discount store for a few other items. He would decide how long his stay would be once he arrived at the house and started his search.

When he arrived, he noticed that the farmhouse still looked dilapidated, but it was nice and clean. The company had done a very good job. Even the musty old furniture had been sprayed to give it a fresh smell. For a fisherman that often carried a fishy/gasoline scent with him, Pete was a meticulously clean person.

He was very glad that he had arranged for cleaners to come as he unpacked his groceries. There was nothing worse than a stinky, old refrigerator. Now it was a sparkling clean old refrigerator. They had done wonders with it.

While he was in town, he had purchased two sets of sheets, pillows, blankets and towels. He told the cleaners to toss out all the linens and bedding his uncle had left behind and spray disinfectant on everything. There was nothing he could do about the old mattress, but it had been sprayed, at least.

The library happened to have been a good place to spend the day. Pete got a library card and checked out a few books. There was no internet or cable at the farmhouse, just an old antenna leaning lopsided on the roof. Luckily there was phone service in the area, so his cell phone worked.

The books Pete checked out were on his favorite subject, stories about Vikings. (Actual Vikings, not the football team.) Pete's father's ancestry was mostly Swedish with some Finnish and Norwegian tossed in. His mother had been one-hundred percent Norwegian. Kolbeck (her surname) meant cold stream or someone who lived by the cold stream. Pete always figured that was one of the reasons he loved Lake Superior - it was certainly cold.

Pete spoke some Norwegian and was also quite familiar with old Norse. He felt it was his heritage and he took the time to learn all that he could. He had been fascinated with Viking lore and Norse legends for most of his life.

When he and his brother Viktor were kids, they would take out their father's old rowboat and pretend they were Vikings sailing across the seas. They made themselves cardboard swords with blades covered in tin foil. One year for Christmas, their dad got them Viking style helmets. It was all he could do to keep the two boys out of the old rowboat until the Spring thaw.

## CHAPTER 3: CASH CANS

What a smart move on his part, deciding to visit the library. Pete now had reading material, giving him something to pass the time in the evening. Normally, on a summer evening, he would either sit outside on his back porch looking at the lake, or visit next door with other fishermen. His house was a hop, skip and jump from the Garvin's store, which boasted a nice boat ramp and public area with picnic tables and benches. Many nights local fishermen would gather on a bench or sit at a picnic table to discuss the day's catch (or lack of one), if the bugs weren't too bad.

If it was a mosquito, flies or no-see-um (gnat) night, the group would gather on Pete's back porch, which was screened in to keep out the pests. Pete always kept a few beers handy for himself and guests. It was a pleasurable way to pass an evening, at least in Pete's opinion. The thoughts made him homesick.

"Oh well, I can catch up on some reading," Pete thought to himself, looking around the old farmhouse where his uncle had spent his life. He actually felt sorry for old Fritz for being stuck here, but then realized one person's confinement is happiness to another. Uncle Fritz probably didn't want to leave the farm any more than Pete would leave his beloved bay. "To each his own," he said to himself.

The library books kept him occupied for the evening, and that night he dreamt of sailing in a Viking ship. In his dream, he was young again, and his brother Viktor sailed with him, along with his daughter Cari. She was a little girl in the dream, and their mother was making them all fish sandwiches.

Pete awoke early the next morning, smiling at his silly dream. He fixed coffee and toast which he ate quickly, as he was anxious to search the house. He figured Uncle Fritz must have left some money lying around, or something else of value.

Sipping his coffee, he rummaged through an old desk in the living room. He found rubber bands, paper clips, pencils, keys, loose change, old papers and canceled checks from many years previous. In a kitchen drawer he found more pencils, numerous twist ties and a few wads of cash, mostly smaller bills. A dresser in the bedroom held some cash as well, nothing but a few fives and tens. He laughed at one item he found in the dresser, a well-used deck of cards with a topless woman pictured on them. Uncle Fritz!

So far an entire day of searching the house had yielded nothing more interesting than a racy deck of cards and about fifty bucks. He took some time to pack up his Uncle's clothes in a box for donation, and another, bigger box for rags. Fritz hadn't spent too much money on clothes, apparently. The assorted bric-a-brac and kitchen items all went into donation boxes as well. Maybe someone looking for antiques would be interested in this stuff. It looked like junk to Pete.

Next on Pete's agenda was the old barn, which he tackled the following day. He wasn't too hopeful, but it was possible Uncle Fritz stashed some cash out there. It was worth a look, anyway.

He overlooked the nasty looking, rust covered farm implements that hadn't been disturbed since Pete's childhood. He kicked around some grubby, loose hay, and many year's worth of dirt and dust. There was nothing much else out here that he could see. Surprisingly, it still smelled like a barn. There hadn't been an animal in here for a good many years, or anything else for that matter. It seemed like Uncle Fritz himself didn't bother to come out to the barn either. Well, it had to be checked out.

Following the barn search was a look around the silo, which for some strange reason was set off by itself away from the crummy barn. It was in a state of disrepair envying the barn. It was packed with stuff. Spider nests and years of dirt and dust covered every inch of the inside. He quickly shut the old door. Outside he noticed some mounds of dirt nearby, which were covered in grass and weeds. The mounds were too large to be hiding places for coffee cans full of cash. He made a mental note to check those out later.

On every search, he had hoped to find some sort of treasure map leading to his uncle's cash stash. No such luck.

Finally, on day three, he decided to tackle the yard. This would be physically taxing, for sure, it was a big yard. If he was right, and his uncle buried cans full of cash out here, like he saw him do that day, it could yield some nice income. The yard backed up to his uncle's farm fields, with a cheap wire fence at the end. Hopefully, Uncle Fritz didn't venture into the farm field. Pete had not planned to dig that much. It brought back memories of the dreaded rock pile. "Well, here goes," he thought, and pushed his shovel into the ground.

After two days of digging, which by the way is very hard work, Pete found three rusty old coffee cans, each holding cash. The first had $240. The second had $390 and the third, $450. Over $1,000, not a bad haul so far. The bills were wrapped in plastic bags and smelled a bit like dirt. "No matter," thought Pete. "Smelly money spends the same."

The cash in two of the cans were older bills from more than twenty years ago, the third contained the newer versions. The cans weren't buried too deep, but Pete was exhausted and his hip was telling him to take a break.

"I gotta take some time off," he thought, wiping his brow. "I'm not getting any younger." It was solitary work, but it was his secret. He would have to dig up that whole damn weedy yard, no matter how long it took.

# Chapter 4: The Stone

Pete had taken an entire morning off to rest, and was feeling better. His hip didn't hurt and since he was smart enough to wear gloves while digging, his hands weren't blistered or sore. He was sitting in a decrepit old chair, thinking about the money that could still be out there in the yard. It was making him restless, and the weather had cooled off considerably. He decided it was a good time to return to his digging, he could get more done if it wasn't hot and humid.

The first can he found following two hours of digging was full of five dollar bills amounting to $175. He was searching in random spots, trying to remember how many paces he had seen his uncle walk all those years ago. He dug closer to the side of the yard nearer the silo trying to figure out a pattern, and wishing there was a map for this. "Uncle Fritz had a method for how he buried the cans, using his compass and pacing off steps. Certainly he had planned to unearth them at some point and noted the locations," he thought. "Was it plotted?" he wondered.

Pete had spent a good portion of the day digging and part of it exploring the house again for a "treasure" map. No luck. The sun was getting low, it would be getting dark soon. Pete was just about to give up when his shovel hit something hard, making his hands sting.

"Oh crap, I hit a rock," was his first thought. Another addition to the rock pile. He reached down to pull out the large flat slab of rock, hoping Uncle Fritz had maybe hidden a cash can beneath it. The rock was larger than he thought, so he decided to leave it alone. Just as he was about to cover the rock with dirt, he noticed it had something carved on it. Ooh, maybe it was Uncle Fritz's map to the cash cans. He brushed the dirt off as best he could and shone a flashlight on it. Pete couldn't believe his eyes...Viking runes!

Due to his interest in Viking lore, Pete was able to recognize that these were actual Viking runes. Had he found a rune stone? It was incredible to think about.

As he tugged and pulled at the slab of rock, Pete recalled the story of the Kensington Rune stone, which had been discovered in central Minnesota in 1898. The gravestone-sized slab of rock had Scandinavian runes (runic writing) etched into it. Pete had the words from the Kensington stone committed to memory.

The old Norse words on the stone read (roughly) "We are 8 Goths (Swedes) and 22 Norwegians on an exploration journey from Vinland (North America) through the West. We had camp by a lake with 2 skerries (small rocky islands) one day's journey north from this stone. We were out and fished one day. After we came home we found 10 of our men red with blood and dead. VIrgin Mary save us from evil. We have 10 of our party by the sea to look after our ships, 14 days' journey from this island. Year 1362."

Kensington, where the stone had been discovered, was about thirty miles or so from where Pete stood. "Could this be another?" he wondered aloud. There had been speculation whether the Kensington stone was genuine, or a hoax. Pete always believed the stone was the genuine article. Now he apparently had located another rune stone. Hoo boy! This could be something valuable.

Pete rooted out the old rock hauling wheelbarrow from the barn. He carefully dug out the whole stone, which was quite heavy, but it was not as large as the Kensington stone. He wheeled the stone as close to the house as possible, then dragged it into the kitchen to clean it off. He had to stop a few times to rest, he was exhausted from the effort. "I'm gettin' too old for this shit," he said to himself, wiping the sweat from his brow.

As he studied it closer, running his hands over the stone, he marveled at the runes etched into it. "This is incredible," he said to himself. "I have found an actual rune stone."

Recalling his knowledge of runes, he read the runic words, which did not make too much sense. It was like nothing he had read or heard of before. The message seemed to be something resembling a curse of sorts. Perhaps he was reading it wrong, so he read it again and again, aloud. Hmmm...

Leaning back in an old kitchen chair, Pete rubbed his chin and looked over the stone again. What could this mean? Just then he heard a rumbling noise coming from near the barn and silo. Glancing out the window he saw something moving around in the dark near the old silo.

"What the hell?" Pete mumbled. Was that some kind of an animal? It was hard to tell in the shadows. He stepped outside and looked around. Nothing. Suddenly something flew close to him. It looked like an eagle. An eagle? Here? No way, he had never heard of eagles living around here. It must have been a barn owl. It flew near him again. If that was an eagle, it exhibited odd behavior. Eagles didn't normally do that.

Pete toddled over to the barn and peeked around the corner towards the silo. In the darkness it appeared as if one of the mounds surrounding it had been disturbed. "I must be seeing things," he told himself. He headed back to the house watching for the eagle/owl that had swooped near his head. When he got into the kitchen, he covered the stone with an old quilt he found in a closet and went right to bed. The stone and everything else could wait until tomorrow, he was too tired to do anything else.

That was the first night, and only the beginning of the nightmare. Pete thought several times about leaving the farm, but he knew there was more money to be found in the yard. Besides, he wanted to find out more about the rune stone he had unearthed. The other 'things'...that kept happening had to be connected, he needed to find answers, but how?

Pete suddenly remembered that his niece Cari, in addition to telling fortunes and doing tarot readings also conducted rune readings. She was very well versed in rune writings and their significance. He decided to call her first to see what she thought was happening here, and what exactly was etched into the stone.

When he reached Cari, he explained to her about finding the stone slab buried in Uncle Fritz's backyard, and told her what he had read on the stone. He also told her about some of the bizarre things that had occurred on the farm lately.

"When I read the runes, I think I'm getting some of it wrong," he told Cari. "It doesn't make much sense to me. It sounds like some kind of curse, but that can't be right," he said. "It's odd, you know."

"How many times did you read it, Uncle Pete?" she asked him.

"Ah...I don't know, a few, I guess," he answered.

"Now this is important, did you read it aloud?" Cari asked.

"Well, I suppose so. I am here by myself, but I'm pretty sure I read it out loud."

"Okay, now when did all the strange things start up?' she questioned.

"Um...let me think...hmmm...I know, it was shortly after I read the stone words. Weird things have been happening ever since. It started with the rumbling noise and that eagle."

"Did you say eagle?"

"Yeah, there was an eagle, very odd for this area. I heard a noise outside, looked out and thought I saw something moving around the old silo. Then when I stepped out, this eagle flew by me, twice. I noticed the next day one of the mounds near the silo had been disturbed."

"I really hope I'm wrong Uncle Pete, but it could be trouble, and I mean serious trouble," she told him quietly, explaining briefly what she thought had happened.

"What should I do now? Pete asked. "Leave? If I go, will it follow me, or will it continue causing trouble here?"

"I'm not sure, but you should stay put for now Uncle Pete. I'm going to make arrangements and come there as soon as I can get away. I need someone to come with me, let me think for a moment."

The phone line was quiet for a minute or so, then Cari spoke up. "I'll be there soon, there's no time to lose. It will get more powerful."

Pete cringed a little at the last words she spoke. "I knew this stinkin' farm was nothing but trouble, and now I've gone and done it. Let me know when you're arriving," he said. "There's a little airport that isn't too far away."

"No need, I'll drive. I would like someone with me, preferably someone with a reliable vehicle. I think it should be Wolfgang. I'm calling him right now."

"Aha Varg! Excellent idea," Pete agreed.

# Chapter 5: Cari

Cari Magnusson, otherwise known as Madame Carishimo (the name she used when doing tarot readings and fortunes in her shop and for on-line clients) was very worried about her Uncle Pete. He was too stubborn to leave the farm just yet, and the "thing" she suspected was causing all the trouble would not just go away. She wasn't sure how they would get rid of it, but maybe her uncle was right. He woke it up - he couldn't just leave it there.

Cari was the only daughter of Pete's brother Viktor. It was hard to believe the two were brothers, they were so different. Her father was more at home in the city, whereas her uncle preferred the big lake and backwoods.

Pete was a fisherman at heart and loved his home in the Upper Peninsula of Michigan. It was a bit wild, remote and somewhat unspoiled, at least where Uncle Pete lived. Cari liked to visit him, especially in the summer. He would always take her fishing, a time they always enjoyed together. Uncle Pete would regale her with stories of Vikings and was proud of their Scandinavian ancestry. He was the first to teach her to read runic writing. He also introduced her to an interesting local lady named Freya Saari, who got her interested in tarot reading.

Cari hadn't seen her uncle in quite a while and regretted not making a better effort. She was surprised to hear from him out of the blue. She and her father had known that Pete had inherited her great-uncle Fritz's farm. It was no surprise. He was the last holdout that still was in contact with old Fritz. They naturally assumed he would sell the farm, Pete was no farmer, and rarely left Michigan.

The shop Cari owned was in Lake Geneva, Wisconsin. She did tarot readings, told fortunes and sold various types of related items. Her on-line tarot readings were very popular and well-known all over the country. She was very successful, which meant she was busy most of the time. "That's no excuse for letting so much time go by without seeing my family," she told herself.

She and her uncle had a mutual acquaintance, Wolfgang Kilmer. His family had a summer home in Trygghaven Bay where her uncle lived, so uncle Pete knew him from the time he was a young man. He had once referred to him as "that good looking boy with all the hair."

By chance, Wolfgang had stopped into her shop, and she had done a reading for him and confounded him when she referred to him as "Varg", a nickname her Uncle Pete had given him. (It meant Wolf in old Norse). Later on, she confessed to being Pete Magnusson's niece, and thus made the connection.

Wolfgang was a cryptozoologist, studying and seeking legendary creatures. He referred to it as his hobby, but recently his "hobby" had gotten him involved in some rather dangerous situations. Most recently in the mountains of Colorado, seeking a Skinwalker, and it had nearly gotten him killed.

Cari and Wolfgang were getting to know each other socially, but taking it slow. He lived on the outskirts of Chicago, and was starting to spend more and more time in Lake Geneva. At first, it was under the pretense of visiting his buddy Ron who resided there, but more often than not, it was to see Cari.

His was the first name to come to mind after her uncle called with his strange story. Cari would take the time to go to the Minnesota farm, but hoped that Wolf would go with her. If she was right, the "thing" that was causing all the trouble would be of great interest to Wolf.

Right after her second conversation with Uncle Pete, Cari called Wolfgang. The call went straight to voicemail, the message saying he was out at sea for his job as a marine biologist and would be out of touch for a few days.

"Damn it, what to do now?" she wondered. She definitely would go to see her uncle right away, but wanted to explain things to Wolfgang, hoping he could join them later.  She could leave him a message, but it was quite a bit to explain, and would sound a tad weird.  "I know what to do, I'll call Ned."

Ned Ferris was Wolfgang's best friend, and had been since they were young, along with Wolf's sister Kyra. Ned and Kyra were something of an item now. The three of them spent summers together in the Upper Peninsula, in Trygghaven Bay, where Ned also had a summer home. Ned, Kyra and Wolfgang discovered what had happened to Ned's father Jake, a retired police detective who was murdered, and in doing so they uncovered a toxic waste dumping scheme.

Since Wolfgang and Cari had been seeing each other socially, she got to know his friend Ned and Wolf's sister Kyra. They all were acquainted with her Uncle Pete, who by all accounts was a local "character", but a likable one. Small world.

Wolf's sister Kyra was a photo-journalist, and was currently on assignment in Vermont, but as far as she knew, Ned was at his home in Chicago and was her best bet to get a complicated message to Wolfgang. Cari felt sure that Ned would be able to get in touch with Wolfgang as soon as he returned. If not, Cari and her uncle would be on their own with the creature.

# Chapter 6: Ned

The phone buzzed and Ned glanced at it a moment questioningly. Cari? Oh yeah, that sultry blonde woman that Wolfgang was interested in. She really was something else. She reminded Ned of Jayne Mansfield or Marilyn Monroe. Unforgettable.

Ned was lost in thought for a second, and then suddenly realized he should answer his phone.

"Hello, Cari, how are you?"

"Fine, thank you Ned. I suppose you're wondering why I'm calling you."

"Um...yeah."

"I am actually trying to reach Wolfgang, but he's out at sea for his job. I want to leave him a message, but it's a bit too complicated to explain in a text or email. Can you help me out and give him my message when he returns?"

"Sure, fire away."

"You know my Uncle Pete, of course."

"I certainly do. I run into him every time I visit Trygghaven Bay."

"So, here's the thing. My Uncle Pete inherited my great-uncle Fritz's farm in Northern Minnesota."

"Yes, I heard all about that from Pete when I saw him last."

"Well it's a long story, but he is in trouble and needs help. Not only from me, but I think Wolfgang too."

"Trouble? What kind of trouble? Shouldn't you call the authorities?"

"This is not the kind of trouble the police can help with. Let me explain."

"Alright go ahead, I'm listening."

"My great-uncle Fritz was a  suspicious old cheapskate and used to bury cash in coffee cans in his backyard for safe keeping. He didn't trust banks, or anyone for that matter, so he hid the cash. Uncle Pete saw him bury money once, so he knew all about it."

"I don't think that's illegal," Ned commented.

"Oh that's not the problem. While he was searching for cash cans (which, by the way, are actually out there). Uncle Pete found a stone slab with rune lettering on it. Have you heard of the Kensington Rune Stone?" Cari asked.

"Yes, as a matter of fact, I have, but I don't recall much about it."

"Good, then you'll understand. The Kensington stone was found roughly thirty miles or so from where great-uncle Fritz's farm is located. There's a good chance that Vikings or other Scandinavian explorers passed through that area. It's entirely possible that a rune stone was buried in what is now the farm's backyard, way back in the 1300's or thereabouts."

"So you think this is another?" asked Ned.

"Oh yes I'm sure of it. Uncle Pete found a rune stone, a big one, but not as big as the Kensington stone. He dug it out, dragged it in the house and cleaned it off."

Cari paused momentarily to let Ned absorb what she was explaining, and to give him the opportunity to ask a question.

"Go on," said Ned.

"Uncle Pete knows how to read Viking runes and is well-versed in Old Norse. Or at least he's somewhat capable. So after he cleaned off the stone, he read the message etched into the stone."

"He read it?" Ned questioned.

"Yes, you see the runic alphabet, or what is known as the "Elder Futhark" has 24 letters. It was the literal alphabet during the Viking age. Runes are believed to hold power and symbolize inherent qualities and be associated with magic."

"Pete knew how to read these, eh?"

"Yes, like I said, he is mostly capable. He was by himself, when he read it, and was having trouble comprehending the message, so he read it out loud, several times, in fact. It was confusing to him, because, like he told me, it wasn't as much a message as a sort of curse."

"So?"

"The writing on the stone, as far as I can tell as he read it to me, is actually a curse. The Vikings who etched the letters on the stone were putting a curse on something, then buried the stone to seal the curse."

"Uh oh."

"Exactly! Right after he read the message on the stone, he heard a loud noise, like a rumbling coming from near the silo. Where, by the way, there are some grassy mounds surrounding it. He looked out and saw something moving around. He went outside and an eagle flew close to him, twice."

"Did he see anything else?"

"The next day he noticed one of the grassy mounds had been disturbed, like it had been dug up."

"Wow."

"Ever since that night, bizarre things have been happening at the farm. Some of them were like practical jokes, and others more dangerous and wicked."

"What do you think it is?" questioned Ned.

"Here's what I think. By reading the curse aloud several times over, Uncle Pete has unknowingly broken the curse and woke up the creature. It's causing havoc at the farm right now."

"When you say creature?"

"I believe it could be a troll. My uncle has awakened a troll!"

# Chapter 7: The Explanation

"Hold up a second, did you say troll?" said Ned. "Like a troll doll or internet troll?"

"No, not like a troll doll or an internet troll. An actual troll. Let me explain," said Cari.

"Each Scandinavian country has their own trolls. For example, Finland has Moomintrolls, basically benevolent. Iceland has Yule lads, mischievous. Norway has a variety of both mountain and forest trolls. In Norse mythology, trolls symbolize danger and power. Vikings believed trolls had magical powers and could transform into different animals, specifically bulls, eagles and dragons. These animals are displayed on the Coat of Arms of Iceland, known as protectors. Trolls were even known to transform into humans."

"Shapeshifters," whispered Ned.

"Precisely."

"This sounds like fantasy," said Ned, (at the same time he recalled what Wolfgang had told him he witnessed in the Colorado mountains - a shapeshifter.)

"I agree it does sound like fantasy, but there are some very unusual things happening that coincide with Uncle Pete reading that message on the stone."

"If this is a troll or something like it, what can you do about it?"

"Trolls have weaknesses like anything else. They are weakened by sunlight, bells drive them crazy and they fear lightning, which, legends say, can kill them, as Thor hunted them, and he is the Norse god of thunder, lightning and storms."

At this point, Ned started laughing.

"Alright, I know this is wild, but what's so funny?"

"Do you know that quite often Wolfgang gets mistaken for the actor, Chris Hemsworth, that played Thor in the Marvel movies? I'm just picturing him in a cloak and armor holding Thor's Hammer Mjolnir and chasing a troll. I'm sorry, I just couldn't help myself."

At this point Cari started laughing as well. "I just realized that he really does resemble Chris Hemsworth when he portrayed Thor. Quite a coincidence."

When they both finished laughing, Cari said her plan was to go to the farm with her uncle, take a look at the stone and perhaps try to figure out how to curse the troll back to sleep again.

"I was hoping that Wolfgang would be able to come along with me. He knows Uncle Pete and he is interested in cryptids, or legendary creatures. I think a troll would be considered legendary, don't you?" she asked.

"I'm quite certain that, if possible, Wolfgang would gladly go along with you. I'm not sure how long he will be gone, though. I can check with his sister Kyra, maybe she knows," Ned explained. "Either way, I will convey your message to him as soon as possible."

"Thank you Ned. I really appreciate it."

"No problem. I am curious, though. What are some of the bizarre things you say have been happening on the farm?" Ned asked.

"Hoo boy, where do I start?" Cari said. "I'll begin with the mischief. First of all, there's been the nightly rattling of farm implements in the old barn. Uncle Pete says around midnight every evening something starts clanging around the old farm tools. Like there are scythes, shovels, hoes, pitchforks, saws, etc. You name it, great Uncle Fritz had it. Everything is old and rusty."

"By something, you are referring to the"troll "?"

"Yes, according to Uncle Pete, it goes into the barn and starts up a ruckus with all the old farm tools. He's in the process of getting the tools all cleared out right now, but there was so much stuff in there, it's going to take time. Not to mention all the junk stored in the silo."

"It sounds to me like it could be some smarty kids playing tricks. Has he actually seen it?" asked Ned.

"No more than a quick glimpse. It disappears as soon as he goes outside. He has described it, from what he could see at a glance, it's the size of a short, stout man with a beard, at least he thinks so. Pete says the creature vanishes so fast that the tools are still swinging on their hooks when he goes into the barn."

"What else?"

"Well, there's been holes dug near the front porch and back door to trip up Uncle Pete as he walks outside. He fell a couple of times already. Now lately it has been collecting junk and piling it up all over the place. Sometimes there's brush piles, weeds, rocks, you name it, scattered everywhere."

"It sounds to me like the troll (or whatever) is trying to get rid of your uncle."

"Precisely. It has been throwing rocks at the house late at night. The only time it's not around is during a thunderstorm."

"Are there any measures other than lightning to frighten it?"

"Uncle Pete discovered that trolls don't like bells, so he bought a variety of bells, which he starts ringing as soon as it gets dark. He bought a loud bell alarm clock and made recordings of his bell ringing. It worked for a while, but the ringing apparently drove the troll crazy, so it got mad, so the mischief got worse. Then unfortunately, Pete came up with another idea on how to get rid of it. He called to tell me everything had stopped, he thought it was over with, and then later on, it started up again. The mischief turned into pulling tricks."

"What kind of tricks?"

"The evil kind."

# Chapter 8: Pete's Stone

Pete was tired. It was nearly impossible to sleep at night, so he had resorted to napping during the day. He was running out of options and couldn't wait to get away from this cursed farm. When it all started, he thought it was all a figment of his imagination.

After the first night when he had read the rune stone, little things began to happen. It began slowly, so he wasn't sure if it was just the result of being here. He was accustomed to being lulled to sleep at night by the waves of Lake Superior. When the lake was frozen in the winter, he would fall asleep to the wind whistling. Here at the farm he began to hear strange clunking sounds at night, followed by the snapping of tree limbs, or rustling noises near the window.

"I must be going out of my mind," he thought. "I have got to get this dump sold and get the hell out of here." He vowed to finish his search for buried money and contact that real estate lady and get this farm unloaded quickly.

Pete spent most of his days searching the yard for buried coffee cans, hoping for more cash finds. He located a few more, but the yard was large and it was very difficult to determine where Uncle Fritz had buried his cans. There was no pattern he could discern, so it was to be random digging for now, and extremely time consuming, not to mention back-breaking work for a man of his age. However, it was a rush of adrenaline when he located a can. Such a strange treasure hunt.

Three nights after he had located the stone (which he kept stored in the extra bedroom), he heard giggling outside in the front yard. He stepped off the old porch to investigate and tripped in a hole that had been dug at the bottom of the stairs.

"Son of a bitch!" he shouted, rubbing his ankle which he had twisted slightly. He hobbled into the house, wondering what animal dug such a deep hole so quickly. "Must have been a squirrel," he thought. "A really big squirrel, or a groundhog."

The laughing sound was confusing, though. It could have been a bird noise that sounded like laughing. This damn farm was starting to give him the creeps.

The next day Pete took a ride into town and went back to the library. He wanted to further research the finding of the Kensington rune stone and to see if there were any others. He found contact information for the museum where the stone was displayed, and decided to take a trip there the next day. Perhaps someone there could answer questions about the stone he had found.

The information he found at the library was nothing new. He got the address of the museum and decided to travel there the next day. When he got back to the farm, he took a few photos of his rune stone, as it was pretty large to tote with him.

Pete hoped the stone he found could be authenticated and perhaps would be housed in the museum with the Kensington stone. He never believed the Kensington stone was a hoax and he felt like his stone was the real thing as well.

The rest of the evening was spent researching runestones. Interestingly enough there had been others found, the most famous, the Stenkvista runestone in Sodermanland, Sweden. It actually references Thor and has a depiction of Thor's hammer, Mjolnir. The oldest stone found was in Norway, the Svingerud Stone.

All this was very interesting to Pete, but he really wanted to find out if his stone was authentic, or a hoax. He was glad to find all the cash cans, but this was a real find, something related to his Scandinavian heritage. He was so excited.

The following day Pete traveled to the Runestone museum in Alexandria. The Kensington Runestone is at the heart of the museum. Pete was intrigued by the slab of greywacke stone covered in runes, which was discovered in 1898, clutched in the roots of an aspen tree on the Olof Ohman farm near Kensington. It's authenticity has been debated for many years. Researchers quest to explain how a runic artifact, dated 1362, could show up in North America.

After viewing the stone, Pete inquired with a staff person, who he could speak to about a runestone he had found. The staffer told him the museum's director was currently out of town and unavailable, but he would convey Pete's contact information upon his return.

Pete knew it would probably take some time to actually find out if his runestone was authentic and get it to the right person. When the museum director got in touch, he would forward the photos of the stone. There was plenty of time, the stone wasn't going anywhere.

It was dark when Pete got back to the farm. When he pulled into the drive, he noticed something stacked up near the front porch entryway. "What the hell?" he said to himself. He got out of the car and when he got closer he noticed it was a pile of rocks, weeds and sticks piled high. He had to clear it away just to get on the porch.

"Argh, vandals!" he said to himself. Off in the distance he heard giggling. That was only the beginning.

# CHAPTER 9: HEADACHE

"Where are you? I know you're out there, you little bastard," Pete shouted into the darkness. "Come out where I can see you!"

"I've had enough," he thought to himself. "I need help." Pete was working on his last nerve with these little tricks and constant noises at night. By the time he had reached his niece, and she told him what she thought was causing the trouble, everything had escalated. It was time for more research.

The first thing he discovered to try and rid himself of the troll was the bells. He bought cow bells, bicycle bells, and an old school bell from an antique store. He made recordings of the bells' sounds and played them over and over. The bells worked for a while, and he had a few quiet nights, but then it seemed to make the creature angry. The mischief became more intense and occurred more often. Pete would wake in the morning to see piles of rocks scattered everywhere.

The more Pete played the bell recordings, the more chaos occurred. One night rocks were being thrown at the farmhouse and farm implements were stacked near the front door. He had to look down before stepping anywhere to avoid tripping in a hole. It was becoming exhausting, and he didn't know how to stop it. The havoc continued for several days. He couldn't sleep and was getting frustrated trying to figure out what to do.

If a thunderstorm with lightning came through it was a blessing. A night free of the rotten little bastard.

"I can't believe I am actually at war with a troll," Pete thought to himself. "Common sense tells me this is the work of vandals tormenting me for some strange reason. I'm a stranger here, why would anyone bother? What would be the end game?" he wondered.

He felt defeated. If he sold the farm and left, he wouldn't have time to dig up more cash. It was hardly worth it anymore, so the buried money was no longer the issue. The problem was, if he did leave, would the troll stay and continue to cause problems here? Would it follow him? The mere thought of that made his blood boil.

Pete began to question his sanity. He wished he had never come here in the first place. If he hadn't found that blasted stone, none of this would have ever happened. The trouble began with finding the rune stone. Why didn't he just leave it alone?

"Wait a minute!" Pete said to himself. "I know what to do."

Pete went to the barn, got the wheelbarrow, and rolled it into the kitchen. He loaded the stone into it and rolled it out to the yard, taking a shovel along with him. He was tired from the effort, but kept on working while it was still light. Finding the approximate area where he found the stone, Pete dug a deep hole, and dropped the stone in. After pausing to catch his breath, he recited the curse written in the runes on the stone. He repeated it three times out loud, then he re-buried the stone.

That night all was quiet. No more noises, no more rocks thrown, no new holes dug. Days passed without further disturbance. "Whew, it's over," Pete told himself.

Pete decided to call his niece right away and tell her how he had corrected the problem, so she wouldn't worry or feel like she had to rush here to help him. She answered immediately and said she would be on her way soon.

"No need to come here Cari. I have solved the problem. I read the runes again and buried the stone where I found it. It has been quiet ever since. I think that I cursed the little devil back into the ground."

Cari was silent after her uncle explained what he had done.

"Did you hear me, Cari? It's taken care of. Now I am able to search for some more of Uncle Fritz's cash cans and sell this blasted farm."

"I heard you Uncle Pete, but it seems too easy," she answered. "I don't want to seem negative on this, but I'm not sure that just a do-over would actually work. I hope for your sake it did, but let me know if anything else happens, and I'll be there right away. Promise me that you'll call if things go awry."

"Oh, don't be a silly girl, I'm sure it's gone. Once I get things settled here, we'll have a nice visit in the bay, and do some fishing."

"Okay Uncle Pete, but promise me that you'll call if you need me."

"Alright, I promise. You take care."

It was so nice to talk to his niece and assure her that all was well. He felt as if things were returning to normal. It was a shame he had to bury that stone again, but he kept the picture on his phone. There was no way he could ever tell anyone about it, because if the stone was dug up again, and the curse broken, the little bastard would be on the loose again, and who knows what trouble it could cause.

Pete spent the next few days digging for cash cans, and finding a few. He was getting tired of digging and decided it was time to rid himself of the farm and go back home. He called the real estate woman, Talia, and asked her to come out the next day and they would discuss the sale of the farm. She agreed to meet him at 10:00 am with paperwork for him to look over.

What a great feeling it was to have this all behind him. It had been a wild adventure, but now it was over. Pete was so relieved that he slept deeply that night. He was so soundly asleep, he didn't hear the giggling outside of the bedroom window.

# Chapter 10: The Farm Sale

The day dawned brisk and sunny. Pete rose early and decided to treat himself to a big breakfast in celebration. The Hovland woman would be here soon, so he made another pot of coffee and had some grocery store sweet rolls to go along with it. She showed up at exactly 10:00 am and he greeted her at the door.

"How nice to see you again, Mr. Magnusson," she gushed. "I think you've made the right decision to sell the farm. The timing is very good right now and we have much to talk over."

"Please come in," Pete gushed back at her. "I have coffee and sweet rolls in the kitchen. We can talk there and then take a look around the farm," he said and escorted her into the old farm kitchen.

"Wonderful. I would love some coffee," she said, flashing her whitened teeth in a big smile.

Talia had already consumed plenty of coffee this morning, but she knew he had gone to the trouble of fixing coffee and she noticed the grocery store bakery rolls on a plate. She would choke a couple of those down with a cup of coffee and talk this fellah into a quick sale.

Over coffee and rolls, they discussed the sale of the farm. Afterward they began a walk around the property, first visiting the barn. Pete wondered why she was wearing expensive looking shoes with high heels to visit a farm.

"I see you have gotten rid of some of the rusty farm implements," Talia told him as they entered the dusty old barn.

"Yes, I've started clearing things out. There is still quite a bit left. How did you know what was here before?" he asked.

"Oh, I did a quick visit out here when we arranged for the cleaning company. I wanted to see if they did everything you asked."

"If he only knew how much time I spent out here on this wreck of a farm," she thought to herself. "I even ruined one of my favorite pairs of shoes."

"Hmm, I see. How very nice of you to go that extra mile, but I don't think they did any cleaning in the barn," Pete said wryly.

After looking through the barn, they peeked into the silo, which was packed nearly to the broken down rafters with dust-covered junk.

"It seems like there's more to be dealt with here," Talia noted, waving her manicured hand at the junk pile. "I can certainly recommend a junk removal service for you."

"Thank you, I appreciate that," Pete replied, and shut the door.

"How odd," she said pointing down at the grassy mounds near the bottom of the silo. "It looks as if something has been buried there. That one seems like it had been disturbed," she added, pointing at the one mound that had fresh-looking upturned dirt.

"Yes, I agree," said Pete. "I don't know why these mounds are here. Maybe my uncle buried stuff under there. It's a mystery."

"It looks as if you tried to find out what was buried there," she told him, pointing at the disturbed mound.

"Nope, not me. I guess it must have been an animal or something."

"Mmm..hmm. I suppose so. Farms always have plenty of critters about," Talia replied. "Let's take a look at the yard behind the house."

As they entered the yard, it was quite noticeable that there had been many spots freshly dug up. Pete would have to explain that somehow. He didn't want to tell her about the coffee cans of cash. When Talia mentioned critters, it gave him an idea. Before she could comment about the yard, he pointed at the holes and said, "Groundhog."

"Oh dear, I think this is the work of more than one groundhog. I also noticed there had been holes covered up all around the front of the house as well. I think you should have an exterminator come and (live) trap those little guys for relocation."

"You are so right Ms. Hovland. What a good idea." He certainly wouldn't tell her about the mischievous creature that had dug some of the holes around the front of the house to trip him. She'd think he was crazy.

"Call me Talia. You know, when I was here before, I didn't notice all these freshly dug holes everywhere. Even near the front porch. It looks like a family of groundhogs moved in when you did."

"Ha ha, I suppose you're right," Pete said, wondering how much "looking around" she did while she was inspecting the cleaning job. He was a bit leery of this woman, she seemed a bit too anxious and nosy for his taste.

"Well, I think I have seen enough of the outdoors, may we return to the farm house so I can take a closer look?" she asked, brushing a stray hair from her face.

Pete figured since she had been here before, the "closer look" had already been done, but he agreed and Pete guided her to the house. He held her arm beneath her elbow so she wouldn't trip in a hole, wearing those ridiculous shoes.

After a look through the house, Talia requested they sit down and go over the sale price she would recommend and what her commission would be, etc.

"That sounds great, Talia, but I'm not ready to commit to anything."

"Oh, well, of course, you take your time. I certainly don't want to pressure you, but don't wait too long," she told him, with disappointment in her voice. "Let's just go over some of this paperwork, and you sign it when you're good and ready."

"Yes, that sounds fine. I appreciate all you have done," Pete agreed.

## CHAPTER 11: DECISIONS

Pete woke up early again the next day, feeling relieved that he could finally sell this old farm and go home. Talia Hovlund went through the sale paperwork with him and suggested an asking price that seemed more than fair. He didn't sign anything yet; he wanted to look it over and possibly discuss it with an attorney. (Maybe the law firm Uncle Fritz used; that Korhonen fellah?) Nah, he didn't know that guy very well, besides, he seemed like a cold fish. The asking price was more than he ever expected to get and the quicker he signed, the quicker he could go home.

It was a damn shame though, that he had to bury the rune stone again. What a fantastic piece of history and he had discovered it.

"What if I dug it back up and didn't read the curse out loud, or didn't read it at all, could I safely move it away from here?" he wondered. It was certainly very tempting.

"If I relocated the stone, without reciting the curse and took it far away from here, it would protect anyone that maybe would happen upon it in the future. The creature would stay dormant or asleep or whatever and I would have a piece of Viking history. Yeah, that's what I should do," he told himself.

Pete thought long and hard about this dilemma. Move the stone? Leave the stone alone? Was it really a troll? Could it have actually been vandals?

If it had been vandals, why did everything stop when he buried the stone again. This was a strange puzzle for sure. Before he sold the farm and left, decisions would have to be made. He would sleep on it and maybe call Cari again and get her opinion.

Since he was up and about, Pete decided to hunt for a few more cash cans after breakfast. He felt invigorated after a good night's sleep. The weather was nice, so why not do a little digging for money.

It took most of the day, but Pete found two more cans containing cash. One had $105 and the other had $150. A nice return for a full day's work. The realtor was going to have to explain the yard being dug up to potential buyers, so Pete figured he could throw on some grass seed and say he was working on improving the back lawn.

When he finished his digging in the yard, Pete wandered into the barn and took a look around to check if there was anything worthwhile out here. There wasn't. Next he ventured into the silo, which was filled with what appeared to be junk, most of which had a heavy layer of dust and a good amount of spider webs and nests.

"Argh...I better get a broom," he told himself. "There's too many spiders in here." He didn't like spiders - one bit him on the forehead once and one side of his face swelled up for almost a week and he was left with a nasty scar at his hairline.

Pete came back with a well-worn broom he found and began to sweep off the piles of stuff (he was determined not to refer to it as junk). "Maybe there's some valuable antiques in here," he thought, but as he began uncovering the items, everything appeared to be junk.

He decided to talk to Talia Hovlund before signing the paperwork and ask her about having an auction here prior to putting the farm up for sale. Perhaps she could put him in touch with an auction dealer and get rid of the items in the silo and barn. There may be someone who wants all the junk.

Here was another dilemma: get the place sold and go home, or keep it a little longer, dig around a bit more for cash cans, have an auction, then sell. As much as Pete wanted to go home, finding over $250 today and thinking about proceeds from an auction, gave Pete pause. He was doing okay financially, and the farm sale money would go a long way. A new boat? Hmm....what to do?

There were some important decisions to be made: sell the farm now or wait and have an auction, dig up the stone and take it with him when he went home. His final decision was to sleep on it. He wished there was someone he could talk to for a second opinion. He thought about calling his brother Viktor, but what if Viktor was disappointed that he didn't get a share of their uncle's farm? Besides, Viktor was traveling abroad right now and he may be hard to reach.

Another option was to call his niece Cari again. She was adamant that he contact her if there were further difficulties with the "creature". He knew she would have an opinion about moving the stone again, and probably would tell him to sell and get the heck out of there.

The more he thought about it, the more he determined that the creature was a figment of his imagination and the tricks were the work of some local vandals that probably got chased off a few times by crabby old Uncle Fritz when he was alive. Imagine - believing in a troll that was cursed by Vikings...crazy! This old farm was making his vivid imagination run wild.

"Oh well, decisions for another day," thought Pete. He was tired from digging and sweeping and fell exhausted into bed. He was asleep in no time, so didn't hear the giggling out in the darkness.

# CHAPTER 12: AUCTION?

The farm sale papers looked inviting on the kitchen table the next day. It would be so easy to sign and go. Forget all about the stone and be happy with the cash and proceeds from the sale. No more worries about what was going on here. Pete loved his home on the lake so much, and he didn't like it here, but...there could possibly be some more money to be made, and who didn't like money?

What would be the harm in staying here just a little bit longer? It was certainly worth his time to look into having an auction, as long as someone else did the majority of the work. He assumed they would take care of everything and take a percentage. Whatever was left for him would be gravy on top.

"Okay, decision made!" Pete declared and called Talia Hovlund to inquire about having an auction. She answered immediately, and from the excitement in her voice, Pete figured she assumed he was signing the sale papers.

"An auction?" she asked. "So you want to auction off the contents of the barn and silo?"

"Yes, there's lots of stuff out there, and maybe some of it could be valuable," Pete explained. "What do you think?"

"I suppose there could be a few items of value, but I wouldn't get my hopes up," she told him. "I can give you the name of an auction service that works in this area and the owner can look over what's there and tell you if it's worth the time and effort."

"That's exactly what I would like to do. If an expert tells me to forget it, then I'll know for sure and get this place on the market quickly."

"A solid plan Mr. Magnusson. You don't want to wait too long. Once the weather turns cold, it may take longer to sell the farm. You don't want to lose any potential buyers."

She gave Pete the name and number of a local auction house and re-minded him to keep in touch with her if he needed anything else. Pete had been leery of her at first, but decided that she was being very helpful and he appreciated it.

Pete called the number Talia gave him as soon as he finished his call with her. A man with a nasal voice answered, "Taylor Auctions, may I help you."

It turned out that the nasally voice belonged to the owner, Dwight Taylor. He agreed to meet Pete at the farm the next day to look over what was in the barn and silo. Things were moving along quickly so far, Pete could be going home sooner than he thought. It gave him a happy feeling.

Depending upon how long the auction would take, Pete figured he would be leaving fairly soon. Actually, why would he have to be here for the auction? He could leave everything to Mr. Taylor and be home before summer was over and get in some good fishing time. Things were looking up.

The next day, Dwight Taylor showed up exactly on time at 10:00 am. He was a big, barrel-chested man with fluffy white-ish hair and a bushy mustache to match. He had an odd way of sniffing, as if he was showing disapproval. Pete showed him the barn and the silo. Mr. Taylor did lots of sniffing, but made no comment until they were finished.

"There are some items that could be worthy of an estate sale rather than an auction, Mr. Magnusson, but the condition of the barn and silo, well, I don't have the staff to deal with that mess. I can recommend a young man that does clean up work for me and he can get things ready."

"Oh, okay. Does he work for you?"

"No, you could employ him yourself to clean up and organize. He's worked on projects like this before, and would know what to do. Here's his card, call me if and when you want to proceed with an estate sale, that is, if everything is in better order."

Pete shook the man's large, damp hand and took the business card he offered. The card read, "Davey's clean up service. No job is too big or small."

Now things were getting more complicated again. He would have to hire a guy to clean up and organize. After he thought about it for a while, it didn't seem like such a bad idea. If the clean-up was done, potential buyers wouldn't have to deal with the mess.

Pete called Davey right away, and a young voice answered. "This is Davey." Following a quick explanation of what he wanted, Davey agreed to meet with Pete in a couple of days when he finished the current job he was working on.

"Ah...now we're in business," thought Pete. "I can have this Davey kid clean up the mess in the barn and silo - sell Uncle Fritz's crap in an estate sale that someone else will organize, put the farm up for sale and get the hell out of here."

Pete was quite pleased with himself after taking care of business. It could be lucrative - and even if it wasn't - he would be rid of the problem. That night when he lay in bed, he didn't sleep right away - his thoughts kept him awake for a while.

The old clock next to the bed read 2:00 am. Pete was finally getting sleepy. He was nearly asleep when he heard a noise outside. It sounded like someone was whispering and giggling. He lumbered out of bed, adjusted his eyes to the dark, peeked outside and saw nothing at all.

"Whoa, I must be tired," he said to himself. "I'll bet I was dreaming."

Pete eventually drifted off to sleep and in between wake and sleep, thought he heard whispering in Norwegian. "Jeg er tilbake, Jeg er tilbake." Translated to English: "I have returned."

# Chapter 13: Coffee, Tea or Creature?

The creature climbed through the window and stared at Pete asleep in his uncle's old bedroom. Pete woke abruptly, saw the creature and couldn't move. He felt as if he was paralyzed with fear and dread.

It was small, maybe four feet tall, but stout and sturdy. It had a large head, beady black eyes, a long nose and a thick beard. It stood at the foot of the bed, not moving, just staring. Suddenly it spoke, its teeth were long and crooked, the voice, scratchy and deep.

"Takk for friheten," it said to Pete. Translated from Norwegian: "thanks for freedom."

"Velbekomme," Pete managed to reply. ("You're welcome.")

"Ikke ferdig," said the creature, shaking its ugly head. ("not finished").

"Hvorfor?" asked Pete (why?)

"du er et  darlig menneske," it replied ("you are bad human")

"Nei!" answered Pete. (No!)

"du er ond mann" it told him. ("you are evil man")

"illr troll!" Pete shouted. (evil troll in old Norse)

"Faen," the creature hissed at Pete. (curse word in Norway for devil). The creature kept hissing the word, then skittered toward the window.

Pete hollered to the creature as it climbed out the window, "ga til hel-vete"

("go to hell")

The creature turned, grinning to show its nasty sharp teeth and said (clearly in English) "you're already there," then he turned and disappeared through the window.

Pete awoke with a start, covered in sweat and shaking. "Whew, what a bad nightmare," he said aloud the next morning. The nightmare was so real, and he attributed it to stress or concern. It was most likely due to what he's been going through lately.

"No worries," he mumbled to himself, (quoting his friend Varg: Wolfgang) as he climbed out of bed, shaking off the bad dream. He glanced around the room, noting with relief that nothing had been disturbed and the window was firmly shut.

Wiping the sweat from his face, Pete ambled to the bathroom and turned on the shower. It took a little while longer to escape thoughts of the nightmare. After thinking about it while showering, he was quite amazed at his remembering the old Norse as well as Norwegian words and phrases. The one word he and his brother could never say was "Faen". It was what the creature hissed at him over and over in the dream. Faen was a bad curse word in Norwegian.

Since that Davey kid wasn't coming until the next day, Pete decided to search for some more cash in the yard. It may be his last chance. He certainly wouldn't do it with other people around. He didn't want to explain that he was digging up a yard for cash left in old coffee cans.

He was tired from staying up too late. That crazy dream left him a bit shaken. It would be good to spend some time outdoors doing some physical labor (digging). Besides, if at the end of the day, it yielded some cash - great.

After two hours of digging, Pete finally found a can. This can was different. It wasn't a coffee can like all the others, but more of a metal box. It was tall and the top was also made of metal and it was in the shape of an octagon. It would be something possibly used as a canister. He looked closely and realized it was a tea container. The container was rusted and hard to read, but it was some sort of Scandinavian tea. When he shook it, something rattled inside.

The top was hard to remove, it seemed to have been sealed shut and then rusted. Pete pulled and twisted until he finally gave up. He'd bring it in the house and pry the damn thing off.

Before going inside, Pete did the best he could repairing the holes he had dug in the yard and put away the shovel and wheelbarrow one last time. He would have that kid clean up everything, do the estate sale and off to Michigan.

While Pete was busy digging, someone watched him from a good distance away with powerful binoculars, until the digging was finished for the day.

It was getting to be late afternoon and Pete was getting hungry. He made a quick sandwich and noticed that he needed some more groceries. A quick trip into town to pick up a few things, return his library books and pick up a few more.

Hurrying into town to get to the library before closing, Pete reflected on how nice it was to be away from the farm. He had to admit that he never liked the place and since he had a run-in with a troll or some rotten vandals, he liked it even less.

The very thought of returning home to the Upper Peninsula was making him feel light-hearted. He longed to sit on his back porch with the spectacular view of the bay. If he closed his eyes and thought about it, he could smell the fresh air and hear the waves lapping on the shoreline. He loved how the morning sun would sparkle like diamonds on the water in the bay.

He snapped out of his daydream and made a quick stop at the library, dropping the books off and selecting a few more. It was such a pleasant afternoon. On his way out he ran into one of his uncle's attorneys, Isaac Korhonen.

"Hello there Mr. Magnusson," said Korhonen in a solemn voice. "I'm surprised to see you are still here."

"Oh, not for long. I'm wrapping up a few things, then I'll be on my way home."

"You've decided to sell the farm then?" Korhonen asked brightly. His demeanor seemed a bit friendlier.

"I always intended to sell the farm. My home is in Michigan. I'm no farmer, and I miss Lake Superior. I stayed to settle a few things before leaving. Say, I've been meaning to ask you - are you Finnish? I noticed your last name is Finn."

"Yes, I am Finnish."

"I asked because I know there are lots of Norwegians in this area. Where I live in the Upper Peninsula of Michigan, we have many Finnish people there."

"How interesting. Well, it's nice to see you again. Let me know if there's anything I can assist you with. Enjoy the rest of your stay here," the lawyer added as he walked away.

"He's always so serious and stoic," thought Pete. "Not unusual for a lawyer," he laughed to himself.

The grocery store was busy and Pete had to stand in line for a while. A tap on the shoulder startled him.

"Hello Mr. Magnusson."

It was Talia Hovlund smiling at him and holding a box of tea in her manicured hand.

"Oh, hello there Ms. Hovlund."

"Talia."

"Hello, Talia. Please call me Pete."

"Okay Pete, have you decided on the property sale yet?"

"I um...well, yes. I don't s'pose this is the place to talk about it."

"You're right about that. I'll call you and we can set up a time to meet. It's wonderful to see you again."

"Yeah, you too," Pete answered, thinking that wonderful was a strong word. He also noticed that the tea box she was holding looked very much like the tea canister he had dug up that afternoon. Coincidence.

It reminded him that he hadn't opened the tea canister yet. He would do that when he got back to the farm. What was rattling in there?

# Chapter 14: Rune Letter

Pete quickly put away his groceries and set his library books on the rickety coffee table. Settling into an old kitchen chair, he started to tackle opening up the tea can. For some reason it made him feel anxious. The other cans he dug up were the same brand of coffee that Fritz had used for years and years. Why was this different? Ah… the old guy just probably ran out of coffee cans and he had some money to bury. The rattling was probably loose change. Ooh, maybe it was a gold coin or some sort of coin that was valuable.

As he struggled to open the can, he wondered again, why this can? It was much rustier than the others. "I bet this was the first can he buried, and then switched to coffee cans."

Just as he was about to take a hammer to the old can, the top gave way and it opened. There was no money inside, but a yellowed piece of paper and a stone. He took out the paper and read the words, written in old Norse. The words read:

"bjarga seidh" Roughly translated: save or protect from dark magic.

The rune letter - a small stone had the runic letter ALGIZ - The Elk: Protection, Shield, Ward off Evil. The letter looked like a Y with a line through the center.

"Well, what the fuck is  this?" wondered Pete holding the yellowing paper and rune letter in his hand.

It had to have been put there by Uncle Fritz. The tea can certainly wasn't put there by Vikings in the 1300's. Pete knew his uncle was familiar with the old Norse and meanings of the runic alphabet. They had talked about it on occasion, but Fritz never really seemed to want to discuss it too much.

Time for more research. Luckily the books he grabbed from the library gave him something to study on. There was no internet here, so he couldn't research that way, not that he had a laptop with him anyway. He could use the computers at the library. But still...what the fuck? Dark magic? What was that all about?

Pete stayed up later than intended trying to work out the reasoning behind the paper and rune letter for protection. He wondered whether Uncle Fritz had also found the rune stone and read the curse. This was puzzling and made for a very restless night. He felt very alone in all this, but didn't want to bother Cari, or anyone else for that matter. It all seemed so unreal. He was the practical sort, this was out of his comfort zone. He just wanted out.

The next morning, Pete was still tired from a restless night, fortunately without any nightmares. He remembered that kid Davey was supposed to be stopping by. They hadn't set a particular time, so he could come anytime. Following a late breakfast, Pete napped in a chair in the living room. He must have been at least partially awake, because he could hear himself snoring.

A loud knock on the front door woke Pete with a loud snort. "Jeez, I hope nobody heard that," he thought, getting up from the chair. "Just a minute, I'm comin'," he shouted, rubbing his hand over his face.

It took him a few seconds to loosen up his stiff joints and amble over to answer the knock. He opened the door and there stood a tall young man with curly red hair and a face full of freckles, smiling at him.

"You must be Mr. Magnusson. I'm Davey," he said, holding out his freckled hand.

"Hello Davey, you can call me Pete. C'mon in and I'll tell you what we're up against out here."

"Sure thing, Mr. um...Pete."

"Sit down, you want some coffee or something?"

"No thanks, I'm good."

"Well, here's what we've got. The barn and silo are full of junk, covered in dust and dirt and who knows what all. Probably some animals living out there and I know there's spiders for sure. What I need is someone to clean up and organize everything. You know, sort it out."

"Okay so far," said Davey, still grinning.

"Well sir, some dealer fellah named Taylor, you know him, is going to put on an estate sale here. He insists it has to be cleaned up and organized first."

Davey nodded knowingly.

"What is good or what's crap is anybody's guess. Right now, he won't look too close, cuz it's nasty out there. You need to de-nasty it all and sort out anything that's for sure trash."

"I can do that."

"Let's go out and take a look at what you're up against and you can give me a quote if you decide to take the job. Sound good?"

"Yep."

Pete and Davey went first into the barn. Pete pointed out all the scary looking rusted farm implements that were still hanging in the barn.

"You know, it's funny, I could have sworn there's even more of this shit than when I first arrived, like it's growing," said Pete.

"Those are some scary looking tools, I wonder when they were used last," commented Davey, touching a rusty scythe that appeared to still be sharp.

"Yeah, I don't know who would want this stuff. Maybe one of those dealers that sells to places for displays, kinda like they have at a Cracker Barrel."

"I don't think a scythe or pitchfork would be a safe decoration," added Davey.

"Hoo boy, you're right about that. If one of them fell on you while you was eatin' lunch, you'd be a goner for sure," laughed Pete.

# Chapter 15: Farm Tools

It turned out that hiring Davey was a fine decision. The guy worked hard and his quote for the job was reasonable. He seemed to be making quite a dent in the mess of junk in the silo. Pete asked him to start there first, considering the huge amount of stuff that had been left behind. Piles of odds and ends were being unloaded into the open trailer that Davey brought with him.

"Do you want to look over any of these things?" Davey asked Pete pointing at a load of junk piled high in the trailer.

"I wouldn't know the first thing about what would be worth saving," said Pete. "It all looks like crap to me."

"Well, I think you're right about that," Davey told him. "I loaded the pieces that need to be disposed of, but I thought I should check with you first. These are mostly broken parts and general trash. None of it would be considered by a scrap dealer - it's just garbage. I'll take it to the dump then."

"Do you need money for the dumping fee right now?" Pete asked.

"Nah, I'll keep track and you can pay me later. It would be easier that way. The guy gives a receipt, so I can turn it into you. Believe me, this won't be the first load of trash that has to be dumped."

"I sure appreciate all you're doing here, Davey. I wouldn't want to take on this job myself."

"Sure thing, Mr. Magnusson. Thanks for hiring me to do the job. I'd better get going before the dump closes. I'll be back later this afternoon to start another load," said Davey as he climbed in his truck and drove off with a friendly wave.

While Davey was gone, Pete decided to do a bit of digging in the back-yard. "No harm in looking for a cash can or two," he thought.

Deliberately staying far away from where he had re-buried the rune stone, Pete began another digging project. An hour later he was sweating and his work had yielded nothing. Davey would be returning any minute, so Pete wrapped it up, and brought the shovel back to the barn.

As he stood looking around, Pete noticed again that there seemed to be more items in here than when he first arrived, especially the nastier looking farm implements.

"Now that I think of it, some of these things weren't here before, I'm sure of it," thought Pete. "Either I'm losing my marbles, or somebody put these here."

There were three scythes, two of them looked very new and sharp to have been hanging in the barn for years. Three pitchforks were mounted on the wall, hanging on rusty nails. In addition, he noticed two sickles (shorter handle and hook-like blade). He was positive they had not been there when he first looked in the barn.

"Where did this come from?" he wondered aloud when he spotted a broadfork that looked newer and very sharp, and a bale spear that seemed to be new as well. "I wonder if Davey brought these here for some reason?"

He decided to ask Davey about it when he returned, but he was quite sure that the items were put there by someone (or something) else.

Pete was walking out of the barn when Davey got back from the dump. He waved the young man over to the barn and asked him if he knew anything about the extra farm tools.

"Um...no I don't, Mr. Magnusson. Why do you ask?"

"I'm sure some of these weren't here before, especially the newer-looking ones."

"So...do you think somebody stole them from another farm and is storing them here?" Davey asked.

"That's a good possibility. I've had some issues with vandalism recently, so that could explain it."

"I'll ask around and see if anyone is missing some stuff," said Davey. "Can you tell me what doesn't belong?"

"I'm not exactly sure. I really didn't look that closely at everything, and I'm not a farmer. I only know what they are used for because I spent time here helping out when I was a teenager. I would assume that anything that looks to be newer isn't the property of this old farm."

"If I hear of anything missing or reported stolen, we can check it out," said Davey. "In the meantime, I'll get back to working in the silo."

While Davey continued working in the silo, Pete shook some grass seed around in the backyard, and suddenly noticed something. The rune stone he had re-buried was partially exposed. He was absolutely sure he had buried it deep enough, but a small corner of it was sticking out of the ground.

# Chapter 16: Accidents Happen

"**S**on of a bitch, somebody is trying to dig up the rune stone," Pete said to himself. "What the hell is going on around here?"

He stood over the exposed corner of the stone, trying to determine how it became exposed. There was no sign of more recent digging since he had buried it. The thought of that creature coming back gave him the chills. He just couldn't go through that again. He needed to sell this dump and get out of here.

Sighing and rubbing his hand over his face, he tried to get hold of himself and not fly into a panic. The extra farm tools, now the rune stone partially uncovered: what did it mean?

"Okay, Pete, think," he told himself. "This is certainly the work of thieves and vandals. They are stealing stuff, putting it all in the barn and trying to scare me away from here. Now that he considered it, things were making sense. The timing of the rune stone discovery was just a coincidence. Maybe someone saw him dig it up and heard him read the curse.

"Aha! I'll just bet someone buried that tea canister with a rune stone in it to scare me. Those thieves are using this farm and want me out of here. Well, I'm happy to oblige!" Pete shouted.

"Are you okay Mr. Magnusson?"

Davey had walked into the backyard just as Pete was talking to himself.

"Oh, sure, sure. I was just trying to figure out why those thieves are putting things in the barn."

"Okay. I just wanted to know if it's alright to keep working today. I'm making some good progress out in the silo, and I had lunch and a nice break in town. I kinda hate to stop when I'm on a roll."

"Sure Davey, you work as long as you like. I think I'll go inside. Do you need some water, pop or coffee?" Pete asked.

"No thanks. I brought along some snacks and drinks for myself. I'm good."

"Alright then, you let me know if there's anything you need."

Pete toddled inside and decided to take a nap. It was late afternoon and he was tired from digging earlier. Since Davey was all set, and working, he could take a much needed rest.

Pete awoke hours later and it had gotten dark outside. He noticed a light near the silo - so Davey was still out there. What a good find that guy was. He leaned into the fridge looking for something to fix for dinner. Hmm...what to have?

Suddenly he heard a loud crash, a shout and a sort of a scream. Was it coming from the silo? Davey?

Pete hurried outside and heard another shout. It was coming from the barn. Davey!

Pete ran as quickly as he could to the barn. What he saw was shocking. Davey was lying on the floor of the barn, pinned down by some of the evil looking farm implements. He was bleeding from his arm and a leg and had a nasty gash on the side of his head.

"Oh no, what happened!" Pete shouted. "Davey are you okay? I'm going to go call for an ambulance. I'll be right back." Davey didn't answer.

Pete rushed back to the house, called the emergency number he had located in the old desk, briefly described what happened and told them to hurry. He ran to the closet, grabbed some towels and a first aid kit.

He raced back to the barn with the kit and an armload of towels. By the time he returned, it appeared that Davey was unconscious. Pete worked diligently to move the farm tools off of Davey and stop the bleeding, hoping that none of the tools had nicked an artery.

Pete continued to work, wrapping towels around Davey's wounds, which to him looked quite bad. He kept talking the whole time - hoping that Davey would be alright.

"I'm so sorry this happened to you Davey, I'm trying to stop the bleeding, you're going to be okay. The ambulance is on the way."

Davey didn't answer.

After what seemed like hours, but was actually less than twenty minutes, the ambulance arrived. The EMT's quickly got Davey on the gurney, prepped him and loaded him into the ambulance. They told Pete to stay there, that the police were on the way, and he could check on Davey's condition at the local hospital.

Moments later the police arrived. Pete motioned them into the barn, where he noticed the blood all over the floor where Davey had lain.

The first officer followed Pete into the barn, the second was looking around outside with a powerful flashlight.

"What happened here sir?" the first officer asked Pete and introduced himself as Officer Larsen.

"I'm not sure. I was in the house and heard a crash and a shout. I ran out here and found Davey on the barn floor with farm tools pinning him down. I ran and called the emergency number and came back with towels and a first aid kit to try to help him."

"Why was that young man in the barn?"

"He's doing some work for me. He has a service doing odd jobs and I hired him to clean out all the junk left here. This was my Uncle Fritz's farm and I'm getting it ready to sell."

"While my partner looks around out here, let's go inside and get your information," Officer Larsen told him.

"What information?"

"Your name, etc. and a complete description of what happened here."

"I just told you what happened!"

"Please calm down, sir. Let's go inside."

"Okay," said Pete, noticing that his hands were shaking as he walked toward the house.

"You should sit down sir, this has been quite a shock," said the officer, motioning to a shabby living room chair.

The officer sat directly across from Pete and pulled out a notebook.

Pete sat with his head in his hands, worriedly rubbing his temples.

"Can I get you a glass of water, sir?" the officer asked Pete.

"Nope, I'm good, let's just get this over with. I'm worried about that young man."

"Of course, sir. What is your name?"

"Pete Magnusson. This was my uncle's farm and he died recently and left it to me. I am staying here now, but plan to sell the place."

"So this is not your permanent residence?"

"No, I live in the U.P. of Michigan in a little burg called Trygghaven Bay," Pete told him, reaching into his back pocket. "Here's my driver's license."

The police officer noted the information on Pete's license and then asked him again what had happened in the barn.

"Same as I told you before. I heard a crash and a scream or a yell, and there was Davey laying in the barn all covered in a pile of those nasty old farm tools. He was bleeding pretty bad, so first I called the emergency number then I grabbed some towels and the first aid kit to see if I could stop the bleeding. That's all."

"Okay, that should be everything I need for now, Mr. Magnusson. Here's the number for the local hospital if you want to check on the young man's condition."

"Thanks. I'm sorry I snapped at you, but this kinda shook me up a bit."

"I understand sir. Are you feeling okay?'

"Yeah, I'm alright. I ain't no spring chicken, but I'm in pretty decent shape."

"Well, please let us know if you need anything else. We're checking out the barn to see why all those tools fell at once. There could be old, faulty hardware holding things up."

"You're probably right about that, everything around here is old and faulty. I just wonder why Davey was in the barn, he was working in the silo and wasn't going to start in the barn until that was finished. If I woulda known he was going in there...um...he shoulda been warned about those farm tools."

"Warned?"

"You see, some of the stuff in the barn wasn't there before. It's like, ah... somebody's been stealing stuff and storing it in the barn. Davey and I talked about it earlier. There's been some vandalism here, you know, rocks thrown, stuff like that and then suddenly these extra farm tools show up. Some of them look sharp and dangerous."

"Tell me more about this vandalism," Larsen requested.

"Hmm...it started shortly after I arrived here. As I said, it was rock throwing, hole digging, stuff like that, but it stopped, so I didn't pursue it. Then I noticed the extra tools in the barn."

"Could they have been there before, and you didn't notice?" Larsen asked.

"I knew you'd say that, but no, I'm sure they weren't there before," Pete answered.

At that moment, the other officer came in and motioned to Larsen. They walked outside and spoke quietly so Pete couldn't hear. After a few minutes the officers came back to the house, and Officer Larsen introduced his partner, Officer Andersen.

"Mr. Magnusson, it appears that the bolts and hangers holding the farm implements have been tampered with. This was no accident, they were detached on purpose. We will be cordoning off the barn, so please don't go out there."

"What? You mean somebody intentionally dropped that shit on the poor kid. That coulda killed him!" Pete exclaimed.

"Please calm down sir, we're going to investigate. Do you feel safe here, or would you prefer to stay elsewhere? We can give you a ride to a hotel if you want," said Officer Andersen.

"Nah, I ain't leaving here. Sumbitch better not try anything else," Pete said angrily.

"Okay Mr. Magnusson, let us know if you need anything and please stay out of the barn until we're finished investigating," Larsen added and the officers left.

Pete sat in a chair - steaming mad. He knew it was that devil troll, he just knew it. He walked outside and hollered into the darkness. "I'll get you, nasty little sumbitch, illr troll (evil troll) you won't get away with this!"

Pete heard a noise coming out of the darkness...giggling. He picked up his phone and called his niece Cari back.

"It's not over," he told her somberly, and she knew exactly what he meant.

## CHAPTER 17: NED & KYRA

While Pete was dealing with unburied stones and falling farm implements, Ned Ferris was trying to relay a message to his friend Wolfgang Kilmer, so far to no avail. Following the unusual phone conversation with Cari Magnusson, he wanted to make good on his promise to her to try to reach Wolfgang. Ned didn't know Cari very well, but he knew her Uncle Pete from Trygghaven Bay.

Ned, along with his friend Wolfgang and Wolf's sister Kyra were all well acquainted with Pete from visiting the bay and stopping by the bay's social center: Garvin's General Merchandise. Pete was a local character and a regular at Garvin's coffee counter.

Although Pete was something of a smart-aleck, (or wise-ass) he had been a good friend to Ned's late father Jake and had helped Ned and his friends out when they needed it after Jake's death.

"I've got to help out Pete," Ned thought. "He'd do it for me. Besides, once I reach Wolf, he's going to want to lend a hand, especially since he's been dating Cari, Pete's beautiful niece."

It was a good time to take some time off. Business was a bit slow at Ned's law practice lately, so Ned made a decision. He would leave the practice in the capable hands of his secretary Phyllis and his law partner Matt. His first order of business would be to talk with Wolfgang's sister Kyra (she was also

Ned's long time love interest). He assumed she was still on assignment in Vermont, but she may have heard from her brother.

Kyra answered the phone immediately. "Ned, how nice to hear from you," she told him.

"Hello Kyra, it is great to speak with you. First of all, I have a question. Have you heard from Wolf lately? I know he has been on assignment doing his marine biology thing, but I need to reach him if I can."

"Hmm...not lately. I know he was planning to visit the U.P. when he got back. Our parents are up there right now staying at the family's summer place. I'm supposed to meet everyone up there when I'm done here in Vermont, which will be in a few days."

"Do you think your parents have heard from him?" Ned asked.

"Doubtful. They have old phones with poor service, and don't care about getting new phones. It's kind of tough to get in touch with them. I think his plan is to go up there as soon as he returns."

"I really need to get a message to him," Ned told her.

"What's up?" she asked.

"I heard from Cari Magnusson, and she's trying to reach him."

"Oh yeah, Cari. Wolf's sexy new girlfriend. What does she want?"

"It has to do with her Uncle Pete. He's in well...trouble."

"Pete's in trouble? What can Wolf do?"

"It's a long, unusual story. Have you got a few minutes?"

"Sure, fire away," said Kyra.

Ned proceeded to tell her the whole story about Pete breaking a rune stone curse and possibly awakening a troll. If not a troll, then (the more likely scenario) dangerous individuals trying to drive him away from the farm he inherited.

"How bizarre," Kyra whispered.

"I know, it sounds crazy, but I think Pete could be in danger. Something scary is going on there. A young man was seriously injured and Pete could be next. He has talked with the police, but there's really not much they can do but check in now and then."

"He could just leave," Kyra commented.

"Yeah, that's what his niece said, but he's worried that the troll will follow him, or that it will cause trouble for whoever buys the farm. He feels responsible for his part in breaking the curse and waking the troll."

"Yeesh, what a mess," she added. "So he actually believes there's a troll? It sounds as if someone wants him out of there, and soon."

"I agree. Cari wants Wolf to go with her to the farm. She believes in the rune stone curse and thinks he could possibly advise Pete."

"Why him?"

"Because he is a cryptozoologist and the troll is a legendary creature. Most people don't believe in such things, but she knows he has an open mind and would also want to help out Pete."

"Cari's right about my brother, he is accepting of the notion of legendary creatures. I'm sure he will be happy to go and see what's going on with Pete and his supposed troll. I'll probably see Wolfgang in a few days at my parent's place. I can explain the whole situation and then he can decide what he wants to do."

"Thanks Kyra, that would be great. I'm going to drive up to northern Minnesota tomorrow. I'll call Cari and see if she wants to ride with me and I can pick her up in Lake Geneva."

"Yeah, that sounds like a plan. I know you're worried about Pete. I'm sure that sexy blonde will be good company on the ride," Kyra said with a laugh.

"Oh, um sure," Ned answered, stammering his words.

"Hahaha, I'm just teasing you," said Kyra. "She's a really nice woman, and I'm glad she and Wolf are becoming an item."

"I wish you were coming along too," said Ned.

"Well, you never know, I might just show up. I can drive over there with Wolf. We can have a shorter visit with our parents, which is the best kind."

"Hey, I love your parents. The Kilmers are great," commented Ned.

"Yeah, they are great, in small doses. They will be gardening and canning, painting rocks and collecting driftwood for their art projects. It's what they love, but not for me," Kyra added. "Besides, I can only take so much of the folk music they constantly play. It sticks in your head for days."

"It would be great if we could all meet up in Minnesota, Kyra. I'll check on local accommodations. I don't think we want to stay on Pete's late uncle's farm."

"I'm with you there. I've met Pete. Nice guy, in his own way, but I wouldn't want to stay with him."

"I know exactly what you mean, and we haven't exactly been invited anyway."

"True. My brother's presence was requested by his lady friend, but neither one of us was."

"When we get off the phone, I'll call Cari and see what she thinks. I'll let her know that you'll be seeing Wolf soon and you two can come to the farm together, once you explain the situation to him.  I will mention that we will all be seeking local hotel accommodations."

"Okay, I'll have Wolf contact you as soon as he gets back. He can get directions to the farm and let you all know when we'll get there, that is, assuming he wants to go, which I am fairly sure he will."

When Ned finished talking with Kyra, he immediately called Cari. She was very happy to hear he was planning to drive to Minnesota and said she would be very happy to ride along. "My car is a bit iffy right now, so I would love to ride with you," she told him.

Ned said he would leave the next morning and pick her up around lunch time in Lake Geneva. Cari had made arrangements for a staff person to run her store while she was gone. She had no upcoming appointments or readings scheduled, so it was a good time to take a break and go to see her Uncle Pete.

Cari was very concerned about her uncle. If what she thought was true about the troll, Uncle Pete was in great danger. She would need her wits about her if she was to deal with the troll. He wouldn't be easily fooled and was probably quite dangerous. If he had been cursed, it was for a reason...possibly many reasons, and many deaths.

## Chapter 18: Minnesota Bound

Ned left after breakfast the next morning, and arrived in Lake Geneva just before lunch. The plan was to pick up Cari at her shop downtown. After finally finding a place to park nearby, Ned entered the shop and immediately noticed how good it smelled when he opened the door. It was a mix of light perfume and a natural scent of freshly cut grass or possibly a lemony-herb.

The shop was bright and cheery. Ned noticed the attractive arrangements of products for sale, which included numerous types of tarot cards, crystals, jewelry, books of all varieties, essential oils and even rune stones. It was very impressive.

While he was looking around, a slim, young girl with big blue eyes and long blonde hair with tinted purple streaks came out from the back room and asked if he needed any help.

"I'm actually here to pick up Cari," he told her.

She nodded politely and called softly, "Madame Carishimo, there's someone here to see you."

"She'll be right out, she's in the storage room," the girl explained to Ned.

Cari entered the store from the storage room pulling a large suitcase. Ned was again taken aback by her beauty. She was a glamorous, sultry platinum blonde, very curvy with a lovely, serene face and amazing green eyes. She had a mystical air about her, especially here in the lovely shop.

Ned had, of course, met her before, but every time her looks gave him pause. He was basically in love with Wolf's sister Kyra, who had long dark hair and was very beautiful, but this woman, well, she was one you noticed.

"Hello Ned. Thank you for picking me up," she said in a mellifluous voice. "I appreciate the ride to see Uncle Pete. As I mentioned, my car is not too reliable, and I haven't had time to get it serviced lately."

"No problem," Ned mumbled, wondering to himself how this gorgeous woman could be related to Pete. Granted, he was a nice guy, but Pete was not exactly a handsome man. Maybe he had been better looking in his younger days.

"Oh, where are my manners, this is my assistant, Sara," said Cari, gesturing toward the young girl. "She's watching over the store while I'm away. Sara, this is Ned Ferris, he is a very good friend of Wolfgang's and is also acquainted with my Uncle Pete."

"It's very nice to meet you," Sara told Ned, reaching out to shake his hand.

"You as well," he replied. The girl released his hand and disappeared into the back again.

"I'm ready to go," Cari said as she pulled her suitcase toward the door.

"Um...er...let me help you with that," Ned stammered. (Jeez, what was wrong with him?)

"Mmm.. thank you, I have another case with my rune and tarot supplies, I'll just get that and meet you outside," Cari commented with a brilliant smile.

Ned laughed uncomfortably as he rolled her case to his vehicle. What was it about that woman that made him act like a goofy teenager? He had to get over it, or the ride to northern Minnesota was going to be awkward.

Once they were settled in and on the road, Cari asked if Ned thought that Wolf would be willing to come to help out her Uncle Pete.

"Like I told you, he's meeting his sister Kyra in the Upper Peninsula to see their parents. Kyra said she will explain everything to him and if all goes well, they'll be on their way shortly after visiting with the Kilmers. I'm sure he will be happy to help in any way he can. Besides, he is always fascinated by legendary creatures, and it sounds like the troll fits that description."

"I certainly appreciate your coming along as well. Not to mention Kyra. I've only met her a few times, and I know she's acquainted with Uncle Pete, but it's very kind of her to volunteer to make the trip."

"Kyra is a great person, and cares about others," said Ned.

"I noticed that she cares a great deal for you," Cari told him.

Ned blushed and explained that they had all known each other since childhood, and he and Kyra had finally started a romantic relationship after skirting around it for years.

"You know, your names are kind of similar, Cari and Kyra. We're going to have to make sure not to get them mixed up," blabbered Ned, immediately regretting his comment.

"If you get confused you can always call me Madame Carishimo. That's the name I go by professionally. Or just Madame C."

"Oh, sure, Madame Carishimo. That's a mouthful, though." (Yeesh, another stupid comment, Ned told himself).

"You know what I think?" asked Cari.

"No, what do you think?" answered Ned.

"I think you are uncomfortable with me and you needn't be."

"You know, um...why do you say that?"

"It's just a feeling I'm getting. I think we could be good friends. You are close friends with Wolfgang, who I'm seeing socially, and you are on the cusp of a relationship with his sister. This trip will give us a chance to get more acquainted."

"Yeah, sure, that sounds good...Madame C."

The ride through Wisconsin was going along fine, and soon they were crossing the border from Wisconsin into Minnesota north of the Twin

Cities to avoid heavy traffic. The scenery was much the same...mainly farmland, but also some very scenic areas on the drive along the border.

It was late afternoon, and Cari mentioned stopping somewhere for dinner. Later on, when they were riding through a small town, she pointed at a small restaurant, and asked if that would be okay with Ned.

"Sure, it looks good to me," he said.

"Great, let's stop then," she added.

They found a booth and a waiter brought them water and menus.

Cari and Ned both ordered cokes, and looked over the large menu.

"I'm trying to decide between a cheeseburger and a hot beef sandwich with fries," said Cari.

Ned looked at her surprisingly.

"You thought I was going to order a salad, didn't you?" she asked.

"No, um...no."

"That's okay, I eat what I want, when I want. Sometimes it's healthy fare and sometimes I like a burger and fries."

"Okay," Ned replied. "I can appreciate a woman with a good appetite."

Cari ordered the hot beef sandwich with french fries, covered with lots of gravy. Ned ordered a cheeseburger and fries (no gravy.)

After finishing every delicious bite, they both ordered hot fudge sundaes.

By the end of the meal, Ned was becoming more comfortable talking with Cari, or as he now called her, "Madame C."

"You mentioned that your other case had tarot and rune supplies, what did that mean exactly?" asked Ned, scraping the bottom of his ice cream dish.

"In addition to tarot readings, I do rune reading as well. I will explain how it works to everyone when we arrive. I think it may help with guiding our way as to how to deal with the troll."

"Do you actually believe it's a troll?," he asked. "It could be someone acting as a troll to scare your uncle. Maybe to get him away from the farm."

"I have considered that, certainly, and have not ruled it out. Whether or not you believe in trolls, or think it's someone pulling tricks on Uncle Pete, it doesn't matter. Someone or something is out to harm him, and chase him off," Cari explained.

"Do I believe it's really a troll? I'm not sure what I believe, but one thing I'm sure of... Uncle Pete's in danger," she continued.

"You really think he's in danger?" asked Ned.

"I have no doubt he is in grave danger," said Kari. "Recently, I talked to my father, who is Pete's brother Viktor. My dad told me that he believes there's something treacherous on that farm, and we should get Pete out of there as soon as possible."

# Chapter 19: Kyra and Wolfgang

Kyra's plane landed at the small airport and she immediately saw her parents waving wildly at her when she disembarked. It wasn't hard to pick them out. Her mother, Jilly had long dark hair, shot through with gray, pulled back in a messy bun. Her father, Jon, had wavy blonde hair, with white streaks throughout, tied back in a small ponytail. Both of them wore "boho" style clothing, which looked quite appropriate on them. They wore it well.

"Kyra, my darling, it's so good to see you," her mother gushed. Her dad said much the same and they gathered her into a family group hug, which smelled like patchouli oil, musk and maybe a little weed.

"I can't believe it," commented Jilly. "All the Kilmer's will be together for my birthday when your brother arrives."

"Have you heard from Wolf?" Kyra asked her parents.

"No, but I'm sure he will let us know when to pick him up," her dad said.

As Kyra waited for her luggage, her phone buzzed. It was her brother Wolfgang.

"Hey Wolf, guess where I am," she said.

"Hey Kyra, I'm guessing you're at the airport in the U.P. Am I right?"

"How did you know?"

"Cuz, my plane just landed and I'm looking at you right now."

Kyra turned around and saw her brother standing there holding his cellphone and smiling wickedly. She ran toward him and he gave her a giant bear hug.

"Wait until mom and dad see you," she told him. "They are going to freak."

At that moment they heard a shriek. Lo and behold it was their mom running through the small airport in their direction. Time for another family hug.

"When did you get here, son?" Jon asked Wolfgang when the family hug was finally done.

"My plane just landed. I was going to rent a car and surprise you, and I spotted Kyra in the luggage area."

"Now you don't have to rent a car," said Jilly.

"Um...yes I do, mom. I don't want to be in the U.P. without a vehicle."

"Well, alright honey. You go and do that, and we'll see you at the Kilmer homestead in Trygghaven Bay," his mother told him.

"Do you want to ride with me Ky?" Wolfgang asked his sister.

"Yes, that would be great. We can catch up," she replied.

"You kids do your catching up. Your mother and I will stop and get some supplies for a big family birthday dinner tonight," Jon told his son and daughter.

"Oh boy, I can't wait," said Kyra, turning toward Wolfgang and rolling her eyes.

"Mmm..mm, I am ready for some home cooking," said Wolfgang winking at his sister.

As they bade goodbye to their parents and walked toward the car rental counter, Wolf leaned toward his sister whispering, "drive thru burgers?"

"You bet!" she answered.

After renting the vehicle and stopping for some fast food, Kyra and Wolfgang quickly caught up on each other's recent news.

"What do you think mom and dad are cooking?" Kyra asked, chewing on her double decker fast food burger.

"Something with unusual root vegetables and some weird, exotic seasoning," Wolfgang answered with a shrug, tipping the last of his fries into his mouth.

"Hide our dinner plates in the usual place?" she asked.

"Of course," he answered.

"Well, I have a bit of extra news to share," said Kyra.

"Oh yeah, do tell," Wolf replied.

"Ned called and told me an interesting story about Pete Magnusson and the farm he inherited in northern Minnesota."

"Pete? You mean old Pete from the bay?"

"Yeah, apparently the farm is home to...get this...a troll!"

"Did you say, troll?"

"Yep, troll."

"This I gotta hear," said Wolf.

Kyra told him the whole story of how when Pete arrived, he had been searching for coffee cans containing cash in the backyard and dug up a rune stone, read the curse out loud and apparently woke up a troll.

"That's a wild story, even to me, and I've seen a skinwalker," commented Wolf.

"I know, right? But your new girlfriend, the sexy Cari, is currently on her way to the farm with none other than our good buddy Ned."

"Ned?"

"Yep, Ned."

"So how did Ned get involved?" Wolf asked.

"Cari called him looking to get in touch with you, or leave you a message. Ned got it in his head that he would drive up there with her and he's planning on us joining them."

"In Minnesota? On the farm Pete Magnusson inherited, with a troll?"

"Yep, Minnesota, farm, Pete, troll," she answered.

"Okay, I'm in," he replied.

"I knew you would be," said Kyra. "Besides, how many days do you think we can spend with Jilly and Jon? Gardening, folk music, communing with nature. I love them, but...well you know."

"Yep."

# Chapter 20: The Farm

The rest of the trip through Minnesota went along fine. Ned and Cari listened to classic rock music and talked about nothing important. When they got close, Cari navigated, as she had very specific directions to the farm, which was located near a small village named Dalton. The road to the farm was in surprisingly good shape. It was dark by the time they arrived, and fortunately, Uncle Pete had left some outside lights on.

No sooner had they pulled up in front of the farmhouse when Pete toddled out the door, crossed the front porch and quickly made his way toward them.

"Cari, my girl, how great to see you," Pete told her, wrapping her in a bear hug.

"And Neddy Ferris, so good of you to come," he said to Ned, shaking his hand.

"Hey Pete, nice to see you again," said Ned. (Pete always called him Neddy, much to Ned's chagrin.)

"C'mon on in you two," Pete told them, gesturing at the front porch.

"I won't stay long, Pete. I have a hotel room booked and want to get checked in," said Ned, as he helped Cari with her suitcase, which she promptly took to the guest room.

"You know you can stay here, Neddy," said Pete.

"Nah, that's fine. I will probably be more comfortable in a hotel."

"Wouldn't we all," Pete replied. "This ain't exactly the Ritz, and that little bastard has started up with his mischief again."

"The troll?" Ned questioned.

"So Cari's told you about our little friend, eh? He's up to something nearly every night, as soon as it gets dark. He almost killed that kid Davey, who was just here cleaning up for me. Luckily it looks like Davey's gonna be okay."

"Well, that's good," said Ned. "You're pretty sure this is an actual troll?"

"I know it sounds crazy, but I seen it with my own eyes."

"Could it be someone disguised as a troll to scare you?" Ned asked.

"I s'pose it could be, anything is possible, but why did it start up after I read the curse out loud? If it was some kids or vandals, like I thought at first, why? Nothing has been stolen, and in fact, some stuff has been left here, in the barn. Stuff (like farm tools) that wasn't here at first, and now it is. Davey was gonna see if anyone around here was missing stuff, but...well, you know, now he's in the hospital."

"Have you seriously considered just putting the farm up for sale and leaving here now?" Ned questioned.

"Of course I have, Neddy. I'm worried that little bastard will follow me, or make trouble for someone else. If it is a troll, I feel responsible for breaking the curse and setting that thing free."

"If the menace isn't a troll, but someone trying to scare you off, then you could be in danger, Pete," Ned added.

"Yah, I thought about that too. If somebody is trying to drive me out of here, there's a reason, and I want to know what it is. This dump of a farm can't be worth much, so...why, then?"

"Do you happen to know if your Uncle Fritz ever tried to sell it?"

"Nah, he always said it was his home, and he wasn't going anywhere. He was pretty stubborn and kinda mean."

"Well, it's certainly up to you, Pete, but I would proceed with caution," Ned advised.

"Thanks Neddy, and I do appreciate your making the trip up here. I know you are a busy guy."

Cari entered the room and suggested that they all convene in the morning to discuss the situation.

"Why don't we meet for breakfast?" Ned suggested.

"Sure, there's a good place right in town, we can meet there," said Pete and gave Ned the diner's name and directions. "How about 10:00 am?"

"That would be fine," said Ned and he bade goodbye to Pete and Cari.

After Ned drove away, Cari took a seat on the old sofa and indicated her uncle should join her. She looked very serious.

"Uncle Pete, I am very worried about you. Dad said this place is treacherous."

"Yer dad always hated this farm. He didn't want nothin' to do with it, that's all," Pete told her.

"He used the word treacherous. What did he mean by that?"

"I don't know, you'll have to ask him. He never said it to me," Pete answered. "Who knows what my brother is thinking. All I know is, he said he'd never come back here and he never did. I was stuck here doing chores for Uncle Fritz all by myself until I got another summer job. Then that old miser had to fork over money to pay a farmhand."

"Have you had any late night disturbances lately?" she asked.

"Not since the incident with Davey," Pete answered. "By the way, is your new boyfriend Varg (Wolfgang) planning to come out here?"

"He's not exactly my boyfriend. We're seeing each other socially, but nothing too serious right now."

"Jeez, you young people and your expressions: 'socially' and 'not serious'. What in the hell does that all mean? You like each other - you are dating. That equals boyfriend and girlfriend."

"We're just getting to know each other, that's all."

"Okay, none of my business, anyway," Pete grumbled. "So is he coming out here or not?"    "I'm not certain. He is supposed to meet his sister and their parents out in Trygghaven Bay for his mother's birthday. They may drive out here after their visit."

"Oh yeah, the Kilmers. Nice people, but kinda flaky," said Pete with a grin.

"Uncle Pete! That's not nice at all. Please don't say anything like that to Wolf or his sister."

"I won't, don't worry. I saw Varg's sister not too long ago. She was at their parents' place with Ned. I think I interrupted something."

"Ned and Kyra are building a relationship," Cari told him.

"Building a relationship, eh? Is that what you call it now?"

"Please don't embarrass Ned by talking about seeing him with Kyra, okay?"

"I am what you would call the soul of discretion, young lady. Good night!"

"Good night Uncle Pete."

A few hours passed when there was a crashing noise coming from outside.

Cari looked out the window just as a brick was being lobbed at the house. She couldn't see anything in the darkness, and the brick hit the house alongside the window she had peered from.

Pete came running from his room, "What happened?"    "Someone threw something toward my window. I think it hit the outside wall, and just missed the window."

"Son of a bitchin' troll!" Pete shouted and hurried outside shaking his fist, with Cari close behind. As they exited the front door, they heard footsteps running away and giggling.

"Hey, Wolf, tell mom and dad more about your adventure in Colorado," said Kyra with a cheeky expression. "You never told them too much about it last time we were here."

"Oh yeah, it was exciting," he started to say, after shooting his sister a dirty look. "I ran away from a murderer, got shot and saw a Skinwalker up in the mountains."

"You are so funny," said Jilly. "I love your stories."

"I really did get shot," he told his mother. "Remember, I explained that to you last time we visited."

"Oh dear, that's terrible. It looks like you recovered well," she said with a frown.

"You got shot? Where, son?" his dad asked.

"Yes, Dad, in the leg. I told you about it the last time we were here. It's healed up nicely and the scar isn't too bad," Wolf repeated, shaking his head. His parents were very poor listeners and easily distracted. On top of that, they may have been slightly stoned.

"You have to stop taking these dangerous trips," said Jilly.

"I agree with your mother," said Jon. "What is a marine biologist doing in the mountains of Colorado anyway?"

"Remember? I was there to see a friend who told me about a creature that had been creating havoc where he was camping. Dad, you know my hobby is cryptozoology. I had to see for myself what he had described."

"So you got shot by the creature?" his mother asked.

"Of course not. I got shot by…oh never mind, it doesn't matter now."

"Did they get the shooter?" asked Wolf's dad.

"In a manner of speaking. He's presumed dead."

"Well, that takes care of that," said Jilly. "How about dessert? I made some zucchini cookies."

"Mmm…boy that sounds good, but I am too full right now," said Wolf. "I'm sure Kyra would like a couple. She barely ate any of her dinner."

"Ah…I'm trying to cut back on the sweets, mom," said Kyra, giving her brother the evil eye.

"No worries, dear. These are made without sugar, just some apple-sauce," her mother said and plopped two big greenish cookies in front of Kyra.

"I'll get you for this…" Kyra whispered to Wolfgang, pointing at the cookies.

"I'm just paying you back for bringing up my Colorado trip," he whispered to her.

"Hey mom, did you know that Wolf is dating a sexy blonde that owns a fortune telling shop in Lake Geneva?"

"Oh my, you must tell me all about her, Wolfgang," Jilly insisted.

"We're just seeing each other socially once in a while," he told his mother.

"Sexy blonde, eh son?" his dad inquired.

Kyra jumped in before her brother could reply. "Yeah dad, she does tarot reading, and that kind of thing. Her name is Cari Magnusson, but she's known on her website as Madame Carishimo. She's quite well-known in those circles."

"I've heard of her," said Jilly. "How exciting. I can't wait to meet her."

"Um...well, we're just getting to know one another," Wolf mumbled.

"Hey, I know that name, Magnusson," said Jon. "Where have I heard that name?"

"Pete Magnusson, from here in the bay is her uncle," Kyra answered.

"Hmm ... .isn't he that big man that smells like gasoline and fish? You know, Jon, the one that sits around at Garvin's lunch counter."

"Sure, I remember him," said Jon. "He likes to fish."

"He calls Wolfgang by a nickname: Varg," Kyra commented.

"I get it - Wolf in old Norse. Very clever," said Jon. "So, you say this girl is a sexy blonde and she's related to Pete? Seems unlikely."

"Can we just cut this conversation," said Wolfgang. "Maybe Kyra can tell you about how her relationship with Ned Ferris is coming along."

"Ned Ferris! Oh Kyra, we love Ned. Are you two an item?" asked Jilly eagerly.

"Mom, please. We have just been seeing each other socially once in a while. A few dates, that's all. Nothing serious," said Kyra as she reached over to punch her brother in the arm.

"I don't see why you kids can't tell us about your relationships," said Jon. "Your mother and I are open-minded. We know what goes on."

"Stop right there, dad," said Kyra. "Ew".

"Alright, alright, I won't say another word," replied Jon, holding up his hands.

"So, we should make some plans while we're all here together," Jilly said excitedly. "We have some great ideas."

"Oh yes, your mother and I have been discussing how to best spend our time together on this trip. We thought it would be interesting to take advantage of the most cherished treasure we have hereabouts...Lake Superior."

"I'm not going swimming, if that's what you're getting at," said Kyra. "That lake is freezing."

"Of course not, darling. We discovered that there's an excursion boat trip that we can take. It will bring us to...wait for it...Stannard Rock Lighthouse!"

"What!," Kyra exclaimed. "Are you kidding me right now? Do you not recall that I was trapped out there, alone, waiting for someone to come back and kill me. Why in the world would I want to go back there?"

"No dear, we aren't allowed to go on to the lighthouse, just ride around it on a boat. It's a luxury ride, and they serve lunch and cocktails. Your father and I both thought it would bring you some nice closure from that frightening event. Besides, it would be cool for the rest of us to see the lighthouse. It has a fascinating history. Do you know that it's called "The Loneliest Place in the World?"

"Yes, mother, I know that. Why don't you and dad just go?"

"We just thought it would be a fun family outing," said Jon. "The four of us can take a nice, long leisurely boat ride, have someone fix us lunch and drinks. It'll be fun, you'll see. When we were together last time, you two were much too busy with your friends to spend quality days with your parents. Besides, it's your mother's birthday and that's what she wants to do."

Wolfgang was trying not to laugh while his sister attempted to argue with their parents. "I think it sounds like a super fun day," he said, grinning at his sister.

"You know it's going to probably be cold out there," Kyra added, with a hostile stare at her brother.

"No worries, we have plenty of warm coats and things," said Jilly. "You can borrow my old wooly poncho if you want, Kyra."

"Fine, I'll go, but they better have lots of cocktails on that boat," said Kyra. "And I won't need your poncho. Wolf is going to buy me a nice, new warm jacket, aren't you dear brother?"

"Sure, sis. It'll be worth every penny."

"Wonderful, I'll make all the arrangements," Jilly said happily.

Kyra turned to her brother and whispered, "Sometimes I really hate you."

"No you don't, I'm too loveable," he replied quietly. "Besides, once we get this boat trip out of the way, then we can leave for Minnesota. You know they were going to plan some sort of family day. It could have been worse. I think seeing that historic lighthouse is very cool. In fact, it's one of their better ideas for a family outing."

"I suppose you're right. On the bright side, someone else will be providing the food, and there will be drinks," said Kyra. "When we get back from the boat 'excursion' tour, then we can explain to them that we're leaving on a trip to Minnesota, and cutting short our visit here."

"All you have to do is tell mom and dad that Ned will be there. They'll get all excited and encourage us to go."

"Dad will want you to see the sultry blonde," Kyra added. "Dad would probably enjoy meeting her too."

"Mom and dad are wonderful people, a bit flaky, and I love them," said Wolf. "But somehow I think visiting a troll might not be so bad in comparison."

# Chapter 22: Neddy

Ned woke up suddenly and realized he was in a strange bed. He soon recalled that he was staying at a hotel in Minnesota and meeting Pete and Cari Magnusson for breakfast that morning. As much as he thought of Cari as a lovely and intelligent woman, he really had his doubts about her troll story. There was more to the recent happenings than a rune stone and a supposed evil troll.

While he was showering, Ned kicked around some alternate theories in his head, none of which involved a troll or a Viking rune stone.

"There has to be a reason for someone to try scaring Pete off of the farm," he thought, trying out different theories. "His uncle was stubborn and wouldn't sell, then he died, leaving the farm to his nephew, who would logically try to sell it immediately. Pete hung on for a while to search for his uncle's stashed cash, and somebody is getting impatient."

By the time Ned finished showering and dressing, he had determined that one course of action was to find out more about Pete's Uncle Fritz and the history of the farm property. It was, in his opinion, the best place to start. As an attorney, Ned looked at situations from a more logical standpoint. He thought the troll story an interesting piece of fantasy, but doubted the existence of such a creature.

Ned stepped outside and was hit with a stiff breeze, laced with a slight tinge of dirt and cow manure. "Dairy air," he said to himself with a smile.

The leisurely walk to the restaurant gave him time to gather his thoughts on how he was going to suggest to Cari and Pete that they look into Fritz Kolbeck and the background of his farm. He didn't want them to think he scoffed at their troll theory, but to consider other alternatives.

When Ned arrived at the restaurant, Pete and Cari were already seated and waiting for him.

"Neddy! Have a seat," Pete said loudly pointing at the chair across from him at their table, which already had a menu and ice water ready.

"Thanks Pete, good morning to both of you," Ned said with a smile.

"I hope you're hungry, they serve a good breakfast here," Pete announced.

The server came to the table and Ned ordered coffee and proceeded to check out the menu. She was the same server Pete had talked to days before, named Patti.

"Say, I remember you. Aren't you old Fritz Kolbeck's nephew?" she asked Pete.

"Right little lady, that's me. You told me that my uncle came in here about once a week for lunch."

"Yes, he always ordered soup and pie. Well up until the last few times he came in, then he ordered bigger meals, like steak dinners or roast beef. He told me it was nearly time to cash in his treasure."

"Treasure?" Pete asked.

"Yep, that's what he said. I figured it was either a joke or some kind of inheritance or something. He told me that he was rich, since enough time had passed. He always talked a little crazy. No offense."

"Oh, you couldn't offend me talking about Uncle Fritz," said Pete.

"Did he have other stories that he told you?" asked Ned, and Pete shot him a questioning look.

"Sure, he had all kinds of stories. He was an older guy and sometimes older folks need to have someone to talk to. I guess he liked talking to me," explained Patti.

"Do you remember any of his stories?" Ned questioned.

"Well, there were a few times he mentioned something evil was after him or after his treasure. I'm pretty sure that was a joke."

Ned asked if there were more stories, and she continued, "Um...he mentioned FEHU - said it was a rune or something that meant wealth, abundance and luck. He told me that the FEHU finally came about after waiting so many years. I'm sorry, but that's about all I remember. He often spoke a little...oddly. Do you think he was a bit senile?"

"Er...could be," Pete mumbled. "Well, let's order. I'm getting hungry."

Cari and Ned ordered ham and eggs with pancakes on the side and Pete ordered eggs, sausage and waffles.

During breakfast, the three of them tried to determine what the treasure was that Fritz referred to. It seemed that he was holding on to a secret that may have died with him.

"Whatever this "treasure" is, could be what is valuable to the farm," said Ned.

"It's probably just his coffee cans. I think he buried quite a few of them," said Pete. "I have to wonder whether he encountered the troll too. Remember, he told Patti that something evil was after him and his treasure."

"What would a troll need with cash?" Cari wondered.

"Then the "treasure" could be just about anything," said Pete.

"I think the key to all of this lies with your Uncle Fritz," Ned replied. "I just have a feeling that he harbored some secrets, and if you can figure out what those were, maybe there's your answer."

"I guess I never thought about it that way," said Pete. "I just always considered Fritz a crabby old curmudgeon that was a bit odd. I suppose he could have been hiding something, he was secretive. If we put our heads together and search, we'll find an answer."

Pete, Kari and Ned didn't notice, but a person at a nearby table was very interested in their conversation and strained to hear what they were saying without being too obvious.

"Hmmm...it might be time for more serious action," thought the eavesdropper.

# Chapter 23: Stannard Rock Lighthouse

I t was a quiet day on the lake, the sun was warm and the breeze was light and crisp. The sun sparkled on the water like diamonds. There was a slight tinge of fish in the air, along with the fresh, clean smell of Lake Superior. Wolfgang sipped his coffee on the early morning boat trip, enjoying just being out on the lake.

Jilly and Jon Kilmer, Wolfgang and Kyra's parents, as promised, chartered a boat trip to the historic lighthouse as a family outing. Kyra had her doubts about going near the structure, as her memories of it were frightening. She had once been trapped out there by someone wanting her killed. It still haunts her.

Roughly a half hour into the trip, the amiable boat captain, Rich, regaled a good deal of the lighthouse's history to his passengers.

"The Stannard Rock light is a lighthouse located on a submerged reef (approx five miles long and about a mile wide) that was the most serious hazard to navigation on Lake Superior," he explained. "The actual rock itself is small, about the size of a couple dinner tables."

"It is located about 24 miles from the nearest land, and  45 miles from where we started.  The lighthouse, also known as the "Loneliest Place in the World" is 78 feet tall and exhibits its light at a height of 102 feet above Lake

Superior. It was built in the late 1800's. The light is currently automated, but was once manned," Rick continued.

"In 1913 the keepers were trapped inside as more than 3 feet of ice covered the lighthouse after a bad storm. It took twelve men a week to pick-ax their way through the icy exterior. Another legend tells of a worker becoming so deranged that he had to be escorted away in a straitjacket," the captain described.

"Tragedy struck in June of 1961 when an explosion of stored gasoline killed one man and injured three others. It took two days before rescue arrived, and the lighthouse was then automated a year later."

At this point, the captain paused and his "crew", a cute, friendly young man with an easy smile by the name of Marty, offered coffee and snacks. Kyra asked when liquor would be available as she accepted a cup of coffee and a fat, gooey danish.

"Anytime you want, ma'am, just ask," Marty said with a flirty wink.

The captain finished his lighthouse history, explaining that Stannard Rock is now run by the US Coast Guard and can only be viewed by plane or boat and is closed to the public. "It also has a new purpose, as scientists have equipment placed around it to measure the evaporation of the Great Lakes."

"I realize the lighthouse is closed to the public, but you know, my daughter Kyra has been on it. She was trapped there all by herself by a criminal," said Jilly.

"Oh yeah, I heard about that. So...that was you. I bet that's something you'll never forget," said Captain Rich. "I'm surprised you wanted to see it again."

"You and me both," said Kyra. "I hope you brought plenty of food and liquor on this trip," she added, holding up her coffee and danish in a mock toast.

The remainder of the boat trip was enjoyable for everyone, including Kyra, who Wolf noticed was pouring the whiskey Marty provided into her coffee.

When they arrived at the lighthouse, all of them were in awe of the structure, which was a marvel of engineering, especially for its time. It was truly amazing that the structure had survived the harsh elements of Lake Superior for so many years.  They were happy to hear that the Superior Watershed Partnership is committed to taking care of the lighthouse and is currently making an effort to restore the  historically significant site. The Kilmer family all agreed to make a donation toward the renovation. Since it would be a significant donation, a plaque with the Kilmer name etched on it will be placed on Stannard where it will live for centuries.

The boat circled the lighthouse slowly and Jon noticed the number of fishing boats around as well and asked the Captain about it. "There are trophy lake trout caught out here," said Captain Rich.

"It's been a popular fishing spot for many years. Most boats didn't have the fuel capacity to make the trip. Fishermen would take barges out here and fish off of rowboats. One of the first captains to make regular trips out here was the late Captain Dave of Kimar's Charters. He was like the "Captain" of the lake, an icon, a Lake Superior legend. He'll be missed," said Captain Rich with tears in his eyes.

As young Marty served drinks, the party toasted Captain Dave. They added another toast to the Stannard Rock Lighthouse and to Jilly, for her birthday. After a few drinks, Marty brought out some delicious appetizers to be enjoyed on the return trip, along with refills on drinks.

When the boat trip was over, even Kyra had to admit she enjoyed herself. "The lighthouse is such an amazing sight. I think seeing it again has chased away the demons," she said (a bit tipsy).

Wolfgang and Kyra agreed that they would tell their parents the next day that they were leaving for Minnesota. Their time spent with Jilly and Jon had been enjoyable so far and they wanted to depart on a good note.

The next morning, Kyra and Wolfgang stopped by Garvin's General Merchandise for some cinnamon rolls and aspirin (for Kyra). Mrs. Garvin was so thrilled to hear they would be seeing Pete soon. "We've all been worried about him," she said. "He's never been gone this long."

"We will give him your best," said Wolfgang.

"Thank you ... Varg," said Mrs. Garvin with a sly smile.

# Chapter 24: Trickery

After their huge breakfast, Ned followed Pete and Cari to the farm. It was a bright Minnesota morning, and the sun was warm, shining down from the cloudless sky. It was a shorter trip than Ned had thought, and in the daylight, the farm looked even more rundown than he expected. He was especially surprised by the enormous rock pile at the edge of the property.

Ned looked everything over carefully as he arrived. The silo, made of brick or brown tile, had seen better days. He would describe it as "rickety". The barn wasn't much better and the farmhouse looked...droopy. Who in their right mind would want this place? There was more to this story, he was sure of it.

Cari and Pete waited on the porch as Ned exited his vehicle. "Why are there holes all over?" he asked. "Is this where you dug for cans?"

"Nope, those are in the backyard, straight out from the silo," said Pete, indicating with his waving arm. "That little bastard troll keeps digging holes out front for me to trip in. Nearly busted my ankle the first time he did it."

"So, you come out here and there's holes dug every day?" Ned asked.

"Nope, not every day, and get this straight, he operates after dark. Some nights he throws rocks or bricks at the house, or piles them up, along with weeds, logs, branches, you name it, he piles it."

"He pulls tricks, then?"

"Yah, it started that way, then he dropped all that junk on Davey. Coulda' killed him with those sharp tools. That ain't tricks anymore."

"I see what you mean, but I'm going to play devil's advocate and look for other explanations that don't involve a troll. You and Cari pursue the troll angle."

"This ain't no angle son. I'm trying to find a way to get rid of it."

"I understand," Ned replied with a shrug. He felt his phone buzz in his pocket. Glancing at the phone, he said, "It's Wolfgang, hang on."

"Tell him we're waiting to see him," said Cari as she and Pete went into the farmhouse.

"Hey Ned, I hear you are in Minnesota with Cari and Pete," said Wolf.

"Yeah, we got here yesterday. There's some strange shit going on. Are you coming?"

"Yep. Kyra and I are leaving tomorrow, barring any hold up. We haven't told our parents that we're cutting short the visit, but we just saw them not too long ago, and my mom's birthday is done, so we should be good to go."

"Do you need me to book you a couple rooms? My hotel is pretty nice and they have space available," Ned offered.

"Sure, that would be great. Let me call you back after we break the news to Jilly and Jon that we're leaving. We had a family excursion boat trip to the Stannard Rock Lighthouse. Kyra got kinda drunk, and now she's a bit hungover and eating cinnamon rolls and aspirin. Tomorrow she should be fine to travel."

"The lighthouse? Wow, no wonder she got drunk."

"Yeah, but she said she is shedding her demons from her experience out there. Like closure or some shit. Hey, by the way, Mrs. Garvin sends her regards to Pete. They're all worried about him."

"Well, they should be. Someone is trying to get to Pete and I think it has to do with the farm property, oddly enough," said Ned. "The place is a dump."

"So you don't buy that there's a troll after him?" Wolf asked.

"You're the cryptozoologist, not me," said Ned. "I don't naturally assume that there's a legendary creature, but I will keep an open mind. Cari has convinced me to do so."

"How was your trip with Cari?" asked Wolf.

"She is not what you'd expect. I really like her, but she is a bit, um... let's say distracting. I mean, c'mon, the woman looks like she stepped off of the movie screen, and I had to make conversation in the car for several hours. I was kind of stumbling over words for a while."

"You'll be fine Ned. Kyra will make sure of that."

"I will be glad to see her, oh and you too Wolf. Cari said to tell you they're waiting for you."

"We will be there soon. In the meantime, get as much info as you can."

"Will do. I think there may be some history with Pete's old Uncle Fritz. He was either crazy or keeping secrets. Maybe both. See you soon, buddy," Ned stated and they disconnected.

After his phone call, Ned walked around the property, noting the areas in the yard where Pete had dug up the coffee cans. He had attempted to fill the holes back up, but it was clear to see where there had been disturbances in the dirt.

Cari came out of the farmhouse and joined Ned on his walk around the farm. Pete was taking a nap, sleeping off his hearty breakfast.

"Do you see the mounds here?" She pointed out the grassy mounds around the silo, and the one that had been disturbed. "That mound was unearthed the night that Uncle Pete read the rune stone."

Ned looked at her questioningly.

"Trolls are buried in mounds. What I find unsettling is that there are more mounds here. That could mean more than one troll. They are creatures that exist in groups or families, not loners."

"Okay, for the sake of argument, let's say there is a troll, what could have happened, how did it get here?" Ned asked.

"There are many different scenarios that could have put the trolls here. The troll(s) could have been here when the Vikings arrived. Maybe they inhabited this area and the Vikings or other explorers arrived and invaded the troll's land. They may have battled it out. According to the rune stone, the troll(s) were cursed, or the one remaining living troll was cursed, and that's the one that Pete accidentally reincarnated," Cari stated.

"Or…perhaps the one troll followed the Vikings here. He could have had an ax to grind with a particular group of explorers and ended up getting cursed into the ground," Ned contemplated.

"Nevertheless, if it does exist, how it got here or how "they" got here may never be known. Our problem is how to reinstitute the curse or somehow rid Uncle Pete of the troll."

"What is your plan?" asked Ned.

"I'm going to do a rune reading - I'll explain it to you when Wolfgang and Kyra arrive. The rune stones may give me further insight as to what we're dealing with and how to get rid of it."

"Wow, a rune reading. This is going to be interesting. How does it compare to a tarot reading? I've had a tarot reading before, but I don't remember much about it," said Ned.

"When did you have a tarot reading?" Cari asked in astonishment.

"Oh, when I was in Trygghaven Bay after my father was killed. Wolfgang and I visited a lady named Freya Saari to ask her some questions about happenings in the bay and she insisted upon it. I don't remember too much because she gave us vodka in water glasses and coffee full of bourbon."

"I know Mrs. Saari," said Cari. "She's the one that got me interested in tarot reading in the first place. By the way, you didn't eat anything at her house?"

"Unfortunately I did. Mincemeat pie that seemed old. Wolf fed his to her dog, but I couldn't because she never took her eyes off of me."

"Oh, that's too bad. I always told her I was on a special diet, so I never had to eat her cooking. So, she still has that dog Skamper?"

"Yes, at least he was still around when I was there. Mean little cuss."

"He was always friendly to me."

"Getting back to my original question, how does rune reading compare to tarot?" Ned asked.

"Tarot is a different type of divination than rune reading. Tarot answers questions and there are several ways that it can be interpreted. There's more for the eye to see on a tarot card; it's personal, more about feelings. Tarot is very complex, utilizing intuition and symbolism," she explained.

"And rune reading?"

"Runes are direct and to the point, more about life. You must understand that runes are a sacred and ancient tool. I believe they should not be trifled with. It's not a game or a Ouija board."

"I see you take this very seriously," commented Ned.

"Yes, I do."

## CHAPTER 25: NED'S SEARCH

As much as Ned appreciated Cari's commitment to tarot and rune reading, he was certain there was a less "magical" explanation for what was happening to Pete. He tried to keep an open mind regarding such things, and he had witnessed more than his share of "unusual" occurrences, but more often than not, there was a logical explanation.

Before he had taken the bar exam and  become an attorney, Ned spent a few years as a private investigator, after law school. He learned a couple things while conducting investigations, and even more from his father, a police detective. Pete and Ned sat at the kitchen table discussing the puzzle before them.

The first course of action Ned suggested, should be a more thorough search of the farmhouse, and possibly the barn and silo. He was quite sure that old Uncle Fritz had some secrets that died with him, but someone out there was privy to them. It had to involve money or something valuable; the "treasure" he referred to on his last visit with Pete.

"The land doesn't appear to have any extraordinary value," Ned noted. "The asking price for the sale of the farm is, in my opinion, kind of high, but I'm no real estate expert."

"I thought so too," said Pete. "Maybe the plan is to start high and negotiate."

"Could be. Do you know if your uncle ever considered selling the farm?"

"Not that I know of. He rarely went anywhere, and spent most of his life here. I could ask the realtor if she knows whether he ever wanted to sell."

"Is it okay with you if I start looking around the house and out-buildings? There may be some sort of paperwork or notations regarding what he referred to as his "treasure.""

"He did tell me that he was leaving me his treasure and whispered to me to "trust no one." I just thought he was being his usual self - a bit wacko."

"The server mentioned that something was after him and he did talk to her about his treasure as well. He could have meant those coffee cans with the cash. I suppose to an older man, a few hundred dollars could be a treasure," said Ned.

Cari came into the kitchen, carrying a handful of wildflowers, which she jammed into a mason jar. She caught the tail end of their conversation.

"If, as you say, there's a secret value to this property, I don't think it could be a few coffee cans. Who would even know about it, and if they did, why bother? It's not enough money to cover the price of an old broken down farm," she commented.

"You're absolutely right, Cari. Even if Uncle Fritz had buried a hundred cans, it still wouldn't equal the asking price, or even close. I don't think the incidents that have happened have anything to do with the farm sale. It has to do with the rune stone and the troll. There's nothing here of value besides a few hundred moldy  dollars buried in the yard. Uncle Fritz was a miser who was a little bit crazy," stated Pete emphatically.

"Well Pete, I appreciate your candor, but do you mind if I do a bit of searching?" Ned asked.

"Of course not, Neddy, you go on ahead and search all you want, but you ain't gonna find anything," Pete answered. "You lawyers always want an explanation for things. Yer dad was the same way, because he was a cop. Search away Neddy. Cari, come with me into the backyard and I'll show you how the rune stone has been partially dug up again."

Ned knew that Pete believed in legends. He was the person that told Ned about the legend of a giant sturgeon in Lake Superior that foretold death. His niece, the lovely Cari, made her living reading tarot cards and telling fortunes. He realized that they believed strongly that the troll was behind every odd thing that was happening here. Ned would continue searching for any evidence of Fritz's secrets while he was still here.

While Pete and Cari were looking at the stone in the yard, Ned began rifling through Fritz's old desk and kitchen drawers. Soon Wolfgang and Kyra would arrive, he thought. Ned knew his friend would keep an open mind about the existence of a mythical troll. Wolfgang was always on the lookout for a legendary creature. His sister Kyra didn't share his interest in cryptids, but she mostly kept her opinions about it to herself.

Pete walked into the living room as Ned was looking through papers. "Did you find anything?" he asked.

"Nope, just old papers so far, nothing interesting," Ned answered.

"I looked through that desk and all the kitchen drawers and dressers, but I was basically searching for cash. I did find a deck of cards with a topless woman on them. That's about as interesting as it got," laughed Pete and went back outside.

The search of the desk continued and Ned noticed that Fritz kept almost everything. The papers went back decades. It would take some time to find any reference to a monetary "treasure" if it actually existed.

The back door slammed, it was Cari and Pete returning from the backyard. Pete wandered into the bedroom for a moment and they could hear him opening the closet.

"Oh say, I forgot to tell you both something," said Pete as he toddled into the living room holding something in his hand. "There was an old tea can buried in the yard and it had this note and rune stone in it."

Pete handed the old yellowing note and the stone to Kari and Ned looked on. The note was in a language Ned didn't recognize, but Kari did.

"What does it say?" Ned asked.

"Bjarga seidh," which in Norwegian basically means 'save or protect from dark magic' Cari explained.

"It's in Uncle Fritz's handwriting. You'll recognize it from all those papers he left behind," said Pete.

"What's that stone?" asked Ned.

"It's a rune letter ALGIZ - The Elk, Protection, Shield, Ward off Evil," Cari explained, turning the stone over in her hand. "Apparently great Uncle Fritz was trying to protect himself from evil or dark magic," said Cari.

"Oh boy, your uncle sure liked to bury stuff," Ned added. "I don't suppose any reference to a treasure will be found in this house. It will probably be buried out there in the yard, or worse yet, in the farm field."

"I remember Uncle Fritz using a compass and pacing off when he was burying money cans. There could be some sort of a map indicating burial spots, but that could be anywhere or nowhere," Pete concluded.

"It might be akin to a needle in a haystack to find anything, especially if he made it out to the farm field, but if he buried everything in metal cans, why don't we try using a metal detector," Ned suggested.

"Now yer talkin' - that's a great idea," Pete agreed. "Oh, I just thought of something. I haven't checked on that kid Davey. You know the one that got hurt while he was cleaning out stuff. I gotta call and see if he's out of the hospital."

Pete returned from the kitchen after making his call and announced that Davey was out of the hospital and recovering at home.

"I gotta send him something. Flowers ain't right. What do you think?" he asked Ned and Cari.

"How about a gift basket with muffins and fruit or cheese and sausage, that sort of thing," Cari suggested.

"That's what I'll do," said Pete. "Maybe I'll take a ride into town and pick out something for him. It'll do me good to get out of here for a while.

Wait,  I just thought of something else, I don't even know his last name or where he lives. How do I send him a gift basket?"

"Who recommended him?"

"Ah...let's see, was it the lawyer or the realty lady? I can't recall. I guess I'll have to stop in and ask them both."

Ned left shortly before Pete, returning to his hotel. Cari said she was going to stick around and explore the farm further while it was still daylight.

# Chapter 26: Talia

After a brief phone conversation, Talia agreed to meet with her new "friend" again at a tavern at the edge of town in Fergus Falls. It was the same bar where they originally met a few weeks ago. It had been an evening to remember. Talia had a few drinks and her new companion had several more. What transpired that evening gave Talia an idea. It seemed quite brilliant and possibly very lucrative. With a drunken slip of the tongue, her drinking buddy let some very important and valuable information leak out, then later must have thought better of it and said it was a joke. She didn't think it was a joke.

The timing was perfect, all she had to do was make the sale happen. She had someone (a partner) all set to make the purchase, and then they could search to their heart's content. The searches she conducted yielded nothing so far, and she had to be careful not to get caught. Talia's first visit was to be a quick appraisal, nothing to make anyone suspicious. She looked in all the obvious places for a clue or a map or something, but there was nothing to be found in the house. This was not going to be easy.

She checked around the property next. Tromping around in the mud and dirt had ruined her best shoes, she had been so angry at the time that she tossed them into her car, planning to dispose of them later. Losing a pair of $300 pumps would be worth it if the ultimate prize her drunken friend blabbed about was found.

Talia wondered for a moment about the old man. His death was sudden, even though he was quite old. "Eh, no"...she thought. He was just old and died of old age, the end. After her tavern companion told her the story, she did reflect on the possibility of foul play, but ruled it out. After all, her friend (dare she say friend?) didn't know for sure what happened to the money. She figured that out all on her own.

A sudden interest in the dilapidated property would create suspicion, so she had to play this out very carefully. She didn't want to push too hard, but timing could mean everything. Through the small town grapevine, and her very own "spy", Talia found out about the niece coming to visit and then some other random friends coming too. All this news made her wonder if something had been found. A map perhaps?

When she saw all the holes that had been dug, her heart sank a little. Pete must have discovered something and was looking for the money. There were holes all over the yard and even some near the front steps. He claimed it was groundhogs or gophers or something else, but she knew better. If there had been a map, why so many holes? If the old man buried it, wouldn't a map give a more accurate location?

Whatever the situation out there was, Talia was quite sure the clock was ticking on her plans. When Pete stopped in at her office today, wanting an address, or something, she pushed him again on the property sale, and he seemed annoyed.

Now was the opportune time to meet her new "friend" at the bar and see if she could garner any more information. She had to tread very carefully, making sure not to give the wrong impression, or bring about distrust.

"Hello, it's so nice to see you again," Talia gushed.

"You as well. You are looking quite lovely this evening."

"I have ordered your drink - here it comes," said Talia, taking the drink from the server and placing it in front of her companion.

"So, you remembered?"

"Of course, top shelf bourbon, rocks. I ordered you a double to save time."

"Why, is there a hurry?"

"Oh no, not at all, but I arrived early, so I thought you may want to catch up," said Talia, taking a sip of her martini, which was mostly water. She needed to stay more sober than her comrade. She had to play this out just right.

"Well, thanks for the drink."

The evening continued on for a while, much the same. Talia tried several times to bring up the story about the money, to no avail. She was trying to be clever and it wasn't working.

Talia couldn't help but notice her companion was wearing glasses and a cap and didn't remove them. She should have been wary, but she was focused on gleaning information about the money, and it was making her impatient and foolish.

Finally, her new friend, after checking the time, bid her goodnight and left the bar. Talia was disappointed, her plan didn't work. It was sort of a desperation move and afterward she wondered if it had been wise. She showed her hand, that was stupid.

Talia finished her final drink and left the bar. Her car was parked in a corner of the parking lot and she dug in her purse for the keys. "Oh hell, where are they?"

she mumbled, searching through the large bag.

Suddenly she felt something tight around her neck, choking her. Her hands went immediately to her throat, as she struggled and tried to shout for help. Kicking her legs back and shifting her weight was beginning to work, she caught a bit of a breath before it was cruelly cut off again.

Her assailant whispered something to her before she breathed her last. "Takk Talia" (thanks Talia). "Now I can find the treasure. Too bad you can't share it with me, but it's all mine."

## CHAPTER 27: THE WOMAN IS MISSING

Returning to the hotel room was something of a relief to Ned. He couldn't help but feel, for the lack of a better word, 'odd' when he was at the farm. He was newly acquainted with Cari and didn't know Pete all that well. The whole deal was a bit strange, all that talk about rune stones and curses and buried stuff.

The strangeness was all very disconcerting to Ned, who was by nature, orderly and analytical. Ned was well-liked by his friends and clients. An attractive man, he always dressed impeccably, and carried his tall slim frame with confidence.

His best buddy Wolfgang was himself, 'movie star' good looking, but in a different way than his friend Ned. He had unruly, longish sun bleached hair and dressed for comfort, sometimes in loud, baggy shirts, board shorts and flip flops. He had been often compared to the actor who played Thor in the Marvel movies, or the one who was Aquaman. Occasionally he was mistaken for a surfer.

"Thank goodness Wolfgang and Kyra would be arriving soon," he thought. His friend Wolf was fascinated with cryptids, but he was for the most part...normal. Kyra was more in line with Ned's personality, but they all got along well, as they had since they were young.

After a good night's sleep, while contemplating breakfast at the diner or just picking up coffee, Ned thought about everything he had learned yesterday. He was certain that Pete's uncle had something else to tell them (from the grave). Ned just didn't know where to look. Before returning to the farm, he would stop at the hardware store and see if he could find a metal detector, or order one.

As he was thinking, Ned's stomach growled and he decided on the diner. It was within walking distance and the food and coffee were quite good. No lumberjack breakfast today, maybe just a couple eggs and toast. When he arrived, the same server, Patti was working and she promptly handed him a menu and water.

"Is anyone joining you?" she asked.

"No, just me, thanks," he answered, ordering coffee to start.

"Did you hear the news?" Patti asked him when she returned with his coffee.

"Um...what news?"

"Talia Hovlund is missing," she explained.

"Who is Talia Hovlund?"

"Oh, I thought you knew since you were in here with Pete yesterday. Talia Hovlund is a realtor. Actually "the" realtor here in town. She is handling your friend Pete's listing of his uncle's farm."

"Er...okay. I wasn't aware of that," Ned mumbled, wondering how this woman knew so much about everyone and everything. (Small town gossip).

"She missed a couple of appointments late yesterday, and wasn't answering her phone. The folks at her office were getting worried. The police found her car sitting on the side of the road early this morning. You know, the area where they found her car isn't too far from the Fritz Kolbeck farm. Her purse and phone were still in the car, but she was nowhere around. It's a mystery, that's for sure."

"Well, that's too bad, I hope they find her," said Ned absently and ordered his breakfast. While he waited for his food, Ned thought about the missing realtor.

Could it be a coincidence that strange incidents occurred recently at the farm, and now the woman has gone missing? Could there be a connection? It was most definitely a possibility. Oh, well, it could be that she had car trouble or a health emergency and left her purse and phone behind. There were many scenarios that had nothing to do with the listing of an old rundown farm. He would give Pete the news when he returned to the farm today.

"I must be spending too much time with my dad's old cop partner, Harry Chan," he thought. "I'm finding crime around every corner."

After breakfast, Ned stopped at the hardware store in town. The owner said he would have to order the metal detector, but it should only take a couple of days.

It seemed like the man was very interested in why Ned wanted a metal detector, but was too polite to ask.

"Here's my phone number, if you would call me when it arrives, I would much appreciate it," said Ned, handing him his card.

"Sure, no problem," he answered, glancing at Ned's business card. "Chicago lawyer, eh. What brings you to our little burg?"

"I'm just visiting a friend," Ned answered, instantly regretting handing out the business card.

"Hey, did you hear the news about our local realtor Talia Hovlund?"

"Yes, as a matter of fact, I did. I just came from the diner."

"Oh yeah, Patti would have known about it. I sure hope they find her."

"Yes, me too," Ned replied distractedly as he exited the store, again wondering what happened to Talia Hovlund. His curiosity was getting the best of him. The entire situation was puzzling.

Lost in thought, Ned drove to the farm, nearly passing up the turnoff while trying to determine where the missing woman's car had been found.

Patti had told him that Talia Hovlund's car was located somewhere near the Kolbeck farm, but he didn't see any indication of a recent police presence anywhere.

When Ned arrived at the farm, he saw Cari near the silo looking closely around the perimeter. It appeared as if she had found something, she was pointing at the ground, shouting and waving to Pete, who was standing on the porch.

Ned hopped out of the vehicle and walked toward Kari, along with Pete.

"What's going on?" asked Pete. "You're waving like your pants are on fire."

"Look, it's a shoe, a woman's expensive dress shoe," said Cari pointing at a high heeled, shiny, beige shoe. "I don't think it has been here too long. There is a little dirt on it, and the heel is broken."

"Hey, that looks kinda like one of them fancy high heeled shoes that the realtor lady was wearing when she visited last time. What's it doing out here?" Pete asked as he reached down to pick up the shoe. "Busted heel," he pointed out.

"Is her name Talia Hovlund?" asked Ned.

"Yeah, I went by her office and talked to her yesterday afternoon, to see if she had Davey's address. She didn't know it and was in a big damn hurry to get somewhere. Got kinda pushy with me about the farm sale, too. Hey, how did you know her name?" Pete questioned, turning the shoe over in his hand.

"I just heard some news from Patti at the diner and the guy at the hardware store. Talia Hovlund is missing. They found her car near here, with her phone and purse inside, but no sign of her anywhere."

"Sumbitch," said Pete. "Things are gettin' crazy."

# Chapter 28: Wolfgang and Kyra

The trip from Upper Michigan to Minnesota was taking longer than Kyra expected. She still hadn't quite gotten over her hangover from the boat trip and it was making her grumpy. Her brother was driving way too slow.

"Can you speed it up grandpa?" she asked Wolfgang.

"No, I have the cruise control set for five miles over the speed limit and that's where it is going to stay. I don't want to get a ticket with my out-of-state plates. Some of these small towns are speed traps."

"You won't get a ticket," she answered.

"How do you know?"

"Because you have never gotten a ticket."

"Unlike you, sis. How many speeding tickets have you gotten?"

"A few. Most of them were not my fault. I was just going along with the traffic."

"Okay, I'll go a little faster, but if I get a ticket, you are paying for it."

"Hey Wolf, let's stop in the next town for lunch. I'm hungry."

"Again?"

"Yes...again. What is your problem?" Kyra snapped.

"No problem - I'll stop in the next town. Do you want fast food, or should we go inside somewhere?"

"Inside. I need to get out of this car."

"Remind me to never spend time with you when you're hungover. You are a crab."

"I'm not hungover and I'm not crabby."

"Okay. If you say so, but I don't blame you for drinking so much on the boat, since you had to face the lighthouse and all the frightening memories."

"Thanks for understanding, but I'm not hungover...much."

A short while later Wolf pulled into a popular chain restaurant that had good sandwiches and salads, not to mention desserts. He knew his sister, and she would want all three.

After Kyra and Wolfgang looked at the ponderous menu, he settled on a piled high ham and cheese sandwich with fries and a salad. Kyra decided on a double decker cheeseburger, onion rings and coleslaw. She put her hand on the server's arm and said, "We will want dessert later."

"So, brother, how long until we reach the land of the Vikings?" Kyra asked between bites of her burger.

"We should be there in about three hours," he answered.

Kyra looked at the fat onion ring in her hand that she had dipped in spicy ranch dressing, contemplated it for a moment, then bit it in half.

"You'll still have onion breath, but Ned won't care," Wolf said, reaching for one of her rings.

"Very funny, and stay away from my onion rings," she told him and grabbed some of his french fries.

"I always thought you were such a healthy eater," said Wolf.

"Not when I have a hang...um...not today," Kyra answered, waving the server over to order ice cream cake covered in hot fudge.

The remainder of the trip was quiet, as Kyra slept through most of it.

"Hey sis, according to the GPS, we'll be arriving at the farm in about fifteen minutes. Do you want to brush your hair or eat a mint?" he joked.

"Ha ha, very funny. Do you have any mints or gum?" she asked, pulling down the car mirror and fixing her hair and checking her make-up.

"In the console, help yourself," Wolf told her.

While Kyra fixed herself up, Wolfgang was taking in the landscape. Farm fields that had been plowed over, and others with acres of something growing in them. The roadside ditches were partially filled with brackish water and yellowing plant life.

"There's pretty much just farmland around here," he said, mostly to himself because he knew his sister wasn't listening. "Reminds me of Wisconsin."

"Hey, maybe you better eat a mint too," Kyra said. "Your sexy girlfriend is there - waiting for your arrival."

"I thought you liked Cari."

"I do like her. She's just...well you know, extraordinarily sexy and good looking and it's a bit unsettling. Hard to believe she's related to Pete. I mean, he's a nice man and everything, but there's no family resemblance."

"I heard that her father, Viktor (Pete's brother) is (or was) a handsome young man and his wife (Cari's mother) is very attractive as well. Pete was probably more of a looker when he was younger."

"I suppose you're right about that. We never knew Pete when he was a young man, or even saw a picture of him. It's not that he's bad-looking; just normal, I guess, and she is really something else."

"You are hung up on looks, sis."

"I am not that shallow. I'm just saying what everyone else is thinking."

"I'm not thinking anything like that," said Wolf. "Cari is an interesting, exciting and intriguing woman and I enjoy spending time with her. She just happens to be very attractive in an exotic sort of way."

"Yeah, that's for sure," said Kyra, popping another mint.

The road to the farm was just ahead and both Kyra and Wolfgang were anxious to arrive. They were surprised at the dilapidated condition of the place and both commented on it.

"Why would anyone want to buy this so badly that they were trying to chase Pete away?" questioned Kyra.

"Good question. Maybe it's superior farmland and someone wants a project. You know, fixer-upper type of deal," Wolf replied.

As they pulled up in front of the farmhouse, Ned, Cari and Pete all came out to greet them.

Wolf and Cari hugged, then Pete walked up to shake Wolf's hand and pat his shoulder. "Varg, my friend, thanks for coming."

Ned hung back a bit and then went in for a hug with Kyra. "Good to see you again," he said, then turned to Wolf. "Both of you."

"Come in the house and we can fill you in," said Pete. "Things are gettin' outa hand around here."

A questioning glance from Wolfgang was answered with a nod from Ned. "He's right, things are certainly getting out of hand."

As they entered the farmhouse, Pete gestured with open arms. "Welcome to the Kolbeck farm, such as it is. Since arriving here I've found old coffee cans buried with cash inside, a racy deck of cards, a rune stone, a lady's shoe and a crafty little son of a bitchin' troll!"

"It sounds like a scavenger hunt," commented Kyra.

"Oh, you don't know the half of it," Pete added. "I've fallen into holes, had rocks thrown at me, a kid I hired to clean up the silo nearly got killed by a bunch of farm tools that fell on him and found out my uncle may have had more secrets than a politician."

"Well, I can't wait to hear more," said Wolfgang.

"There's more," said Ned. "The realtor that's handling the listing of the farm has turned up missing, and we found one of her shoes out by the silo."

"Uh oh," said Kyra and Wolfgang in unison.

# Chapter 29: Getting the News

Pete apprised Wolfgang and Kyra of all that had occurred, some of which they already knew, regarding the discovery of the rune stone, and the possible presence of a legendary troll.

"Pete, my friend, this has been a lot to digest," said Wolfgang. "Do you feel safe staying here at the farm? Maybe you and Cari should also get rooms at the hotel in town."

"Nah, I ain't gonna let no stinkin' troll chase me away," Pete answered with a dismissive wave. "What about you Cari?" he asked.

"Nah, I ain't either," she answered with a wink and a grin. "I'm here to help Uncle Pete either get rid of the troll, or discover what else it could be. I can't do that in a hotel room."

"You and your sister go get checked in at the hotel and come back out here tomorrow," Pete insisted. "Ned can show you around town. Get some rest and meet here in the morning. Mebbe stop in at the diner for breakfast and see if the server Patti has heard any news about that Talia lady. You can bring me a cinnamon roll or two. They're not as good as Ginny's, but they ain't bad."

"Tomorrow I will show you all how to do a rune reading. I think that will be the first step toward getting rid of the troll, if that's possible. We'll show you the rune stone that Uncle Pete found. He buried it again, but it's been partially dug up."

"Aren't you concerned that someone may remove it?" asked Kyra.

"No. I don't believe anyone is aware of its existence besides us," Cari answered. "Besides, it would take some effort to dig up and remove. Anyone doing so would be noticed."

"But you said it had been partially exposed. Someone did that unnoticed," Kyra added.

"Only a small portion of the stone is visible. It would take a lot more digging to get it out. Right Uncle Pete?"

"Yah, took me a good while to get that out of the ground, and I had to hoist it into a wheelbarrow. If anyone tries to remove the stone, we'll know it."

"Well, okay then, we'll see you in the morning," said Ned.

"Kyra, why don't you ride into town with Ned, and I'll follow," Wolfgang suggested. "We've been traveling together all day and could probably use a break from each other."

"Yeah, he says I'm crabby, can you believe that?" said Kyra.

"Not possible, Wolf. Your sister is never crabby," Ned replied as the three of them bid goodbye to Pete and Cari.

On the ride into town, Ned explained to Kyra his doubts about the actual existence of a troll, and what scenario he felt was more likely. "There's some unknown value to the farm and these incidents are attempts made by real people (not legendary creatures) to chase Pete away and get him to sell the farm sooner rather than later."

Kyra agreed, but said she felt like more of an impartial observer, as it really was none of her business. "I'll try to keep my opinions to myself, unless they're backed up by facts. That is, unless I get a look at the troll, then all bets are off."

Wolf and Kyra got checked into their rooms and said good night to Ned. They planned on an early morning breakfast at the diner and hoped to find out more about the missing Talia Hovlund.

The hotel bed was very comfortable, but Wolfgang had a hard time getting to sleep. His brain was working overtime contemplating all that he had heard. He knew Ned was skeptical about the troll, as he expected Kyra would be as well. Wolf, however, was not so skeptical. He had seen things over the years that renewed his belief in legendary creatures; a true cryptozoologist. It was in his nature.

Over the years, he had seen firsthand: a giant sturgeon, a wolf-like beast and a skinwalker. None of those creatures, in his opinion, were faked, but others would most certainly disagree. He couldn't prove their existence, but he believed they did exist. He was acquainted with other cryptozoologists that had seen things that could not be easily explained away. "Seeing is believing."

Wolf was anxious to see what Cari had planned with the rune reading. Her broad-mindedness was what first attracted Wolf to her. She was a woman of mystery. From the time they first met, quite by accident and she referred to him by a name Pete had called him: "Varg", he was intrigued. He found out later that she was Pete's niece and put it together. Varg is the old Norse word for Wolf and she had figured it out when her uncle mentioned "the boy with all the hair."

For most of his life, Wolf had been somewhat of a loner. He had friends and family that he cared about, but with Cari he could share his unusual hobby of studying cryptids and she didn't judge. In fact, she was fascinated by it. He didn't know what (if anything) the future held for them, but for now it was fun. He wondered if she knew what their future was; after all, she did tell fortunes for a living.

"Hoo boy, my brain is working overtime," thought Wolf. He got up and turned on his laptop and began to research trolls, Viking runes and the history of this part of Minnesota. Of course, the Kensington Rune Stone came up, and the possibility of Vikings or other Scandinavian explorers searching this part of North America.

Finally, sleepiness won over and Wolf shut the laptop and fell asleep.

The sharp buzz of his phone woke Wolf from a deep slumber. He reluctantly picked it up, noticed it was Ned calling and mumbled hello.

"Breakfast in a half hour?" Ned asked brightly.

"Um...make it forty five minutes," Wolf answered and clicked off. He stumbled to the shower and vowed to get to sleep earlier and not do research so late.

Awakened and refreshed, Wolf met Kyra and Ned in the hotel lobby. The three of them walked the short distance to the diner discussing breakfast choices.

The regular server, Patti, was not the one who seated them, but Ned noticed she was working, just waiting on other customers.

After leaving them with water and menus, the other server chatted with Patti and left the dining area. Hopefully Patti would take over and they could ask her if she knew any more information on the missing realtor.

As luck would have it, minutes later Patti approached their table with her notepad and a coffee pot. "Are you ready to order?"

"Yes, thank you Patti," said Ned. All of them wanted coffee. Kyra ordered fruit and oatmeal, Ned and Wolfgang chose pancakes with sausage.

After Patti had written down their orders, and poured coffee, Ned asked if she had heard anything new about the disappearance of Talia Hovlund.

"I haven't heard much, but apparently one of the last people to see her was your friend Pete. I think the police are going out to the farm to ask him some questions. Have you talked to Pete yet?" she asked eagerly.

"Um...no, not since last night," Ned answered.

"Do you folks know Pete?" she said, turning to Wolfgang and Kyra.

"Yes, we do," answered Wolf.

"Say, aren't you somebody from the movies?" she asked Wolf.

"Nope, no movies," said Wolf.

"That's too bad. You look like a celebrity, I just can't think of who. Hmm... Oh for corn sakes, I haven't put your order in yet," Patti added, hurrying away with a quick apology.

"Does that ever get old - being mistaken for Thor or Aquaman?" questioned Ned.

"Very funny and yes it is a little disconcerting. I think it must be the hair," Wolf answered.

"Maybe you should get yourself a haircut," Kyra commented.

"Nope, not gonna happen. Perhaps just a trim," said Wolf, smoothing his wavy blonde tresses.

"So, I wonder what the police are going to ask Pete?" Ned wondered.

"Since he was possibly the last person to see her, maybe she mentioned where she was going. Remember Pete said she was in a big hurry when they spoke," said Kyra.

"They also found that shoe. Pete thinks it could be one of her shoes, but he's not sure," added Ned. "The heel was broken. That could mean any number of things."

"The question is, was she wearing those shoes when she disappeared?" Ned asked. "If in fact it is her shoe, and not someone else's."

"You don't think they could suspect Pete of anything?" Kyra asked.

"No, he hardly knows her. The shoe turning up by the silo is weird though," said Ned chewing on his lip.

"What shoe?" asked Patti, who had suddenly turned up at the table with their breakfast order.

"Oh, Pete just found a shoe near the silo at the farm. We don't know who it belongs to," Kyra answered as Patti handed her a bowl of oatmeal and another of fruit.

"Do you think it could be one of Talia's shoes?" Patti asked excitedly.

"Probably not," said Ned. "Who knows how long that shoe has been there. Maybe some animal carried it there."

Patti quickly put the plates and syrup on their table and rushed off.

"Uh oh, I think we started the gossip mill," said Kyra. "She sidled up to the table so quickly, I didn't notice."

"It's probably nothing anyway," whispered Ned. "But to be on the safe side, we shouldn't discuss anything else here in the diner."

"I guess we'll find out more when we head out to the farm after breakfast," said Wolf, digging into his pancakes.

The three of them rode out to the farm together, anxious to discover what the police wanted with Pete.

"What is it about small communities and gossip in restaurants?" Kyra wondered. "In Trygghaven Bay, visiting the Garvin's lunch counter is like a news report."

"Restaurants, diners, lunch counters, coffee shops and bars are all places where people gather and talk, particularly locals, so it's just natural, I guess," Wolf stated.

When they arrived at the farm, they saw two police department vehicles parked in front, and an officer was heading toward the silo, leading a big dog on a leash.

"Oh shit," said all three of them in unison.

# CHAPTER 30: FOR PETE'S SAKE

Wolf, Ned and Kyra hurried toward the farmhouse. Cari opened the door for them and ushered them inside. She gestured toward the kitchen, where Pete was talking with a police officer over cups of coffee. When they walked into the kitchen, Pete was shaking his head at the officer, then stopped suddenly.

"Hey, did you bring the cinnamon rolls?" Pete asked loudly.

"Right here," said Kyra, handing him a white bag.

"Officer Larsen and I are having a little discussion about that missing realtor lady. I think we could use a couple rolls with our coffee," said Pete.

Pete introduced Kyra, Wolfgang and Ned to the officer, explaining to him that they were friends of his from Michigan.

"Having some kind of a little reunion here folks?" he asked, his eyes narrowing with suspicion.

"Something like that," Wolf answered. At that moment Cari walked up to him and gave him a kiss on the cheek and quickly glanced at her uncle.

"Ah...Wolfgang here is my niece's, um...I guess you could say boyfriend," Pete explained to the officer. "And Kyra here is Wolfgang's sister and her um...er... boyfriend is Ned over there," he added.

"Oh, okay. I got it," said Officer Larsen. "As I explained to Pete, we think he may have been one of the last people to see Talia Hovlund, at least that we know of. The office manager said you two had "words". We are trying to determine where she was going when she disappeared. The two appointments she had scheduled were nowhere near the area where her vehicle was found."

"Like I told the officer here," said Pete. "She was in a big dang hurry and all I wanted was Davey's last name and his address to send him the gift basket. She put me off and said I needed to make up my mind about the farm. I told her not to pressure me. I guess those were the 'words' that girl was talking about. We didn't have an argument, she just ignored my question about Davey's last name and address and bugged me about the farm again, that's all," explained Pete.

"I ended up having to go ask the lawyer, Korhonen, for Davey's information. I guess he was the one that had recommended Davey, or now that I think about it mebbe it was that snobby auction fellah, Dwight Taylor. I can't remember. Anyway, long story short, the lawyer's secretary gave me Davey's last name (Connor) and his address," Pete continued.

"Speaking of Davey, he is recovering well at home, but he can't recall much of anything; at least not yet," Officer Larsen explained. "Getting back to the shoe found near the silo, you said it appeared to be a similar type of shoe that Ms. Hovlund was wearing when she visited here last," Officer Larsen said to Pete.

"Yup, it sure looked like the same shoe, but what do I know about fancy ladies shoes? I was wondering why she would wear pricey high heels to trudge around the farm. They looked expensive and not very practical."

"Officer Andersen, my partner, is part of the K-9 unit, and he has his dog (Bear) out there sniffing around, just in case there's anything else to find," he stated.

Pete related to everyone that both of the officers had been here days before when the young man Davey had been injured in the barn. "This is the most I've ever talked to police in my life, other than yer dad, Neddy."

He turned to Officer Larsen and briefly explained that Ned's father Jake had been a police detective and was also a friend of his.

"Funny thing is, I don't even live here, I'm just here temporarily since Uncle Fritz died and now the shit's hittin' the fan and I'm caught in the middle of it."

"I'm sorry to have you troubled with all of this, Mr. Magnusson, but we're quite anxious to find Ms. Hovlund."

"Of course you are, and no need to apologize. I sure hope you find the lady soon, and I'm happy to help however I can," said Pete before taking a big bite of his cinnamon roll. "I just wish I had more to tell you," he added between bites, wiping the sticky frosting from his hands.

Moments later, Officer Andersen returned. He and Bear hadn't found anything else near the silo or leading away from it.

"We'll be on our way, Mr. Magnusson," said Officer Larsen. "Please let us know if you think of anything else that could be helpful. Thank you for your time."

"Sure thing," said Pete. "Any time."

As the officers drove away, Pete sighed and dropped to the saggy old couch in the living room. "I wish I'd never come here at all," he said. "I shoulda just put the farm up for sale and collected the money."

"It's too late for that, Uncle Pete," said Cari. "You're here now and we're all here to help. I'm sure that the missing lady will be found, and it won't have anything to do with the farm sale."

"Let's hope so, Cari," Pete answered. "I'm more worried that it has something to do with that little bastard troll." He paused for a moment and looked at Cari.

"We didn't tell the police, because they wouldn't believe us anyway, but the troll showed up last night. I saw him and so did Cari. It was dark, but we noticed him moving around the silo and he was carrying a sickle. I couldn't say for sure, but in the moonlight it looked like it might have had blood on it."

Ned, Kyra and Wolf were wide-eyed with shock by what he had said.

"You know the worst part. When he saw us looking at him, he stared back at us with an ugly grin and giggled."

# Chapter 31: Rune Reading

The story Pete and Cari told startled both Wolf and Ned into silence. Kyra was saying over and over again that they should get out of there right away.

"I know what you mean, it's kind of shocking," said Cari. "Maybe you're right. We're okay during the daytime, trolls only come out when it's dark. The problem is, if we're going to get rid of it somehow, we have to find out where it lives during the day."

"What are you suggesting?" Ned asked.

"One of us follows it after it comes out at night - to see where it goes."

"Then what?" Wolf questioned.

"We trap it and curse it back to kingdom come," Cari explained. "I think I may have an idea how to do it."

"If it isn't an actual troll, but a real person, then what good would a curse do?" Kyra asked.

"In that case, we'll find out what or who it is, trap it and then call the police and let them handle it, and leave this place behind."

"Works for me," said Wolf.

"I'm going to do a rune casting. I will explain rune reading to you all, come up with a curse and then we make a plan," said Cari and she excused herself and left the room. Moments later she returned, holding a small velvet pouch in one hand and a plain white cloth in another.

"Ned and I briefly discussed rune casting, and will tell you all about it as well. I take this very seriously. Rune casting is an ancient and sacred tool, not a frivolous game. If you are skeptical, I completely understand, but please believe that it is meaningful to me."

Kyra nodded and turned to Cari, using her professional name. "Should we leave the room Madame Carishimo?"

"It's not necessary," said Cari. "Unless this makes you uncomfortable."

"No, no, not at all," Kyra replied. "I promise, I will try to keep an open mind and a closed mouth."

"Same here," said Ned.

"Please continue," Wolfgang added. The room became silent as Cari spoke.

"Runes are an ancient form of oracle used by those seeking advice, dating back to ancient use by Germanic and Nordic tribes. The word rune simply means secret or mystery. The runic alphabet used on runes (the oldest) is known as the "Elder Futhark" which contains 24 runes. Each rune symbol, being a letter of the runic alphabet, also has symbolic meanings. The intention behind each symbol is relevant," she stated.

"When the rune is cast - it is not fortune telling. The idea behind how the runes work is that you first think about an issue or even ask a question; focusing your conscious and unconscious mind. The runes cast are not just random, but are choices made by your subconscious," Cari explained.

"Doing a rune reading is not about seeing the future or definitive answers. It's about looking for possible causes and effects and seeing potential outcomes."

Cari very carefully placed the small white cloth on the table. "I will concentrate and ask the runes about our situation," Cari said. "The runes are about life, direct and to the point." She told them she would do a three rune layout. If the stones were upside down, they would indicate a negative tone.

"I'm doing a three rune layout utilizing the concept of "Wyrd" - actions affect the past, present and future, they are interconnected," she began.

"The Norns" in Norse Mythology are the goddesses of fate. The first Norn, weaves the "Wyrd" destiny, the second spins it, the third finishes it - the fulfillment. The Norns are more powerful than the gods in Norse mythology because the gods are subject to fate," Cari continued. "The Norns are weavers of fate itself.  Three sisters: Urd, (past) Verdandi (present) and Skuld (future), aged gray haired hags respected by all for their immense power."

While Cari continued her explanation, the room became eerily soundless, but for her mellifluous voice explaining the three sisters that lived beneath the world tree, weaving the tapestry of fate. Everyone in the room could not help but be impressed by her knowledge of Norse mythology.

The others remained quiet as Cari held on to her velvet pouch and focused on her question for the runes. Her face was a mask of calm. After a few moments, she shook the pouch, then reached in and chose one stone at a time. The stones were amethyst, each with a different rune symbol etched upon it.

The first stone she picked from the pouch was placed to the right side of the cloth. That stone would represent the situation or issue. The symbol looked somewhat like the letter P. The rune was THURISAZ (Thorn) Reactive Force, Danger, Defense, Conflict. She quietly contemplated the stone.

Cari then pulled the second stone out of the pouch, which she placed in the center of the cloth. It represented the obstacle or challenge. The symbol looked somewhat like the letter N. The rune was HAGALAZ (Hail) Wrath of Nature, Destruction, Uncontrolled Forces. The casting of that stone gave her pause.

The third stone she selected from the pouch was placed on the left hand side representing a possible course of action that could be taken. The rune looked like the letter M. The rune was EHWAZ (Horse) Harmony, Teamwork, Trust, Loyalty, Friendship, Movement, Progress. Cari slightly nodded her head when EHWAZ was revealed. She looked to her Uncle Pete, who smiled at her.

"It seems as if we already have our friends with us, Uncle Pete. They are here to help, just as the runes have indicated," said Cari quietly, and explained the rune reading's significance to everyone.

"I have a plan I am working out in mind," said Cari. "Give me a little time to think about it and do a bit more research, then I'll go over it with everyone."

The group agreed to trust Cari's instincts and give her time to mull over what the rune casting indicated to her.

Ned thought quietly about some research he was going to do himself that had little to do with runes or trolls. He would discuss it with Kyra later on. In the meantime, he would be supportive and keep his mouth shut.

# CHAPTER 32: DIGGING UP THE STONE

Pete suggested they all take a look at the rune stone he had discovered in the backyard. It was only partially exposed, but some of the runes etched on it were visible.

"Should we dig it up again?" asked Wolfgang.

"I don't suppose it could hurt," answered Pete. "That ugly little sumbitch is still out there somewhere. Reading the curse and burying the stone again sure didn't get rid of him."

"You know, Pete, I didn't realize how knowledgeable you were in Norse mythology, and runes. It must be quite difficult to read all this," said Wolf as he stooped to brush dirt away from the exposed portion of the large stone.

"Yah, my brother Viktor and I were fascinated by Vikings and everything Norse. I have studied it all of my life. I am quite versed in Norwegian and Old Norse as well."

"I know you corrected me regarding the nickname you gave Wolfgang," said Kyra. "I told him that the word for Wolf in Norwegian was Ulv, and Varg was in actuality Swedish for Wolf. Pete then explained to me that in old Norse, the word for Wolf is Vargr (or warg) like the wolf Fenrir from the battle of Ragnarok."

"I'm impressed you remembered all that, young lady," Pete said to Kyra.

"Oh, I won't forget that conversation…ever," she replied.

"Varg is preferable to "that boy with all the hair," laughed Cari.

"It was quite a surprise when I went into her shop," said Wolfgang. Cari (or Madame Carishimo as she's known there) did a tarot reading for me, which was quite accurate by the way. When I was leaving, she called me Varg. You could have knocked me over with a feather. I didn't know at the time that she was Pete's niece."

"I wasn't completely sure it was you, but I remember Uncle Pete talking about 'that boy with all the hair' that he nicknamed Varg. I took a chance," Cari said. "I'm sorry for the subterfuge, but I couldn't resist."

"It's a small world," said Ned. "Your shop is in Lake Geneva and Wolf's friend Ron lives there. Maybe you were meant to meet."

"We could have met in Trygghaven Bay," said Cari. "I do visit Uncle Pete there now and then."

"You haven't visited me in quite a long time, my girl. You and your parents should come to the lake," Pete commented.

"You're right Uncle Pete. I will tell mom and dad that we must visit the bay very soon."

"I haven't talked to Viktor in a long time," said Pete. "I regret that we haven't kept in touch regularly over the years. He went his way and I went mine. We talked a bit after our mother died, but not too often since. I think it's about damn time we reconnected."

"Did you have a falling out?" Kyra asked guardedly.

"No, not at all.  We are just very different people. He prefers the city and traveling around the world. I like my life in the bay, visiting with my friends and fishing," Pete replied.

"You know, dad would probably enjoy some time spent out on the lake with you Uncle Pete. You may both find out that you're not so different after all."

"Maybe you are right, Cari. When this is over, I'm calling Viktor and we are going to set aside some time to spend together," Pete told his niece.

"So...getting back to this rune stone partly buried here...should we dig it up again and you can explain what it says and how it is significant," said Wolfgang.

"Sure thing Varg. This time I'll let you young folks dig that stone out. It's fairly large, about the size of a small gravestone. It wasn't easy for me to dig that thing out the first time."

"No worries, Pete, we'll get it out of there," said Wolf.

"There's a couple of shovels leaning up by the side of the silo that you can use," Pete told them. "I will go get the wheelbarrow for you," he added as he toddled off to the barn.

Wolfgang and Ned went to grab the shovels and Cari was taking a closer look at the exposed stone, brushing dirt away from it and telling Kyra what the first symbols meant.

"It's a little hard to explain in exact words, but it starts out roughly, "Ten comrades of Scandinavian warriors did battle with the evil troll enemies in the darkness. FIghting to the death. One most evil troll survived.""

"That's where it drops off, I can't see anymore until they dig it back up. Uncle Pete read the rest of it to me when he first discovered the stone. I've committed it to memory. It's basically those who etched the stone, cursing the evil one to death, or barring that, permanent sleep."

"So are you sure it's a troll?" asked Kyra.

"Yes the curse calls the evil one a troll, of many trolls. I suspect, since there's more than one mound near the silo, that there was at one time more than one troll, and the Vikings encountered them and had some sort of battle. The remaining troll has taken revenge on those Vikings left alive. For some reason they weren't able to kill or destroy it, so that's where the curse came in," said Cari.

"What I'm telling you is a lot of guesswork, but that's how I translate it," she added.

"Do you think there are trolls buried in those mounds by the silo? What if they were all cursed and can somehow return?" Kyra speculated.

"You're right, it could be more than one troll, but according to the stone, only one was cursed. At least I think that's what it meant. I assumed the others were dead or destroyed somehow. Again, this is purely conjecture, but what I have seen and heard tells me I may be on the right track."

At that moment, an eagle flew very close to Cari's head, made an odd whistling noise that sounded like laughter, then disappeared.

"Good, it saw me," mumbled Cari.

"What?" Kyra asked.

"The eagle. Trolls are shapeshifters, one of the creatures it can shift into is an eagle. It must be seeking something out for it to fly during the daytime. We're getting close," she said.

"O...kay," Kyra replied, trying not to roll her eyes.

"Don't worry, I know this sounds unbelievable to you, but I know what I'm talking about."

"Sure," said Kyra with a doubtful expression. "I'm sorry if I seem, well, you know, skeptical."

"Please don't concern yourself. I am used to it in my line of work. You and Ned should continue your investigation into Fritz. That could most certainly be valid."

"Um...how did you know?" asked Kyra in surprise.

"I just knew. Like I said, it could be valid. Great Uncle Fritz had secrets, and didn't trust anyone. Oh look, here comes Ned and Wolf with the shovels. Let's get this stone out and you will witness something truly amazing."

Kyra was already amazed. Her next thought was to immediately get her camera. Although she was still very skeptical, it would be worthwhile to get photos of the stone. It could be a piece of history.

Wolfgang placed his shovel off to the side of the stone very carefully, so as not to damage it. As he pushed the shovel into the dirt, they heard a shouted swear word from the barn, followed by a loud crashing noise. Pete!

# Chapter 33: Trouble

Wolfgang and Ned ran quickly to the barn, followed closely by Cari and Kyra. They discovered Pete lying on the floor. He was holding a hand to his face and his head was bleeding.

"Damn bird, flew right at me," Pete mumbled as he wiped blood from his face and struggled to sit up.

"Hold on Pete, take it easy, we'll help you up," said Wolf as he and Ned rushed to assist the big man to his feet.

"Help me get to the house, would you?" said Pete. "That eagle might come back."

Ned and Wolfgang supported Pete on either side and helped him into the farmhouse. They carefully guided him to the couch and Pete dropped to the old sofa with a grunt and a sigh. Cari ran ahead to get the first aid kit and Kyra went to the kitchen for a towel.

"What happened out there?" asked Wolf. "We heard you shout."

"I was looking through the barn and noticed things had been moved around again. Suddenly I heard a weird sound, like a high pitched whistle, then this great big eagle flew at my face. I bet it had at least a seven foot wingspan. I put up my arm, but it caught me on the side of my forehead, and that's when I fell down. It all happened so fast."

"Do you want to see a doctor, Uncle Pete?" asked Cari as she carefully tended to the wound on his head.

"Nah, I think it's okay," answered Pete. "Squirt some disinfectant on it." He then looked at Cari and asked her if she thought the same thing he did about the eagle.

"Yes, I believe it has shifted. It flew close to me outside - quite unusual during the daytime, it must be getting desperate."

"That's the second time I've seen that eagle," said Pete, "This time it flew much closer and last time it was at night.  I think you're right, it's getting desperate."

Ned and Wolf looked confused so Kyra answered them. "She thinks it's the troll. Apparently they can shape shift into eagles."

"Shape shifters, oh yeah, I remember you told me about that," Ned said to Cari. "Wolf, you are familiar with a shape shifting creature, what do you think?" he asked.

"Frankly, I don't know what to think, but one thing I'm sure of, Pete is in danger," said Wolfgang.

"Maybe you should leave now Pete. If the situation is becoming dangerous, why stick around?" asked Kyra.

"I agree with you," said Wolfgang.

"Me too," said Ned.

"I would say they are right Uncle Pete. We can pack up and be out of here by tomorrow morning. You can contact the realty office and tell them to sell the farm whenever they can," Cari stated.

"You are all probably right about it, I should leave, but the thing is...I can't," Pete answered. "The police, as nice as they were to me, strongly requested that I stick around until they have determined what exactly has happened to Talia Hovlund."

"What! They don't suspect you, do they?" Cari questioned.

"Not yet, but it all seems suspicious. First, that kid Davey is seriously hurt in the barn and then my realtor, who had been out here discussing the property listing with me, has turned up missing. I may have been one of the last people to see her, and her abandoned car was found nearby. Oh, and what could turn out to be one of her fancy shoes turned up near the silo."

"Hmm...I see," said Ned. "You are a stranger here, and these events happened after you arrived. You may need an attorney."

"You are an attorney, right Ned?" asked Cari.

"Yes, but not the type your uncle needs," Ned answered.

"Wait just a doggone minute," said Pete. "I haven't done anything wrong, and the police just asked politely that I don't leave just yet. We don't have to jump the gun."

"I will stay here with you Uncle Pete," said Cari.

"As will I," Wolfgang added.

"I'll stay around as long as I can," said Ned.

"Me too," Kyra added.

"Well, you young folks are really something else. I guess the rune casting got it right when it EHWAZ turned up. Teamwork, loyalty, trust, friendship, that says it all," said Pete wiping away a stray tear. "Other than Cari, all of you folks are my acquaintances. We don't even know each other all that well."

"You were always a friend and a great help to my father when he was alive," said Ned. "That counts a lot for me."

"Hey, we are all at least part time residents of the bay," said Kyra. "We stick together!"

"You are right about that sis," said Wolfgang. "I'm in it for the long haul."

Pete again expressed his gratitude and said he would stay at the farm, not at a hotel in town. Cari reiterated that she would remain at the farm as well. "That's the only way we can rid ourselves of the troll," she added.

"If you will excuse us Pete, I think we have a rune stone to dig up," said Wolfgang. "I'll go get that wheelbarrow out of the barn."

Cari stayed in the farmhouse with Pete to make sure he was feeling okay after his ordeal. Kyra went to the car to grab her camera. She wanted to get photos of the rune stone being removed from the ground for the second time.

Ned proceeded to the yard to begin unearthing the big rune stone. He was shocked when he immediately noticed that it had been mostly covered up again. While they were in the farmhouse, someone (or something) took the time to re-bury the stone. Only a small portion of it remained above ground.

"Hey, Wolf, look," he shouted to his friend, pointing at the small edge of the stone that was exposed.

"What the hell?" asked Wolf.

"My sentiments exactly."

A few moments later Kyra approached with her camera and saw them holding shovels and staring at the ground. Then she noticed the exposed stone was now barely exposed, and scratch marks surrounded it.

"Did you do this?" she asked.

"Nope, it was like this when we came out," answered Wolf. "It's been mostly re-buried."

"Wow, that's weird."

After a few more moments of contemplating what they just saw, Ned and Wolf shrugged and started digging out the stone. Perched on top of the silo, out of sight, a large eagle watched them.

Another, (this one a human) watched them from afar through powerful binoculars. The human was quite upset and excited to see the people digging. "Did they find it?" the watcher wondered.

# CHAPTER 34: STONE COLD

Once they had gotten the stone mostly uncovered, Ned and Wolf yanked it out of the ground and carefully placed it in the wheelbarrow. Kyra photographed the stone from different angles as they brushed away the dirt.

"Hard to believe that Pete and Cari can actually read the runes etched on the stone," said Kyra. "It looks like a bunch of symbols. Color me impressed."

"Yep, you just never know about people," commented Ned. "There's more to Pete than the smart aleck fisherman that hangs around Garvin's snack bar."

"A great lesson to be learned about judging others," Wolfgang added. "I know much of Pete's personality quirks are an act. He's one smart cookie."

While they were wheeling the stone to the farmhouse, Wolfgang's phone buzzed.

"Hey, it's Ron, I gotta take this," he told Ned and Kyra looking at his phone. They told him to go ahead and continued toward the farmhouse with the wheelbarrow carrying the rune stone.

"Ron Chalmers, Wolfgang's friend from Lake Geneva, right?" asked Kyra.

"Yes, he's the one that Wolf went out to see in Colorado."

"Oh, of course. Wolf told me about his adventure out there. I spilled the info to our parents about him getting shot. They didn't seem all that surprised."

When they got to the farmhouse's kitchen door, Ned shouted to Pete and Cari. "Where should we put the stone?"

"Put it on the kitchen table, I've put some old towels on there to rest it on," Cari answered and walked into the kitchen as Ned and Kyra were removing the stone from the wheelbarrow.

"Here, let me help you," she told them, and the three of them carefully set the stone on the table.

"Where's Wolfgang?" Cari asked, brushing more dirt from the stone.

"He's on the phone with his friend Ron," said Kyra.

"Oh yes, Ron, that fitness fellow that lives in Lake Geneva. We've met," she answered.

"We've got the stone inside, Uncle Pete," Cari said.

"Good, give me a minute and we'll look it over again," he answered, toddling into the kitchen. "Where's Wolfgang?" he asked, plopping into a kitchen chair.

"He's on the phone with his buddy Ron," Ned answered.

"Who is he again?" Pete asked.

"Ron is Wolf's friend from Lake Geneva," Ned repeated. "He is a fitness and outdoor tour guide. He was recently in the mountains of Colorado and Wolf went out there to visit. They encountered what was termed a Skinwalker or shape shifting creature and Wolf, of course, had to see it for himself. The cryptozoologist in him was intrigued. It ended up being pretty dangerous for all of them. Ron's girlfriend Lelani was there with him too."

"I've heard her name before," said Pete.

"Sure you have, she's Harry Chan's daughter. You know Harry, he was my dad's partner. They were both police detectives," explained Ned. "Actually, Harry also ended up going out to Colorado. He was worried about Lelani."

"Of course I know him. He visited the bay a few times. I even took him over to see Mrs. Saari. She gave him a tarot reading. It was a hoot," Pete smiled at the memory, then turned toward the table "Well, I guess you all want to check out the stone," he sighed. "Where the trouble all began."

The stone loomed large on the kitchen table. Cari, Ned and Kyra got their first close look at it.

Cari spoke first, gently running her fingers over the runes etched upon the stone. "I am awestruck. If this is genuine, it's an important piece of history."

"Wow, do you think it's actually a rune stone left here by Vikings?" asked Kyra.

"Perhaps, or some Scandinavian explorers," said Cari quietly.

A few moments later, Wolf entered the kitchen and he too was in awe of the stone that lay on the table. Pete and Cari were silently reading the rune letters, to see if they agreed on what the runes conveyed.

Ned, Kyra and Wolfgang adjourned to the living room to give Pete and Cari a chance to concentrate. After a brief discussion about the stone, Ned turned to Wolfgang and asked him how Ron was doing.

"Oh yeah, I almost forgot. Ron and Lelani are engaged. He called to let me know. They're having dinner with Harry tonight to give him the news. I told him what was going on here in Minnesota. Actually, he didn't seem all that surprised."

"So, you told him about the troll, the buried rune stone and everything else, and he wasn't a bit surprised?" asked Ned.

"Nope. Ron said nothing that I tell him shocks him anymore. I think it was after we saw the Beast of Bray road in Wisconsin. He's sort of immune to my unusual encounters with creatures now."

"That says a lot about you, and your life on the edge" commented Kyra.

"How long do you think they're going to be looking over that stone?" asked Ned.

"I'm kind of hungry."

"Here's an idea," said Wolf. "Why don't we drive into Fergus Falls and get some takeout. That will give them time to confer over the stone and we can meet up later."

"Good idea," said Kyra.

Moments later Cari strode into the living room and suggested they all return to their hotel and meet back at the farm the next day.

"Are you sure you two are going to be okay?" asked Wolfgang.

"Yes, we have things for dinner out here, and I'll make sure Uncle Pete doesn't venture out after dark. We are taking our time with the stone, to be sure we are as accurate as possible. Please go and enjoy a nice dinner in town and we'll see you tomorrow. Don't worry, we will be fine."

They bade good evening and during the ride into town, debated on what type of food they wanted for dinner.

"Not the diner," said Kyra.

"I'm with you," said Wolf.

"How about somewhere with a bar?" said Ned. "I could use a drink."

"Wonderful idea. How about Tex-Mex with jumbo Margaritas," said Kyra.

"Agreed!" they all shouted.

They found a place in Fergus Falls that served Tex-Mex fare and as luck would have it, jumbo Margaritas.

"This has been a weird little trip so far," mumbled Kyra over a mouthful of tortilla chips she had dipped generously in salsa.

"I concur," said Ned, with a mock toast and a large sip of his margarita.

"Not to me," said Wolf, chewing on a tortilla chip as he reached for his drink. "I think the real weirdness is yet to come."

# Chapter 35: The Curse

"I think we may be right, Uncle Pete," said Cari as they continued to examine the rune stone. The translation, as close as they could determine read as follows: "Tiu (ten) Nordman (Northern men), Ragnar (warriors), Bardagi (fighting), Hjaldr (battle) atta (eight) Nordmen thola (Northern men endured) illur trolls  (evil trolls) fander (devil) fjanddin (enemy) myrkr (darkness), endelaf troll (last surviving troll), banamaor (killer),  seior (magic) Galdr (sorcery, spell), bolva, (curse) troll, svefnugr (sleep). Volva (seeress) bolva (curse) troll, svefnugr (sleep) troll, dauoi (death). bolva,(curse). It sort of dropped off after that.

Cari and Pete read the passage over and over again, finally agreeing on the rough translation.

"Ten Norse men, warriors battled with their enemy trolls. Eight of them survived.  The last and only surviving troll, apparently a killer, was unable to be killed itself, so was cursed to sleep or death, by a Volva, a seeress, or witch."

"So the Norse men brought along a witch on their voyage?" asked Pete.

"The Viking Volva was a powerful seer and highly respected practitioner of Seidr magic. Their prophecies and magic guided them. It would be entirely possible they traveled with a witch," Cari explained.

"You know, it's entirely possible that the troll can be cursed to sleep once again," she continued.

"By whom?" questioned Pete.

"By another practitioner of magic," Cari answered with a slight smile.

"You?" Pete asked in surprise.

"Have you heard the tales about a Hulder or Huldra? She is of the underworld, a supernatural, seductive blonde forest creature."

"Yeah, with a cow's tail," said Pete. "Do you think you can trick the troll into believing you are Huldra? She is from folk stories, you know."

"It's worth a try," she answered. "Besides, folk stories come from somewhere."

"Then what?"

"I'm not sure yet, but I'm going to do some research and at least make an attempt."

"What if everyone else is right, and this is no troll, but an actual person?"

"Then we'll know for sure."

"No. It's too dangerous. We don't know what happened to Talia Hovlund. What if someone did her harm or worse. The same could happen to you. Remember what happened to Davey? He was seriously injured. No, absolutely not Cari."

"I'll be careful, Uncle Pete. Besides, you'll be close by, and so will Wolfgang."

"I think we just wait and see what happens with the search for Talia Hovlund and when they clear me, we just get out of here."

"You don't think the troll will follow you? Or harm others?"

"I'm not sure, I don't know what to do Cari. Please, let's just hold off on any plans just yet."

"Alright Uncle Pete. In the meantime, I will continue my research into magic and do another rune casting on my own."

"You do that Cari. Even though I believe that the troll exists based on what I've seen and heard, I do have lingering doubts."

"Of course you do, so do I," she answered.

"Whether it is a troll or the work of a human, whoever is doing this is evil. The situation has become menacing, and whatever is behind it - there's a reason. The missing realtor, the attack on Davey - these are not coincidences."

"I know Ned is looking into my great Uncle Fritz's somewhat shady past. He was harboring secrets and that could be the catalyst," said Cari.

"Ned is a lawyer, and was once a private investigator, so he has good instincts, but does he know what to look for?" questioned Pete. "We need more help. A cop, a detective to help figure this out."

"The local police are working on finding Talia Hovlund and who injured Davey, but right now, they are focusing on you, Uncle Pete. I hope they look elsewhere."

"Yep, we need a detective, and I know just who to call," Pete said definitively with a slap on his knees.

"Who?" she asked.

"The fellah who has a daughter that just got engaged. I will give him a call tomorrow and congratulate him. Then I will give him some details about what's happening around here and I think he'll be interested enough to come out to help."

"I know exactly who you mean," she said.

"Yep, Harry Chan."

# CHAPTER 36: HARVEY

Harry's phone buzzed and he looked at it in surprise. Pete Magnusson? Why in this world would Pete be calling him? He knew.

"Hello Pete."

"Harvey, good to talk to you."

Harry smiled at the way Pete always called him by the wrong name. He knew that Pete was fully aware that his name was Harry, but he never called him that.

"I'm calling to congratulate you on your daughter's engagement."

"Oh, that's very kind of you. I just found out about it yesterday, how did you know?"

"Um...Varg told me. Your soon to be son-in-law Ron called him to share the news."

"Is Wolfgang in the Upper Peninsula right now?"

"Nope, and neither am I. We are in Northern Minnesota. Varg is here with me along with his sister Kyra and Ned Ferris."

"Hmm...interesting," said Harry. "It sounds to me like there's much more to this story."

"Yes, there is Henry. I am in a bit of trouble here. I inherited my uncle's farm, so I came out here to settle things and there's been (pardon the expression) a real shitload of difficulties ever since."

"I'm going to stop you right there Pete. Ron, my soon to be son-in-law, filled me in yesterday after he talked to Wolfgang. I was just messing with you, I know all about your trouble. By the way, I don't believe in trolls."

"No need to buy the troll story, Herby. I know you are a skeptic when it comes to legendary creatures and such. I myself think there is a troll hereabouts, but I can't be sure. I've seen it, but not close up. My niece and I have studied the legends and read the rune stone. Everything started after I dug up that stone. We are working on a plan to deal with the troll."

"Okay."

"Right now I'm also concerned about discovering what my uncle's secrets are that make everyone so damn interested in this dump of a farm. He would have never sold it. I suppose because it was his home. I was ready to sell, I had no plans to keep it. I just wanted a little time to look for the cash he stashed away"

"Stashed away?"

"Yup, he was a miser and buried some cash in coffee cans in the backyard. He didn't trust banks, or anyone else for that matter. So far it has only added up to a few hundred bucks, not a big fortune by any means."

"That is strange, but I have heard that long ago, some people did that," said Harry. "By the way, how did your uncle die?"

"The official cause of death was old age. Oh, and I don't know if Wolf told Ron about the police asking that I don't leave here since the disappearance of that realtor lady. They ain't found her yet."

"He explained that as well. You must be well-liked by those young people. They are all very concerned about you," said Harry.

"That's a nice group of young folks, they don't come much better. Did Ron tell you that my niece Cari is dating Varg?"

"Yes, actually my daughter Lelani has told me all about it. She is a big fan of Madame Carishimo and was so excited to meet her. Small world."

"Well, why I'm calling...um...since you know about my troubles, I need to ask you a favor, Harvey."

"Go ahead."

"Well, you see, Uncle Fritz may have been up to no good. I think mighta' did something bad and somebody found out about it. There's been a couple of hints that he had a "treasure", but I don't know exactly what that is or what it means."

"By something bad - you mean?"

"Stole something, I think."

"And you want me to look into it? You do realize that I am a "retired" police detective and I have absolutely no jurisdiction in Minnesota, or anywhere for that matter."

"Yeah, but you got cop friends still on the job, right? Mebbe they can help you do some research or have ideas. I'm at the end of my rope Herbie, and I gotta say it's getting a little scary here. Can you help?"

"I don't really think I would be much help, but I suppose I could come out there for a couple of days. I have one request first."

"Anything."

"Say my real name correctly."

"Okay, arghh...Harry."

"Thank you Pete. I should probably tell you now, after Wolfgang talked with Ron he called me. Then last night - Ned called me. They both asked me the same thing you did.  I am packing as we speak and will be leaving tomorrow morning. I even have a hotel reservation."

"Oh, Harvey, you are a tricky one."

Harry continued packing after talking with Pete. He knew the man from his visits to Trygghaven Bay in the Upper Peninsula. Harry spent many vacations visiting the bay, where Pete lived, as the guest of his cop partner, Jake Ferris, Ned's late father. Pete was clever and hid his intelligence behind a veneer of smart aleck fisherman. He was a bit of a social chameleon.

Harry was retired, but still kept his mind sharp by assisting in cases whenever possible. It was hard to admit, but he liked working on cases. Retirement didn't mean he completely turned off his instincts as a detective. He was a quiet and somewhat reserved sort, who had been described as having the appearance of a dangerous man, despite his age; a label he secretly delighted in.

His packing was nearly done. Harry filled a small suitcase and a large garment bag which contained a number of his trademark suits, every one of them green. The garment bag kept them from becoming wrinkled, but as soon as he wore one, it became rumpled. Another trademark.

After he had spoken with Ron, he began thinking about the "trouble" Pete had landed in. Shortly afterward, Wolfgang called him and further explained the situation they found themselves in at the farm in Minnesota. Wolfgang was a cryptozoologist, so he certainly considered the possibility of a reincarnated troll, but he was also concerned that there was more to the story, connected to  humans.

A while later, Ned called him as well. Harry had to laugh at how these young people seemed to not only find themselves involved in situations, but how often Harry himself became involved. Retirement was certainly not boring.

Ned gave Harry more information on Pete's uncle Fritz Kolbeck and that set Harry to start doing research. So far he had found nothing outstanding, but there had to be a connection and Harry assumed it would be a local one. Small towns had secrets, but those secrets were often hard to keep.

"Nobody is invisible," he told himself. "Some trace has been left behind."

# CHAPTER 37: HARRY ARRIVES

The drive from Chicago to northern Minnesota gave Harry a chance to think over all the details he had gotten from Wolfgang, Ned and Pete. He was certain there was some undiscovered value to the Fritz Kolbeck farm, and some parties unknown were doing their best to chase Pete away. If that person or persons had been a bit more patient, Pete would have left on his own.  Aha! That was the key.

What was the hurry? Why suddenly did Pete have to be chased off the farm? Clearly the old uncle had been there for many years. According to Pete, his uncle would not have sold the farm, (because it was his home). Or was there another reason? Did the uncle actually die of natural causes? There were questions to be answered, but would Harry be able to get the answers? Some small towns were notoriously close-mouthed about local issues. The police may be helpful, but would they resent an outsider (with only a retired badge) asking questions?

There were a great deal of variables for Harry to mull over during his drive. He had to admit to himself that the investigation was intriguing. Retirement had been great so far, but Harry felt like he still had more to give - his skills were still sharp.

Farm country everywhere he looked. Fields of...hmmm...what? He didn't know, unless it was corn. Everyone knew what corn looked like.

Harry had a great appreciation for farmers. It was hard work and success could depend upon weather. Dairy farms, also hard work. Taking care of farm animals every day, with never a day off. (Not to mention the smell). Yes, he respected farmers.

Finally Harry crossed into Minnesota. Tired of driving and needing a break, Harry stopped at a restaurant/pub in a dusty little town, or more like a wide spot in the road. When he stepped inside, there were a few patrons at the bar and a couple of others seated in the wooden booths. A young lady greeted him at the door and asked if he was there for lunch, and did he want a booth or to sit at the bar.

"Booth please," he answered.

"I'll be right back with a menu. Would you like anything from the bar?"

"Hmm...a beer please, whatever you have on tap."

The server returned with a frosty mug of beer and a single page menu. Harry glanced at it and decided on a barbecued pork sandwich and seasoned fries.

"Good choice," she told him and sauntered away.

Harry was relaxing in the booth when he noticed a "breaking" news report on the television above the bar. A woman's body had been discovered floating in a pond a few miles from the small village of Dalton.

"Oh oh," thought Harry. "That's the community nearby Pete's farm. I wonder if it could be the missing realtor?"

Harry stayed glued to the television, but no further updates were reported on the identity of the woman or if foul play was involved. The news reporter was promising more details as they became available.

The server brought his sandwich and commented on the news report. "Things like that never used to happen around here, it's getting scary," she said as she set the plate in front of Harry. Then she asked if he wanted another beer and when he declined, she wandered away, leaving Harry lost in thought, and worried for his friend. The sandwich looked delicious, but he couldn't taste anything.

The remainder of the drive could have been through any terrain or any sort of scenery, Harry wouldn't have noticed. His mind was firmly focused on what he would discover when he arrived at the farm.

Following his GPS took Harry right to the front doorstep of the old droopy farmhouse. The first thing he saw was Pete, sitting on the front porch with his head in his hands. "He knows," thought Harry.

Harry pulled up and as he exited the car waved a greeting to Pete and a very lovely young blonde woman standing nearby, seeming to console him. "The niece," Harry recalled.

"Harry, how good of you to come," said Pete, reaching out to shake Harry's hand. It wasn't lost on Harry that Pete used his correct name. The man was probably not in the mood for his running joke right now.

"I'm glad to be here Pete," said Harry. "I take it from your demeanor that you have heard the news about a woman's body found in a pond near here," he continued. "Has there been any further developments on identifying her?"

"Nope, but I'm pretty sure it's Talia Hovlund," Pete answered. He went on to introduce his niece, Cari, to Harry and they both remembered meeting at some time in the past, most likely when they were both visiting Trygghaven Bay.

"What am I gonna do Harry?" Pete asked. "I would never harm anyone, and have no reason to. I can't believe they suspect me of anything."

"I wouldn't get too worried yet, Pete. The police are just doing their due diligence. The body hasn't been identified yet, but if it turns out to be Ms. Hovlund, according to what Ned told me, you may have been the last person to see her. For now, think of yourself more like a witness or a key to evidence they may need for the investigation."

"Harry, I know you probably don't believe it, but what if she was murdered and it was the troll that killed her? I'm the one who broke the curse."

"Um...I can guarantee that you won't be convicted for curse breaking."

# Chapter 38: Suspect

The pressure was getting to him. Pete generally fancied himself bullet-proof, indifferent to most situations. Nothing really bothered him a great deal, but now he was in a peck of trouble. He was sure that if the dead woman discovered in the pond was Talia Hovlund, and foul play was involved, he was going to be the number one suspect.

Sleep was nearly impossible. He was grateful to Harry Chan for making the trip here, but would he be any help? Harry said himself that he was a retired detective and had no jurisdiction here. Pete was pinning his hopes on any assistance that Harry could provide. The police were probably busy building a case against Pete.

Everyone with the exception of himself and Cari, had left for their hotel rooms.

The farmhouse was eerily quiet and there were no disturbances outdoors. Pete sat alone in the shabby living room, wishing once more that he had never come here and just put the property up for sale, sight unseen. His brother Viktor had the right idea. Once he walked away from the farm, he never returned. Now this trouble he found himself in was spilling over onto his friends and family. He was quite sure that Cari had better things to do, just as everyone else did.

Pete jumped when he heard a slight noise. "Uncle Pete, are you okay?" It was Cari coming in to check on him.

"Sure, I'm okay. I'm having a bit of trouble getting to sleep," he answered.

"I understand," she said. "There's nothing helpful in worrying, but I know you can't stop. Listen, you know you haven't done anything wrong. If it is Talia Hovlund they found, maybe she just fell into that pond. If she was killed, then there must be other people around here with a motive to harm her. What would your motive be?"

"You're right, I don't have a motive to harm her, she was just trying to sell the farm for me. Harry's probably right - the police just want me to stick around because I may have been one of the last people to see her."

"Yes, that's it," she agreed.

"You know, I thought of something. Those cops were suspicious when they talked to me about what happened to Davey. They kept asking me questions. Maybe Davey has remembered more about what took place in the barn the night he was hurt. I should go talk to him," said Pete.

"I'm not sure that's such a good idea, Uncle Pete. "Wait and see what the police come up with before you do that. There's more information they haven't released yet. Besides, you can give him a little more time to recover."

"You're probably right. I do want to visit him when he's feeling better. I would like him to come back and finish the job if he's willing (and able). He did a lot of work while he was here, and there's more to do."

"That's what you should do then. Focus on getting this farm sold and what has to be done for the auction. It will take your mind off of things, and I can help."

"You've done enough, young lady. I think all of you should go back to your lives and let this all play out. Harry will work on it, if there's anything to investigate. You young people get back to your homes and jobs. Leave this to me."

"Oh Uncle Pete, you know I can't do that. We still have to try to get rid of the troll. He's still out there," said Cari.

"Is he?" questioned Pete.

"If not a troll - then someone or something else is still out there and I intend to find out what it is, no matter what you say. Now, go get some sleep," she insisted and gave her uncle a hug.

Pete returned to bed and finally fell asleep. He tossed and turned and awoke to find the troll standing at the foot of his bed. Its pointed teeth bared in a hiss.

"Illur troll," (evil troll) said Pete, unable to move, only speak.

"Nei," the creature replied. (no)

"Acwellan kvenna?" (killed woman?) Pete asked.

"Hefnd" (vengeance) the creature hissed at Pete and climbed out the window.          Pete hurried out of his bed to watch the creature, who stared back at him and giggled before it disappeared in the darkness.

Pete awoke once again in a cold sweat, not sure if he had another dream, or if he actually spoke to the troll. He felt as if he was losing his mind. Fortunately, he was able to fall asleep again, this time with no nightmare to haunt him.

The next morning while making a pot of coffee, Pete wondered if he should share the details of his nightmare with Cari, or simply try to forget it. When she entered the kitchen, she paused for a moment and then asked him what had happened. It must have shown on his face.

"Another nightmare. The troll was in my room again. I accused him of killing the woman and he replied, "vengeance" in old Norse. I feel like my sanity is slipping away, Cari."

"Maybe we shouldn't stay here anymore, Uncle Pete. We can get rooms in town."

"You go ahead. I want to stay here and face the creature. I  want to find a way to rid myself of it."

"Well, you aren't going to do it without me," she answered. "Let's find out more about what happened to Talia Hovlund. Harry can check some things out with the police and I can proceed with my plan to trick the troll, if he is out there."

"You are stubborn," Pete said, shaking his head.

"I'm not the only one," said Cari, reaching for a coffee cup.

The rest of the morning was spent discussing Cari's plan for ridding them of the troll. They agreed not to share the details with anyone else, except possibly Wolfgang. He would be the one person that would believe in the likelihood of the existence of an evil troll.

"Describe it to me once again, Uncle. What you saw in the dream," Cari requested.

"It was short, maybe four feet tall and stocky.  It had a big head, a long nose, beady eyes and long crooked teeth, almost like fangs. When it spoke, the words came out deep and scratchy, then it made a hissing sound. I don't need to tell you that...thing, if it is the troll - it's scary."

"Here's what I think. Great Uncle Fritz must have either seen the troll or read about it. He had the tendency to bury things, and I'm sure he buried the rune stone, ALGIZ for protection, to ward off evil. Remember the message he wrote, "bjarga seidh" save or protect from evil magic. The tea can it was buried in is something from this century - so why did he feel the need for protection?" Cari wondered aloud.

"You may be onto something there," said Pete. Uncle Fritz is a part of the scenario, we just have to figure out how."

"Remember the server at the diner said he talked about FEHU, which means wealth, abundance or luck. What if he discovered something out there that the troll was trying to protect?" said Cari.

"The treasure Uncle Fritz mentioned?" asked Pete.

"Precisely. He dug up or found some sort of treasure and somehow it involved the troll. What would be valuable to a troll?"

"Where does Talia Hovlund enter into this? Or does she?" said Pete.

"You said she was out here snooping around after Uncle Fritz died, before you arrived.  Maybe she found something and came back for it. That's why her shoe was left by the silo."

"She did ask me questions about all the holes I had dug - as well as the ones left for me by the troll. I said something about groundhogs, but I don't think she bought it."

"The troll had a sickle - maybe it killed her," Pete thought out loud. "Why her?"

"We have more questions than answers right now," said Cari. "Maybe your retired detective can discover what Uncle Fritz was up to and we can figure out how the troll fits in."

# Chapter 39: Mayhem?

Wolf and Harry met at a small coffee shop a couple blocks from the hotel. Over large cups of steaming brew, the two of them chatted about their thoughts on the very strange occurrences at Pete's farm and the possible killing of his realtor.

"I am reasonably sure this is all connected," said Harry. "Not to be doubtful regarding the existence of an evil troll, but I think there's something rotten going on here and it started with Pete's uncle. His secrets are what set this all in motion. My guess is that he has (or had) something valuable or information concerning something of value that in his old age...he got a bit too talkative about."

"Yes, he did blab to the server Patti about a treasure. He was old, maybe he was senile and talking nonsense," replied Wolfgang.

"Certainly a possibility, but why the accidents (or incidents) on the farm? From what Pete said, they began shortly after his arrival. His discovery of the rune stone could be coincidental, or part of an elaborate hoax. However, I don't believe the rune stone was part of any scheme, as finding it would cause Pete to stay, not leave," Harry said.

"He was digging around the yard looking for those cash cans his uncle buried. That would cause interest or suspicion. Then the incidents started and escalated,   including the very serious one that hurt that young man," Wolf pondered.

"The digging! That's probably the catalyst," said Harry. "Pete was seen digging in the yard and someone assumed he found out about Fritz's secret, whatever that is, and decided to chase him away. I'm sure it wasn't about a few hundred dollars buried in coffee cans. There's something else on that farm and it's got to be valuable enough to kill for."

"You got all that from Pete digging for cans? You must have been quite the detective Harry."

"I may not be right, but it's a start."

Harry and Wolf were getting refills on their coffee when Ned and Kyra walked in the coffee shop. They shared their thoughts about Pete's dilemma, and the four of them continued the discussion.

"I suspected right from the get-go that there's something connected to Pete's Uncle Fritz. His ramblings about treasure and wealth, plus his secretive demeanor got me wondering," said Ned.

"He was an old man and had that farm for many years. Anyone could have robbed him a long time ago if he had anything valuable," Kyra stated.

"Sure, you're right about that, but what if the "treasure" had been discovered recently. Maybe just before the old guy died. I know he was old and purportedly died of old age, but what if he didn't?" questioned Harry.

"You think he could have been murdered?" asked Ned.

"It's possible. Talia Hovlund may have been murdered as well. Maybe she knew too much."

"I don't think it's safe for Pete and Cari to stay at that farm. They should get out of there now," said Wolfgang. "At least stay in a hotel at night. Who knows what could happen."

"I agree with you," said Harry. "But Pete is very stubborn, and his niece won't leave him there alone."

"I can stay out there with them if they won't leave," said Wolf

"I will too," said Harry. "Or we can take turns. Besides, I'm armed."

"You are?" asked Ned

"Of course. You don't think I'd come to Minnesota and tackle a troll without my firearm," said Harry with a wry smile. "I keep it in a lock box in my vehicle, just in case such a thing happens."

"Harry, you shouldn't joke about the troll in front of Pete or Cari. They both believe it exists and claim to have seen it. Pete actually thinks the troll may have killed Talia Hovlund," said Kyra.

"I know. I will watch what I say in front of them. Wolfgang here is aware of my skepticism, in spite of the things I have seen when he's around."

"You're right mate. You're still a doubter, even after seeing a Wolf-Beast, a Shape-shifting Skinwalker and getting shot by a witch. I admire your reserve."

"Correction, I didn't see the Walker, I just heard it. The mayhem was actually caused by a man, not a monster," stated Harry. "So, only a Wolf-Beast and a witch."

Ned got up to get a refill and caught Kyra's eye, motioning to her to join him.

"What?" she asked.

"I don't know about you, but this whole conversation is getting pretty weird for me," he whispered.

"Really? You and I know Wolfgang - he thrives on weird things. Now he's got Harry in his back pocket," she said quietly.

When Ned and Kyra returned to the table, Wolfgang and Harry asked them both how long they would be able to stay before they had to return to their jobs.

"We can handle this, and you both can go back home if you have to. We'll get you back here if we need you, but you can't stay here forever," said Wolf.

"I suppose you're right," said Ned. "I do have to get back to work sometime. Are you sure?"

"No worries, mate. You and Kyra take off and let us take care of this."

"Not until we find out a bit more information," said Kyra. "I think Ned and I will start out with that kid Davey. Maybe he knows something."

"Good idea," said Ned. "We'll find out where he lives and pay him a visit. Harry, you look into Uncle Fritz's past and Wolf, you help with the troll hunt."

# CHAPTER 40: TROLLS AND SUCH

Wolf spent most of the afternoon at the hotel researching trolls and the legends and folk tales surrounding them. At the same time, Harry was researching any news stories that had happened in the area within the last twenty or thirty years. It was a small community, not too distant from other small communities, so the news stories were generally quite benign.

"Hey Harry, I've been reading about trolls, and I found out there's a troll called 'Brunnnmigi' which translates to 'pees in a well'. Apparently that's one of his tricks, to spoil your well water," Wolf told him.

"Makes you think twice about drinking any water out at Pete's farm," said Harry. "I think I will bring my own water bottle with me, just in case."

"Not a bad idea, just to be on the safe side," Wolf agreed with a smirk.

Harry stretched and rubbed his neck. "I've been going through news stories, going back several years, but I haven't found anything seriously criminal here. I have to say, there's not much going on around here, besides the usual small town stuff."

"I have found a lot of information about trolls and also folk stories about them," said Wolf. "Much of what I've read, Cari told me too. Trolls fear lightning, because they fear Thor. They hate bells, because they don't like churches and will throw stones at church buildings. Trolls are shapeshifters and shift particularly to bulls or eagles, and even dragons, represented as protectors," explained Wolf.

"And they may pee in your well," Harry added.

"Yeah, and that too," answered Wolf.

"So, any new theories?" asked Harry.

"None of this information helps me understand more about why a centuries-old troll has reappeared to hassle Pete Magnusson, but it's interesting nonetheless," said Wolf. " I suppose what's written on the rune stone explains it best. The explorers had a battle of sorts with the trolls and their seeress (or Volva) cursed the remaining troll into a dormant state and somehow Pete's reading the curse broke it.  I suppose that troll doesn't know the difference between some Viking explorers and Pete."

"A human is a human - no matter who it is," commented Harry.

"Good point."

Since they had done enough research for the day, Harry and Wolf agreed to head out to the farm to check on how things were going. They would mention to Pete and Cari their suggestion to Ned and Kyra that they head home soon.

Before we leave, let's pick up something we can all have for dinner, maybe like a bucket of chicken or some tacos," Wolf suggested.

"Now you're talking," said Harry. "All that research is making me hungry."

The ride out to the farm seemed to take longer because the vehicle smelled like fried chicken and biscuits. It was distracting to say the least.

"I wonder if Ned and Kyra got in touch with that Davey guy? Maybe they'll wait and have Pete go with them. They would be strangers to him and he may not want to talk to them," said Harry.

"Haha, you underestimate my sister," said Wolf. "She is very charming when she wants to be. Ned is a smooth talker too - he is a lawyer after all."

"I suppose we'll find out soon enough," said Harry. "I didn't volunteer to talk to the guy because I've been told that I give off a "dangerous man" vibe. I don't get it, but it probably is a result of all those years as a detective."

"No comment," said Wolf.

The ride through the country on the way to the farm was pleasant enough in the daytime and the sun was bright and warm today. Miles of farmland continued on both sides of the road, with the occasional farmhouse, silo and barn in between. Usually the houses were surrounded by large trees and the fields of whatever grew on either side and behind the homes. Quite often the house sat on a small hill and rose above the fields. Harry wondered if the home's locations were planned that way. A few of the farms looked abandoned.

The two were quiet during the ride, each lost in thought about what had been occurring in this tranquil locale and the odd circumstances surrounding it.

"I think I'm going to expand my search," said Harry. "If something happened that involved old Fritz, maybe it happened somewhere else."

"Not a bad idea, Harry. Too bad you don't have a narrower timeline. It could take a while going back years and years. That guy was pretty old."

"The communities around here are all fairly small, so any news item would stand out if it was criminal in nature. If I have to widen the search to include bigger cities - I may be out of luck," said Harry. "I wish I knew more about what I was looking for."

"The key here is 'something of value' I think," said Wolf. "What kind of value is the question? If it's money, and people are looking for it, then maybe it's time to look for the money. If it's something else - like what the troll wants - we would have to discover what would be valuable to a troll."

"Simple enough," said Harry. "We should go out after dark and ask it what it wants. Maybe it will answer."

"You know, I think you have something there, Harry."

# Chapter 41: Davey's Story

Ned turned on to the residential street, which was made up of mostly ranch style homes. The lawns were well-kept as were the homes. The neighborhood looked family-friendly. The GPS told him they had arrived at their destination.

Davey's house was much like the others on the street. A small white ranch style with a tidy little front yard, two car garage and probably a tidy little yard in the back. A privacy fence extended alongside the garage and house.

"I hope we're not bothering him," said Kyra. "I feel like we're intruding."

"The basket of muffins may go a long way toward getting us inside," said Ned. He expected that Kyra's pretty face and pleasant demeanor would get them in the door quicker than a basket of muffins.

Ned indicated that she should knock on the door and he stood alongside. After a minute or so, the door opened and a tall young man with a head full of curly red hair, and a bandage on his forehead stood there leaning on crutches and grinning.

"Hello, can I help you?" he asked.

"Hello, my name is Kyra Kilmer and this is Ned Ferris. We're friends of Pete Magnusson. Are you Davey Connor?" she asked, knowing from Pete's description that this had to be Davey.

"Oh sure, Mr. Pete, he's one of my customers. What can I do for you?"

"Well, I brought you these," she said, holding up the basket of muffins.

"Hey, thanks. C'mon in," he said, gesturing to his small living room with one of his crutches.

"Thank you, we're sorry to bother you, but do you have a few minutes to answer some questions?" asked Ned.

"I've got lots of time, in fact it's pretty boring just sitting here. I've been watching too much TV and reading, so I could surely use some company."

"That's great, can I put these in your kitchen?" asked Kyra, holding up the muffin basket.

"Sure, go ahead. It's right through there," he answered.

Kyra returned quickly and Davey invited them both to sit down.

Davey maneuvered himself into a comfy looking chair across from the couch Ned and Kyra shared. He offered them tea or a soft drink, which they declined. They complimented him on his nice home and asked how he was doing?

"I'm getting much better, thanks. The doctor says I should be able to get back to working in a couple weeks. I'm a good healer, I guess."

"That's good to hear. We are very sorry about what happened to you. Pete just feels terrible," said Ned.

"Aw, he shouldn't feel bad. It wasn't his fault that I got hurt. I heard that he came out and helped me and got the ambulance there quickly. He saved me."

"Well, he will be glad to know you feel that way," said Kyra.

"You said you had some questions for me," said Davey. "Ask away."

"Do you remember anything about what happened before the farm tools fell on you?" asked Ned.

"You know, the police asked me the same thing. I didn't really remember much at first, but after I started thinking about it, I remembered hearing a noise in the barn. You see, I was out working in the silo, sifting through the junk out there."

"So you weren't working in the barn?" asked Kyra.

"Nope, I didn't go into the barn until I heard the noise."

"Do you recall what the noise sounded like?" asked Ned.

"Hmm...now that you mention it, the noise was like a snake. I remember now, thinking there could be a snake. I'm not scared of snakes, but I thought it could be a rattlesnake. I wouldn't want to surprise a rattlesnake. Did you know there are rattlesnakes in the Midwest? They're not common, but they do exist."

"It was a rattling sound?" asked Kyra

"Oh no, it was a hissing sound. It must have been a big snake, because I heard it from the silo. It was quiet outside and I have good hearing, but it must have been big."

"Did you see a snake?"

"Nope, never did. I started to go into the barn to  look around, then bam! I was barely in the door and all that stuff fell down on me. When I woke up I was in the hospital."

"So, you heard a hissing noise coming from the barn, you went out there and then the stuff fell on you as you entered the barn," said Ned.

"Yep, that's about it," said Davey. "That's all I remember."

"You didn't see anyone around by the barn or silo before you heard the hissing?" Kyra asked. "Take your time, close your eyes and think about it," she added quietly, looking directly at Davey. "Picture yourself in the silo."

"Hmm...let me think for a minute," he said, leaning back and closing his eyes.

Minutes passed, the wall clock ticking loudly. Ned wondered if Davey was going to doze off.  Suddenly he sat up. "The bull!"

"Did you say bull?" Kyra asked.

"Yeah, I was hauling a pile of junk out to the trailer to cart away to the dump and I saw a bull out in the field. Just a bull all by itself, standing there, then it snorted and pawed at the ground. Weird huh?"

"What happened then?" asked Ned.

"Nothing. I turned around and threw the junk in the trailer. When I looked back, the bull was gone."

"It was a bull, not a cow?"

"Yep, I didn't see it close up, but it was a bull for sure. He must have wandered off and ended up at Pete's. I suppose he walked away when I wasn't looking."

"Anything else you remember?" Ned asked.

"Nope, just the bull, then the hissing noise, then bam!"

"Well, thank you for taking the time to talk to us, Davey," said Kyra.

"Sure, no problem. Say, do you know if Mr. Pete needs me to come back and finish the job when I can work again?"

"I'm not positive, but I think he wants you to come back to work as soon as you are able. I know Pete will be in touch with you soon, and you can ask him about it."

"That's great. Hey, thanks for the muffins."

"You're welcome Davey. I hope you feel better soon," said Kyra, lightly touching his arm. Don't get up, we'll see ourselves out, and thanks again."

Driving to the farm, Ned and Kyra discussed what they had heard from Davey. "First he sees a bull, then hears a hissing sound coming from the barn. Those are both characteristics of a troll, according to what Cari told me," said Ned. "Either someone is posing as a troll, which seems unlikely, or it was a troll, which seems impossible."

"How would anyone know to pose as a troll?" Kyra wondered. "No one is aware of Pete's discovery of the stone and the subsequent incidents."

"Coincidence?"

# Chapter 42: Comparing Notes

Ned and Kyra returned to the farm to report what they had learned from their visit with Davey. Pete and Cari both listened intently to the story Davey told of seeing the bull and hearing a hissing noise from the barn.

"I think we're dealing with a troll, all the signs are there," said Cari. "For some reason it wants to rid itself of Uncle Pete, or perhaps any human that is here at the farm. This area may have been inhabited by trolls, then human explorers (Vikings) invaded and the trolls fought back. The one surviving troll may have been more powerful than the others and wasn't able to be killed, so the seeress cursed it to sleep, maybe thinking she had killed it."

"I think we're getting close," said Pete. "If we can somehow trick the troll and trap it - maybe the curse will work again. Especially if you read the curse, Cari. I would compare you to a seeress."

"That is certainly a stretch, Uncle Pete, but it's worth a try."

Ned and Kyra glanced at one another, but didn't comment. During the ride back from their visit with Davey, they surmised that someone attempted to lure the young man into the barn for reasons unknown, then tried to either injure or kill him by loosening the bolts holding the farm tools and letting them fall on Davey.

"The hissing could have been produced to distract him, or…what about a noise from a tool used to loosen the bolts. Perhaps that made the hissing sound," said Ned.

"That makes sense," said Kyra. "The bull? I think that's a coincidence. He didn't see the bull again, and it had nothing to do with the accident."

Neither Ned or Kyra were surprised when Pete and Cari went immediately to blame the troll. They were nearly certain that it was a legendary creature causing the havoc.

A short time later, Harry and Wolfgang arrived. They told the others that they had spent much of the day researching. Wolf researched trolls and Harry was looking into criminal activities that had occurred in the area. Neither of them had come up with anything new to report. Ned and Kyra told them what they heard from Davey about the hissing sound and the bull.

"I think we may be at a bit of a stalemate," said Wolfgang. "Unless you want to try to reason with the troll."

"We figured to go out at night and see what's there and deal with it," Harry added.

"Our thoughts exactly," said Pete. "We want to trap the troll and see if we can curse it to oblivion."

"If it turns out not to be a troll, but something more human in nature, then we can try to trap the human," said Harry.

"It's worth a try," said Ned. "Why not tonight? Kyra and I will be leaving soon, so let's do this while we have more sets of eyes to keep watch."

Everyone agreed to the plan.

"We should get some of the cars away from the farm, so it doesn't look like so many people are actually here," said Kyra.

Wolf drove his vehicle back to the hotel. Ned followed in his and Cari drove Pete's. They all returned in Pete's vehicle, which was now the only one visible at the farm. Hopefully it would appear as if Pete was alone at the farm if anyone or anything was watching.

Dinner was takeout that Ned and Wolf picked up in town. When they returned to the farm, everyone ate quietly and kept their voices down to keep up the appearance of Pete's being alone.

The sky darkened showing different shades throughout the farm. Clumps of thick weeds looked nearly black and the expanse of farm fields turned from brown to dark blue. Undercover of darkness, each of them crept out carefully to conceal themselves.

Wolf and Cari silently inched their way toward the silo, staying close to the wall of the barn. Harry and Ned scurried toward the other side of the barn and Kyra skulked along the side of the farmhouse with Pete. They were dressed in dark clothing and spoke in whispers. When each of them reached their specified area, they settled in to wait and watch.

Minutes passed silently in the darkness. After what seemed like hours, a strange sound could be heard coming from the field. It was a whistling, chirping sort of noise, and then a large eagle flew around the farmhouse, diving at each of them, then emitting a sound of laughter. As quickly as the eagle appeared, it was gone.

Each pair waited to see if the eagle would return. Cari whispered to Wolf that it was the troll - it had shifted to the eagle and was watching their every move. Harry and Ned both said, "what the hell?" and then stayed quiet. Kyra and Pete did much the same. Everyone held their positions and waited.

More time passed and nothing else happened, until another sound was heard, again coming from the field. This time it was a snort, followed by a louder snort, and hooves pounding in the ground.

The bull charged toward the barn, it suddenly turned away sharply, then was gone. Everyone held their breath, waiting, but the silence returned. After a few minutes, Pete spoke up. "Tell me that wasn't a dad-blasted troll."

# CHAPTER 43: ENEMIES

Ned and Kyra finished packing and were getting ready to return home. Ned had to get back to his law practice, and Kyra had a photo assignment to prepare for. On their way out of town, they stopped by the farm to say goodbye.

"Are you sure you don't need my help anymore?" Ned asked.

"Or mine?" Kyra added. "That bull coming out of nowhere was pretty scary."

"No, you kids return home and get back to your normal lives. We'll handle this," said Pete. "Cari and Wolf are here and so is Henry, we'll be fine."

"If you need any help, we are just a phone call away," said Ned.

"Wolf and Harry should be out here this afternoon. We said our farewells over breakfast this morning," Ned explained. "It's been interesting to say the least," he added, shaking Pete's hand and giving Cari a light hug.

"Same here," said Kyra, hugging Pete and Cari. "Call if you need anything at all."

"Yeah, we'll do that," said Pete. "Thanks to both of you for coming here and helping me. I sure appreciate it. If there's anything I can do for you, let me know."

"Listen if we don't see you beforehand, let's meet up at Garvin's in the bay and the cinnamon rolls are on you," said Ned.

"Agreed. I will also take you out fishing sometime."

"Sure Pete, see you soon. You all be careful, okay? Something or someone is out to get you, and it could be dangerous," said Ned

"Exactly," said Kyra. "Don't take any chances, and take care of yourselves."

Pete and Cari waved them off as they drove away.

"I don't think they believe there's a troll out there, Uncle Pete," said Cari as they walked back into the farmhouse.

"I'm sure they don't," Pete answered. "Whatever it is that torments me, I swear we'll find out what it is."

"We most certainly will, Uncle Pete. I think we had too many people out there last night. Maybe I will just go out alone tonight and watch for the troll."

"Nope, that sounds too dangerous."

"I'll be careful. Besides, all of you will just be a short distance away here in the farmhouse. I can shout for help if I need it. We need to get this thing to come out."

"I know what you're thinking Cari. You want to pose as Huldra and lure the little demon out. Huldra is the stuff of folk stories."

"Folk stories start from somewhere, passed down through generations."

"Or made up in somebody's imagination," Pete retorted.

"It's worth a try. Let me at least give it a go."

"I'm not on board with this plan, but I know better than to think I can stop you, once you have your mind made up. Promise me you'll be careful and shout for help immediately if things go badly."

"I promise, Uncle Pete. I will be wary of whatever I see or hear and keep myself safe."

"You had better, young lady. If anything happens to you, my brother will kick my ass."

Pete and Cari hugged and decided it was a good time to search around the barn and silo for anything out of place or unusual. Everything looked different in the daylight and Cari wanted to explore the area further.

"Are you done searching for Uncle Fritz's cash cans?" she asked, poking around in the backyard.

"Yah, I think so. I've had just about enough digging for a lifetime. If there's a few more cans buried out there, let someone else find them."

Pete and Cari walked the perimeter of the backyard, then returned to the old broken down silo. The grassy mounds remained intact, save for the one that was opened up after Pete read the rune stone.

"This mound that was disturbed seems to be filling back in naturally. I think that this may be where the troll was located, but I wonder where he goes in the daytime," said Cari.

"Trolls don't like daylight, so he has to go to a place that's at least partially in the dark. Maybe there's an old cave hereabouts, or an abandoned building. The old farms around this area have plenty of old sheds and outbuildings that were left to rot," Pete answered.

"Yeah, he could find all kinds of places to hide, and if I'm right, he shifts when necessary. That eagle came out of nowhere, and so did the bull, then both of them suddenly disappeared. It all occurred very quickly," said Cari.

"One way or another, we have to find out why this is happening," said Pete. "I know Harry is looking into Uncle Fritz, in case he had been up to something, but Fritz was good at keeping secrets. We may never know what he was hiding."

"If he was hiding anything. We don't know that for sure. He may have had his own altercation with the troll, and that was his secret."

While Pete and Cari poked around the yard and silo, they were being watched. Powerful binoculars enabled the observer to keep a close eye on them from a safe distance.

# CHAPTER 44: MURDERED

Wolfgang and Harry were finishing their coffee after breakfast with Ned and Kyra who were getting ready to leave.

"Are you going back to the U.P to visit with mom and dad?" Wolf asked his sister.

"You can't be serious," Kyra answered. "As much as I love them, I should get back to work. I have to make a living and I can't pass up an assignment."

"A likely story, but I'll let you slide," Wolf commented.

"Harry, it has been good to see you," said Ned, shaking Harry's hand. "Try to stay out of trouble. Remember, you are going to have a wedding to get ready for."

"Don't remind me," said Harry. "I do like Ron, but I'm not convinced he's the right man for my daughter. It's her decision, though, and I support her."

"Ron can be a bit...hmmm...you know, but he really is a great guy," said Wolf.

"I've known him for many years and I think he'll be good to Lelani."

"I'll take your word for it," Harry replied with a shrug. "In the meantime, we need to figure out what is going on here in farm country, or maybe just leave it behind us when Pete is able to return home."

"Leaving it behind may be the best plan of action," said Ned.

"I agree," said Kyra. "But I see how stubborn Pete can be. Maybe when the police find out what happened to Talia Hovlund, he can just return to Michigan and leave the farm with a for sale sign in front."

"Let's hope so," said Wolf.

The friends all said their goodbyes and agreed to keep in touch. As Ned and Kyra drove away, Harry and Wolf returned to their booth with one more coffee refill and to discuss the plans for the day.

The morning was bright, sunny and warm. Wolf suggested they take a ride around the area surrounding the Kolbeck farm. There were country roads criss-crossing everywhere and his thought was to look for anything out of place. For instance a bull that was wandering loose or a nearby eagle nest.

Before leaving town, Wolf and Harry returned to their hotel briefly. Harry had left his phone in his room and wanted to check for messages. As soon as they entered the hotel lobby, they noticed a crowd had gathered around the lobby's television. Wolf and Harry joined the crowd.

The news banner across the screen read, "Breaking News". The news anchors reported that the woman found in the pond had been positively identified as local real estate agent, Talia Hovlund. The anchors further reported that according to police, Hovlund's death had been ruled a homicide. She had been strangled and dumped into the pond. When she was left in the pond, she was already dead.

"So, it was her after all," said Wolf.

"Yes, I'm not surprised, but I had hoped it would be someone not connected to Pete," said Harry.

"Her connection to Pete was purely professional," said Wolf. "She was his real estate agent, and hadn't even been that for very long."

"True, he really has no motive, as he barely knew the woman. Like I explained to Pete, the police just wanted to interview him because he may have been the last person to see her."

"And what about the shoe?" asked Wolfgang.

"If that is her shoe, which we don't know for sure yet. If she was missing a shoe and the other matches the one found by the silo, that may set off a red flag. In addition, her vehicle was located fairly close to the Kolbeck farm. That is why the police requested that Pete stick around."

"I guess we'll have to wait and see what happens with the investigation," said Wolf.

"We do," said Harry. "That poor woman was murdered, and I have to wonder if there's some connection to the farm. Strange things have been happening, and it seems like there's more to the story. It has to have something to do with Pete's Uncle Fritz."

"I think you're right about that Harry. Then there's the added puzzle of the troll. You know, Pete believes that the troll may have harmed Talia Hovlund, so he's going to come off as guilty."

"Yeah, he blames himself for the reincarnated troll, and the possibility that the troll was responsible. I hope the police discover who murdered her, or Pete may just become a suspect."

The ride through the country roads was put off, as Harry and Wolf realized they needed to get out to the farm right away. If Pete hadn't heard the news about Talia Hovlund, they needed to tell him immediately.

The ride to the farm was made in silence, both of them deep in thought. Harry suspected that the police would be arriving at the farm soon, and felt it necessary to prepare Pete for their visit. He had to convince him that Hovlund wasn't killed by a troll. A human killed that woman and there was no reason for Pete to feel guilty about his perception of awakening an evil troll.

Harry was sure that the Kolbeck farm was the center of some sort of criminal activity and Hovlund may have been deeply involved in it. Perhaps she had discovered something in the farmhouse when she visited before Pete arrived.

On the other hand, the woman's murder might have absolutely nothing to do with the farm or the recent odd happenings. It may all be a coincidence. She could have been killed by a random mugger or someone she was involved with. Truth be told, Harry knew very little about Talia Hovlund. He could be merely jumping to conclusions. He sincerely hoped that was true. The shoe could have belonged to anyone. It could have been there for a long time. If it was her shoe - what was it doing near the silo?

The fact that her vehicle was found nearby wasn't nearly as much of an issue. The country roads were a perfect place to leave an abandoned vehicle. The pond was nearby, so the car would be as well.

While Harry's mind was running at full speed, Wolfgang was thinking about much the same thing. He wouldn't rule out the presence of a troll. In his mind the existence of such a creature was possible. He had seen stranger things in his past. He did wonder, however, what would a troll gain by murdering a real estate agent?  If a troll truly did exist, and was awakened by Pete's reading of the curse on the stone, it wouldn't have a reason to kill her - would it? Wolf felt that a troll would want Pete, or any other humans gone from the farm - thus the tricks. But murder? Unlikely. If murder was the end game - in all probability, Pete would have been the victim.

As they pulled into the driveway of the farmhouse, both Harry and Wolfgang were relieved to note that the police weren't there...yet. Pete and Cari were roaming around near the silo and waved greetings. It looked like they hadn't heard about Talia.

"Hello there," Pete shouted. "Ned and Kyra stopped in to say goodbye. I'm glad you two are here, we are making another plan to deal with the troll."

"Hi all," Cari added. "We're snooping around out here, but no signs of a troll."

"So, you haven't seen the news today?" Harry asked.

"Nope. Why? Is there something we should see?" Pete questioned.

"Yes, they identified the dead woman as Talia Hovlund. Her death has been officially ruled as a homicide. She was strangled and was dead when she was put in the pond," Harry explained.

"Well, shit," said Pete, rubbing a hand over his jaw. "That's terrible news. I didn't know her very well, and she was kind of pushy about selling the farm, but this is a shock."

Pete ambled slowly into the farmhouse and sat heavily on the couch. He was clearly upset and distracted.

"Are you okay, Uncle Pete?" asked Cari.

"Yah, I just need a moment," he answered, staring off into space. Harry and Wolfgang gave Pete a few minutes for the news to sink in. The silence in the old house was punctuated by the ticking of the clock on the wall. The mood was somber.

After some time had passed, Harry reminded Pete that the police would presumably be stopping in soon to ask him more questions now that Talia had been found murdered.

"You don't think…I mean, they wouldn't believe I had anything to do with it?" Pete asked. "I barely knew the woman. Why would I kill her? Wait, the troll!"

"Pete, my friend, forget about the troll for a moment," said Harry. "That woman was not killed by a troll. It was a human that murdered her and drove her car to the area near the pond and left it there. If such a thing as an evil troll exists, and it wanted to kill someone, why didn't it kill you?"

"It tried to kill Davey," Pete whispered.

"You don't know that," said Wolf. "Perhaps the same person that killed Talia tried to hurt Davey, and is making it look like you were involved. The news report said that she was strangled. You were concerned about the troll holding a bloody scythe, which was not a murder weapon."

"There are still many questions that need to be answered," said Harry.

"Like about the shoe?" Pete questioned.

"We aren't sure if that was her shoe. If the shoe belonged to her, was she even missing that particular shoe when they found her body?" said Wolfgang. "I'm sure the police will inform us soon."

Cari had been listening quietly to their conversation and trying to figure out how she could help her uncle. She was determined to complete her plan to deal with the evil troll, and if the troll turned out to be of the evil human variety, then she would deal with that. At her first opportunity, she would sneak out after dark, without telling anyone, and find out where the troll was.

The rest of the day rambled on, with more questions than answers. There had been no word from the police. The hope was that they already had a person in custody for the murder of Talia Hovlund. Pete said that after an appropriate amount of time had passed, he would find out who would be taking over the sale of the farm. He wanted nothing more to do with it and couldn't wait to leave.

After sharing a light dinner with Cari and Pete, Harry and Wolfgang returned to their hotel, promising to return the next day. Pete said he was tired and just wanted to read. He had a thick book about Viking explorers and planned to spend the evening perusing it.

Cari was quietly doing a rune reading, and told her uncle that she was tired as well and planned to go to bed early. Once Pete had retired for the evening, she would slip outside and see what happened out there after dark. She didn't expect to see anything right away this evening, but if she was patient, the creature might reveal itself soon.

About an hour passed, and Cari heard her uncle snoring. She dressed in dark clothing and covered her hair with a scarf. Since the front door was loud and creaky, she slipped out of the back door from the kitchen and stayed close to the house, nearly invisible in the darkness.

The evening was quiet, an occasional rustling of night creatures scrambling around and the lonely hoot of an owl were the only sounds that night. Cari could hear herself breathing, and it seemed quite loud. Time was passing slowly, she wasn't sure how long she had been out here. The light from a phone would give away her presence, so she merely guessed at the time. It didn't matter anyway.

Very carefully, Cari slid herself down the outside wall of the farmhouse. She had been standing still for so long and was getting tired. Dry leaves and grass crunched and crackled beneath her and it sounded like a symphony. Startled, she paused, holding herself completely motionless for a few minutes to determine if she had alerted anyone or anything of her whereabouts. She strained to hear - there was no sound or movement.

There was barely a breeze and the night air was humid. After a while she felt something crawling down her back. Was it a spider or other insect, or was it sweat streaming down? It took every bit of nerve she had not to slap at her back. Slowly reaching back, she felt rivulets of perspiration and breathed a sigh of relief. She wasn't afraid of bugs, but the thought of them crawling on her was troubling.

More time passed and Cari wondered how long she would actually wait out here in the dark. The evening was largely noiseless. Nothing crept out here except for Cari herself. There would be other nights, this was her first attempt.

Not realizing how tired she was and how late it was getting to be, Cari dozed off. A snap of a twig woke her suddenly. Something was moving around. It had to be larger than a possum or racoon to snap a twig that loudly. Shaking herself awake, Cari peered into the darkness and saw it move. It was bigger than she thought, but she could see the outline. It was the troll. She gave an involuntary gasp and the troll's head shot around in her direction. It had spotted her.

"Okay, Cari, think." More time passed, what to do? The troll hadn't moved.

"Troll!" Cari shouted and tore the scarf from her head, shaking out her white- blonde hair.

The troll turned to her and hissed, showing its sharp, pointy teeth.

"Jeg er Huldra!" (I am Huldra) she shouted.

"Huldra? Nei," the troll hissed.

"Ja, Jeg er Huldra," (yes, I am Huldra). The silence that followed was deafening.

The troll paused for a moment, then surprisingly bowed toward Cari, then it quickly ran off. It was headed for a small cluster of trees and moved unexpectedly fast. Cari took a deep breath and ran after the troll. She was catching up, but tripped in a hole, falling heavily to the ground. When she got up, the troll had disappeared.

Limping toward the farmhouse, Cari covered her hair, then tiptoed into the darkness. If it was watching, she didn't want it to see her go inside. Waiting in the gloom near the back of the house, Cari quietly calmed herself, and slowed her breathing. The night once again became soundless and she silently slipped back into the house, hobbling on her left foot.

"What were you doing?" said a voice in the dark kitchen, startling her. It was Uncle Pete, but he was speaking in hushed tones.

"Oh Uncle Pete, you startled me," she said. "Um...I went out to see if I could spot the troll, and you'll never believe it, but I did. I spoke to him, claimed I was Huldra and he bowed to me before he ran off. I tried to chase him, but I tripped in one of those damn holes out there," she rattled on. "He spoke to me, he actually believes I am Huldra."

"Calm down, young lady. Let's go sit down. You're covered in dirt and I see you are favoring your ankle. Did you hurt yourself?"

Cari looked at her ankle, which was already starting to swell. She had to lean on the kitchen counter to keep her weight off of it. "Yes, I guess I did," she answered.

"C'mon, let's go take a look. I wonder if Huldra trips in holes and hurts herself. Hopefully the troll didn't notice," said Pete, helping Cari to the sagging couch.

Once Cari was settled, Pete grabbed a bag of frozen peas for her swollen ankle and a damp cloth to wipe the dirt off.

"You probably know this as well as I do, but I think you sprained that ankle," said Pete. "You won't be chasing trolls for a while."

"It thinks I am Huldra, we can't give up now," she answered.

"I know, but we'll figure out another way. You can't run after it, but maybe someone else can follow it to see where it goes."

"You're thinking Wolfgang, right?"

"Exactly, but I think we should wait until you are at least able to stand up. First things first, we get your ankle checked out tomorrow, then we discuss a new plan. This time don't sneak out while I'm sleeping please."

"How did you know I was out there?"   "I didn't at first. I got up to get some water and I heard you shout, "troll!"

For a second there, I thought I was dreaming. I couldn't see anything out there, it was so dark, but I knew it was your voice."

Cari adjusted the bag of frozen peas on her ankle and apologized to her uncle for sneaking out and not telling him.

"It's okay, Cari, but remember, we're in this together. I couldn't forgive myself if anything happened to you."

"I know, and dad would kick your ass. I promise - I won't take any more chances and keep you in the loop."

"That's all I ask. Now let's get you to bed. We have plans for tomorrow," said Pete, helping Cari from the couch to her room.

"You know what your dad would say - you are as stubborn as he is," Pete added, hugging his niece.

"Nope, he would say I'm as stubborn as you are, Uncle Pete."

Pete was worried about his niece as well as his friends that were here trying to help him. All he came here for was to get this farm sold and dig up a few cans with cash inside. Everything was unraveling and Pete didn't know what to do about it.

He felt like the situation was coming to a head and danger was in the future. Talia Hovlund was dead, Davey had been seriously injured and Cari chased a troll into the darkness. What was next?

# CHAPTER 47: COINCIDENCE?

Harry was at his wits end. There was nothing he could find that would connect Fritz Hovlund to some form of criminal activity. Surely there had to be something, but where to look?  He slept poorly last night, trying to put this puzzle together. His phone buzzed, startling him out of his reverie.  It was Wolf.

"Good morning Harry. Do you want to go have some breakfast? We had a light dinner last night and I'm hungry."

"Sure, where to?"

"How about we drive to Fergus Falls and try another restaurant there? The diner is good, but I'd like to try something different."

"Sounds good, Wolf, give me about ten minutes and meet me in the lobby."

On the drive, Harry told Wolfgang of his frustration with his so-called investigation of old Uncle Fritz.

"It may be time to give up and forget about it," said Wolf. "The police will surely let Pete leave town soon, and we can put this all behind us and move on."

"You're probably right. This was a needle in a haystack search anyway. We've all been over that farmhouse and Pete even dug around in the yard.

There's nothing to find except some old rusty cans with a few bucks inside. End of story."

The first restaurant they saw looked inviting, and advertised home style fare.

There were quite a few cars in the large parking lot, which they assumed meant good food.

"This looks fine if we can get a table," said Harry. "It looks busy."

"Let's give it a try," said Wolf. "We're in no hurry, after all."

The hostess seated them right away, in a comfy booth near a window. She gave them ice water and menus. She said their server would be with them shortly. Minutes later, a younger woman with a very large tattoo of a flower on her arm asked if they wanted coffee and took their breakfast order. She lingered a bit near Wolfgang, so Harry figured they would be getting lots of attention and good service this morning.

While they were sipping their mugs of coffee, suddenly they heard a loud, booming voice say, "Is that Harry Chan?"

Following the voice, they saw a large man approaching the table. He was tall, well over six feet, with thinning brown hair going gray, and a friendly smile.

"Mike? Is that you? Mike Barkley?" said Harry, standing up and shaking the big man's hand. "What a surprise, it's great to see you."

"You too Harry, how long has it been - 15 years or more?"

"At least. Mike, this is my friend, Wolfgang Kilmer. Wolf, this is Mike Barkley. We worked together in Chicago. He left shortly after I became a detective."

Mike shook Wolf's hand and accepted their invitation to join them. After a few minutes of catching up on old times, Harry explained to Mike that Wolfgang was a good friend of Jake Ferris' son Ned.

"Mike knew Jake even before Jake and I were partners," Harry explained.

"Yeah, I heard about Jake's passing. I couldn't make the funeral, my wife was having surgery. I was so sorry, Jake was a great guy."

"He sure was."

"So Harry, what are you doing here?"

"I'm retired and I'm here visiting a friend. He inherited some farm property near Dalton and is having some difficulties."

"Oh, sorry to hear that, I hope it gets sorted out."

"Me too. So, Mike, do you live around here? I remember when you left the force you said you were moving to Minnesota to be closer to family. How did that turn out?" Harry asked.

"Actually, everything turned out pretty good. I'm the Chief of Police in Alexandria now. I worked my way up through the department and made it to chief. I'm off today, and came to Fergus Falls to pick up some stuff from my mother in law's house. She's moving into an apartment and is getting rid of a few things."

"Chief of Police. Congratulations! I knew you would do well," said Harry.

"It was a tough go at first. I wasn't here for two weeks when there was a bank robbery. Who would think when you move to a small town from a place like Chicago that there would be a bank job to investigate."

"Did they catch the robber?"

"Yep, we got him. He's still in prison as far as I know. We thought he had a partner, but never found that person, and never found the money."

"The money was never recovered?" asked Harry. "What did the robber say?"

"He went to prison claiming he was innocent, but one of the bank tellers recognized him. He was wearing a mask, but she was able to definitely identify him."

"Did she recognize him through his mask?" asked Wolf.

At that moment, the server came by with coffee refills and her tattooed arm made Mike smile at a memory.

"Here's how she recognized him," said Mike. "Get this, his mask didn't cover his neck completely and she saw the tattoo on it, and knew who it was right away."

"Poor planning on his part," Harry said.

"No kidding," said Mike.

"Hmm...if this was your guy, he must have hidden the money somewhere," said Wolf.

"Yeah, that was his defense. He said he didn't have any money or any time to get rid of it. He was picked up within hours of the robbery," Mike explained. "If he had a partner that was holding the money, he never gave them up. Went to prison without saying a word."

"Do you remember his name?" asked Harry.

Mike looked at Harry questioningly before answering. "It was Ed, something I think. I don't recall his last name. Possibly started with an H. That's all I can remember."

"I know this sounds odd, Mike, but could I come by your office sometime and look over the case?"

"Sure thing Harry, but why?"

"It's a long shot, but I'm looking into something that could be related."

"From Chicago?"

"Nope, from my friend's farm."

"You are going to have to explain this to me, old friend."

"If you have the time, sit back and drink your coffee. This is going to take a while," said Harry. "It all starts with a man named Pete that we know from Trygghaven Bay. He inherited his uncle's farm not too far from here. As soon as he arrived, things started happening, strange things."

Harry went on to explain the whole story to his old friend, telling him that he was certain that Pete's Uncle Fritz was harboring a secret and that was the reason the old farm was considered valuable. It all culminated with the murder of Talia Hovlund. Harry said he was convinced that it was all connected.

"That's quite a story you're telling me Harry," said Mike. "I'm not too sure that it has anything to do with a 15 year old robbery, but come by my office and we'll go over the investigation details together. We have been acquainted for many years, and one thing is true - you have an instinct for this, and you are usually right."

"Thank you Mike, I know this is a long shot and would be one hell of a coincidence, but I have a feeling."

Harry and Mike agreed to meet at his office the next morning.

## CHAPTER 48: STORIES TO TELL

Pete assisted Cari as she hobbled to the car. He found an urgent care center in Fergus Falls and despite her protests, insisted they get her ankle checked out by a doctor first thing in the morning. Wolf had called earlier and Pete told him briefly what had happened to Cari, and that they were heading to urgent care.

"Do you want me to meet you there?" asked Wolf.

"Nah, we'll be fine. I'll give you a call when we're done and we can meet you guys for lunch or something," said Pete.

"It'll just be me. Harry had somewhere to go this morning. I'll explain it to you later. There's a restaurant that Harry and I went to yesterday, we can meet there," he told him, explaining the name and location of the place.

Two hours passed until Pete called Wolfgang. They agreed to meet for lunch shortly. Wolf waited at the restaurant and saw Pete entering the place behind Cari, who was traveling awkwardly on crutches. It was a new look for her, she was always so 'put together'. Wolf thought it made her seem more real, but felt sorry that she had injured herself.

"Hello, what do you think of my new accessories?" Cari asked Wolf.

"I was just thinking that it was a new style for you. It's not often you see such grace and elegance," said Wolf.

"Aha, you are full of it," said Cari. "Once I get used to these things, I'll show you grace and elegance."

"I'm sure you will. Seriously, how are you feeling?"

"I feel foolish that I tripped in a hole and sprained my ankle while chasing that nasty troll. Otherwise not too bad. I've been told to stay off it for a few days and rest, ice, you know the drill."

"Chasing the troll?" Wolf asked credulously.

Pete and Cari maneuvered into the large booth and further explained what had happened the night before, giving more details of Cari's interaction with the troll creature.

"So you believe it thinks you are the legendary Huldra?" asked Wolf.

"Possibly," said Cari. "He bowed in my direction before he ran off."

"Hmmm...interesting. I don't think you can chase him again for a while," said Wolf. "Do you two have another plan in the works?"

"Not yet, but I suspect we'll think of something," said Cari. "Uncle Pete, you've been awfully quiet. Do you have another plan in mind?"

"Yes, I do. We are all getting out of here, sooner rather than later. We're moving to the hotel in town and as soon as I can, I'm going back home and so are the rest of you," said Pete determinedly. "No one else is getting hurt on my account."

"Can we talk about this later?" said Cari. "You're upset now, but it's not really necessary. I fell in a hole, that's all. It could have happened anytime or anywhere. Please calm down and think about this rationally."

"I am being rational, and it's about time," Pete argued quietly.

"Like I said, we can talk about this later," Cari answered. "Now I'm hungry. Let's get some lunch and Wolf can tell us where Harry is. He looks like he has a story to tell and I want to hear it."

"How do you know I have a story to tell?" asked Wolf.

"I can see it written all over your face. So am I right?" she answered.

"Yes, as a matter of fact you are right. Yesterday Harry and I came here for breakfast. Harry said he was unable to find any sort of criminal connection to your Uncle Fritz and quite frankly, was ready to give up," Wolf explained.

The same server from the previous day came by their table to take a drink order. They all settled on raspberry lemonade, the place advertised as homemade.

They took a moment to look over the menu and then Wolf continued his story.

"We weren't here very long when someone recognized Harry. It turns out it was his old police officer friend from Chicago. He is now the Chief of Police in Alexandria. Apparently, his first case was a bank robbery, about fifteen years ago. The perpetrator was caught and sent to prison, but the money was never recovered and the guy wouldn't say if he had a partner or what happened to the money. He just claimed he was innocent and was found guilty and incarcerated."

"So what does that have to do with anything?" asked Pete.

"Harry went to the Chief's office today to look over the case file. He said he has a funny feeling there's a connection. Pure instinct."

"Oh, I get it. He thinks great Uncle Fritz has a connection to the robber, right?"

"He didn't say for sure, but it seems like that's the direction he's going in."

"My Uncle Fritz was a lot of things, but a bank robber? That doesn't seem likely," said Pete. "I assume Harry thinks the money is hidden on the farm or some paperwork or a map is there to tell its location. If Uncle Fritz had all that cash hidden away, why leave it there for so long? Fifteen years is a long time, and Uncle Fritz would have still been pretty old when the robbery happened. Besides, he barely knew anyone, he had no friends that I knew of. Who would he be willing to help rob a bank? Nope, sorry, I think Harry is barking up the wrong tree."

"Wait a minute, Uncle Pete. Harry could be on to something," said Cari. "It certainly won't hurt for him to look over the case file, and it would explain why there's such an interest in the farm and getting rid of you."

"What about the troll? He certainly had nothing to do with it," said Pete.

"No, but it explains why Talia Hovlund was so interested in that crummy farm and maybe why she was killed," Cari added. "Is it so unusual to believe that story, but not that you awakened a troll?"

"You're right, young lady. I will keep an open mind," Pete agreed. "Excuse my bad language, but I don't know what to fuckin' believe anymore."

Wolf considered what both Cari and Pete said. He wasn't positive about the troll's existence, or Harry's theory of robbery cash hidden on the farm. What he did know was that someone was trying to harm Pete and get him away from the farm.

When the server came back to the table to take their lunch order, Wolf was reminded of the story Chief Barkely told of the teller recognizing the robber's tattoo, which showed on his neck, and ultimately sent him to prison. He related Mike's story as to how the robber was identified.

"Do you know what the tattoo was?" Pete asked suddenly.

"No, he didn't say. I suppose Harry will tell us after he looks over the case file."

"Did he tell you the robber's name?" Pete questioned.

"Um...he wasn't sure of the last name, but thought his first name was Ed."

"Ed or Fred?" asked Pete.

"I'm pretty sure he said Ed," answered Wolf. "Why do you ask?"

"I just remembered something, but I'm not completely sure. It was a long time ago and my memory is a bit fuzzy."

"Now you have my curiosity piqued," said Cari. "Spill it."

"No, sorry Cari, but I will have to wait until we hear more from Harry. If I'm remembering things correctly, Harry is on to something. I hate to say it, but he could be right."

# Chapter 49: Shoe

After they finished a very nice lunch of hearty chef salads, Cari, Pete and Wolf departed for the farm. Wolf dropped his vehicle at the hotel and rode with them, knowing that Harry would be joining them later when he finished his meeting with Chief Barkley.

Even though Cari pestered her uncle relentlessly to find out what in the world he was recalling about someone named Ed or Fred with a tattoo, Pete would not budge. He explained that he didn't want to start making assumptions before talking with Harry about his meeting with the police chief and subsequent information. She finally gave up when they pulled into the farmhouse driveway.

Before they even got out of the car, a police cruiser pulled up behind them. At first Wolf thought it was Harry catching a ride, but soon noticed it was the two officers that had visited the farm recently.

"Look who's here," said Wolf.

"Oh boy, they didn't waste any time getting here, did they?" Pete commented.

"Don't worry, Uncle Pete, they're probably just here to pass on some new information, and maybe tell you that you're free to leave town."

"Let's hope so," answered Pete as he lumbered out of the vehicle.

Pete turned immediately to the officers to invite them inside. He wanted to know why they were at the farm and didn't want to wait any longer. The two officers greeted all of them in a friendly manner and followed Pete inside.

Cari and Wolf exchanged glances before entering, wondering if they were going to hear some news - good or bad. "Fingers crossed," Wolf whispered.

The two officers and Pete were seated in the kitchen. Cari and Wolf peeked in and asked if it was okay to join them. Officer Anderson told them it was fine, since they would find out everything soon enough, and this was so far to be purely an unofficial visit.

"It has been determined that Talia Hovlund was murdered by strangulation and then left in the pond near Bagley Road, which is less than a mile from here. Her vehicle was found on that same road, close to the pond.  It appears that she was strangled by some sort of rope or cord and the perpetrator drove her car to the location before putting her in the pond. The  time of death - as close as can be determined was around 11:00 pm on the twelfth. She was found wearing both of her shoes."

The sigh of relief by Pete, Cari and Wolf was audible. "So the shoe we found near the silo - has no connection?" asked Cari.

"It doesn't seem to have any connection. If she lost the shoe out here, it was most likely sometime before she was killed, probably when she made a trip here related to the sale of the farm," Officer Anderson said.

"So, I can leave the area, free and clear?" asked Pete.

"We can't keep you here, Mr. Magnusson, but would appreciate it if you could stay around a few more days. You did have a 'heated' discussion with her before she disappeared and we are putting together a timeline. By the way, where were you on the twelfth, around 11:00 pm?"

"I was here on the farm, probably sound asleep, or close to it," Pete answered. "For the record, it wasn't a heated discussion, just a regular one. I just stopped to ask a question, which she ignored, then pushed me on the farm sale, that's all. I have no wish to speak ill of the dead, but that's how it went."

"He's right, he was here at the farm the evening of the twelfth, and so was I," Cari commented.

The officer looked at Wolfgang, so he answered. "I was not here."

After turning down the offer of coffee, the two police officers departed with their thanks for everyone's time. They requested that the information they shared not be discussed publicly, even though it would be news soon enough.

"Wow, I'm sure glad she had on two shoes when they found her," said Pete. "I was getting a bit concerned about the shoe thing. There really was no good way to explain why it was here, if she was missing a shoe when she was found."

"If that was her shoe, she must have lost it out here before you arrived," said Wolfgang. "I wonder how often she was out here? I know realtors do a close inspection of the property before helping you come up with an asking price, but she wasn't officially your realtor yet."

"You are right about that. She was just supposed to get me a cleaning service, and then I met her at the office and we discussed the farm sale at that time. I wonder if she was up to something?"

"I think her involvement was a little more than being your realtor. There's a connection, I'm sure. When Harry gets back, we need to go over everything," said Cari. "Besides, I'm stuck in the chair with ice on my ankle, so I can't go chasing the troll. Not yet anyway."

"I'm still serious about us moving out of here," said Pete.

"Not yet, please Uncle Pete."

"Okay, but if one more thing happens - we're gone, no argument," said Pete.

Wolf was quiet, but suspected there would be at least one more thing that would happen. He was quite sure of it. The story wasn't over yet.

# Chapter 50: Theory

Harry arrived at the Alexandria Police Station at 9:45. He was anxious to talk to Mike and look over the case file involving the robbery. Since the case had been closed years ago, and the perpetrator jailed, Harry assumed the files were in a box in the station's basement storage, if they had one. Although, fifteen years was not that long ago, perhaps the case files could be found stored in the computer as well.

"Good morning sir, may I help you?" said the officer at the front desk. A very young looking woman, with a pleasant demeanor.

"I'm here to see Chief Barkley, we have a 10:00 am appointment," Harry answered.

"Please have a seat, and I'll let him know," she answered.

Harry sat down and took the time to glance around the police station. It was really quite nice, at least in the waiting area. He didn't see any other people besides police officers. There were phones ringing and everyone looked busy.

"Harry, welcome," said Chief Barkley, reaching out to shake Harry's hand.

"Thank you Mike, I hope you're not too busy this morning."

"Not at all, I have most of the morning free so far. I have meetings scheduled for this afternoon, but nothing right now. Come on in my office and we can talk."

From what Harry could see, it looked like an efficiently run department and he was glad for his old friend. He knew Mike was a top notch officer when he was in Chicago and would bring his expertise with him. It was certainly a lucky break to run into Mike yesterday. What a terrific coincidence.

They entered Mike's office, which was nicely put together, without being too pretentious. "Have a seat Harry, and I'll tell you what I've found so far."

Mike pecked away at his computer and found the file he was searching for.

"We have all of the information here in the computer database, but we also have paper copies of everything as well. We can discuss what is here and then have a look at the hard copy files if you like."

Moments later an officer tapped on Mike's office door. He was carrying a file box. Mike waved him in and indicated he should put the box on the small conference table. He thanked the officer and told Harry the files he wanted were in that box.

"Let's take a look then," said Harry. "I won't have to look over your shoulder at your computer screen and I can peruse the files if that's alright with you."

"Of course, Harry. Let's have a look. I can tell you what I've found so far, and see if there's anything that could help in your, well...I don't want to say investigation, um, how about...search."

"Fine, search it is," said Harry. "I suppose I am searching for the truth."

"Well put," said Mike as he joined Harry at the conference table and they proceeded to look through the files.

"So the robber's name is Frederick Helms. He had no previous record, and knew at least the one bank teller who identified him by the tattoo on his neck. Not too smart on his part," said Harry, as he studied the file in front of him.

"Yes, and Mr. Helms served his full term and has been released from prison," said Mike. "His release was nearly six months ago and he is listed as living here in Alexandria."

Harry paged through the papers in each file. "It looks like he worked at a local lumber mill at the time of the robbery," said Harry. "There's no indication of a close connection with any co-workers. There were several interviews done, but no one came up as a person of interest that could have helped him."

"No, not one. He claimed his innocence right up until his release. He refused to admit to the crime, even when the offer of a shorter prison sentence was being considered," said Mike.

"Has he been on the radar since his release?" asked Harry.

"At first, yes. The detective that took over the case had him watched for a few months. There was no unusual activity. He got a part time job back at the lumber mill and no red flags," said Mike. "If he hid that money, he sure didn't go on a search for it that we could see."

"That is an unusual tattoo," said Harry. "I can see how the teller noticed it."

"I know, we couldn't figure out why someone would get that tattoo, it just looked like a big X," said Mike. "Then one of the officers said that Helms talked a lot about rune letters. Are you familiar with Viking runes?"

"I am now - you wouldn't believe it," said Harry. "Is this a popular thing here in Minnesota?"

"There are certainly folks hereabouts who study this stuff, and since it is Viking related, it does garner special interest in this part of the state," said Mike. "Are you familiar with the Kensington rune stone?"

"Yes, as a matter of fact, I am. My education on all things 'rune' is fairly new, but I am learning," Harry answered.

"That's good, then I don't have to explain it to you," said Mike. "We do have the museum here that houses the stone, so there are a great number of people aware of the rune stone and the meaning of Viking runes. I myself wasn't one of them, (remember, I'm from Chicago). Since Helms mentioned runes in passing, the officer asked his girlfriend, who was quite well versed in Viking runes, and came up with the meaning."

"Well, what does the big X mean?" asked Harry, paging through the documents.

"According to what my officer found out, the symbol, which to the average person just looks like an X, is the rune GEBO," Mike explained.

"GEBO, eh? So tell me, what exactly does that mean?" Harry questioned.

"Roughly translated, it means: 'contracts and partnerships'. I thought that was an interesting element," answered Mike.

"No kidding, this fellah apparently takes partnership seriously. He never gave up the person that helped him. Quite the twist of fate, how the symbol he had tattooed on his neck is the one thing that gave him away," said Harry.

"I suspect he was protecting the money more so than the partner. If the person who helped him out doesn't have the money anymore, then I suspect there could be a big problem," said Mike.

"No kidding, after all these years in jail, I'm betting he wants to get his hands on the cash," said Harry.

"After I read through the file this morning, I sent an officer over to Helms' apartment. He wasn't there. The officer checked with the building manager, and he said that Helms still lives there, but left recently. The manager said that Helms told him he was going out of town for a few days, and hasn't returned. The officer questioned the lumber mill manager, and he said Helms was a no show for several shifts, and was fired. He hasn't been seen and didn't come by for a final paycheck.

"He's going after the robbery money," said Harry.

"Yeah, I think you're right. We probably should have continued watching him, but so much time passed and nothing happened. We only have so much time to spend on cases, and this was an old one that was basically closed. We're going to pursue this case now, believe me."

"If you don't mind, could you keep me posted on anything you discover?" Harry asked.

"Of course, Harry. If it wasn't for you asking about the case, we may have missed something. We'll be looking for Helms and alerting the other departments in surrounding communities to watch for him as well. Right now, he hasn't done anything illegal that we know of, but we want to know where he is. I suspect he will lead us right to his partner, and the money, if we can find him."

"I have a theory, but I have to ask a few questions first. Give me a day or so and I'll get back to you Mike."

"Sure thing Harry. I know that once you get your teeth into something, you don't let go. I'll trust you on this, but remember, you're retired. Let me or another police officer in on anything you find out, and right away."

"I will Mike. No worries."

# Chapter 51: Uncle Fritz

Harry's mind was racing after he left the police station. He stopped at a drive thru to pick up something for a late lunch and ate in his hotel room. In case he was going to be gone for a while, he tossed a few things in a bag and departed for the Kolbeck farm. He was very anxious to talk to Pete, Wolf and Cari. He had a lot of interesting information to share.

Harry had the feeling of being rushed, but at the same time felt the need to ride around the country roads near the farm. He had a strong hunch that something was going to happen and he wanted to have a lay of the land first. The police found Talia Hovlund's vehicle on Bagley Road. Less than a quarter mile away was the pond where her body was discovered. The police hadn't released any information on where the murder occurred. Perhaps they weren't sure yet.

"I don't think she was killed out here. I'm sure her body was moved," thought Harry. "If she was murdered elsewhere, the killer would have had to drive the car out here, leave it, put her in the pond and somehow get back to town? That seems like a lot. Maybe the killer was in the car with her, but then would still have to get back to town. It's not that far, but it would be quite a walk. Unless...the killer is somewhere around here. There are a few other farms, and some look quite abandoned. Any one of them could be a good place to hide."

Harry's mind continued to mull over all different scenarios as he drove around. He finally decided it was time to get back to the farm and go over his findings with the others. When he pulled into the drive, Wolf was standing on the front porch with Cari, who was leaning on crutches. He immediately wondered what had happened to her.

"Harry, I'm glad you're back," said Wolfgang. "We have plenty to talk about."

"We certainly do," said Harry. "First of all, what happened to you Cari?"

"I fell in one of those holes that are everywhere on this farm and sprained my ankle. It was dark and I was chasing a troll."

"Mmm hmm...so nothing unusual about that," Harry replied wryly. "So, are you okay?"

"Yes, I'm fine. I just have to elevate it, rest, ice, and stay off of it for a while. I'm not too happy about the situation, but there's nothing I can do about it."

"Let's go inside and we can all share our information," said Wolf.

"Most definitely," said Harry, "I have some interesting details to divulge."

"As do we, particularly Pete. He said he won't share some specific knowledge until you arrived to share what you learned," said Wolf.

They entered the living room and Pete joined them, carrying a tray with a pitcher of iced tea and some crackers, cheese and cookies.

"Hello Harry. I fixed us all a snack, because I think we're going to be talking this out for quite a while," Pete said, setting down his tray. "Let's get comfortable and hear what you have to say Henry."

Everyone found a seat, helping themselves to tea and snacks. The conversation began with Harry, who proceeded to tell them everything he had learned from Chief Barkley. When Harry mentioned Frederick Helms, Pete stopped him for a moment.

"I think we have found the connection to Uncle Fritz," said Pete. "I believe he was hired as a farmhand after I told my uncle I was going to take another job. Uncle Fritz hired a man named Fred."

"Pete, this is important, did you ever see this Fred fellow?"

"Yes, I saw him once when I visited here."

"Do you remember, did he have a tattoo?"

"Sure, how did you know? He had a tattoo of the rune letter GEBO on the side of his neck. You know, Cari, GEBO is the symbol that looks like a big X. I thought at first it was just an X, but when I mentioned the tattoo to Uncle Fritz, he said it was a rune letter."

"Helms was arrested for a bank robbery that happened about fifteen years ago. He was sent to prison, but the cash was never recovered. It was assumed that he had a partner that kept the cash all this time. Helms proclaimed his innocence and never gave up his partner. He served his whole term, and is out of prison," Harry explained.

"So you think Uncle Fritz was his partner?" Pete asked. "If he was, then the money could be here somewhere and that guy Helms is looking for it."

"What do you think Pete? Is it possible?" questioned Wolfgang.

Pete rubbed his hand across his stubbly whiskers and sighed. "It's possible, I s'pose."

"Uncle Pete, my dad may not have told you this, but he came back to the farm, once, when Uncle Fritz was ill."

"Oh yeah, I remember now. He came here at our mother's request to check on Uncle Fritz. I wasn't able to travel at the time, because I was in the middle of a business deal. I had forgotten all about Viktor visiting here."

"He saw Uncle Fritz without his shirt on, when he was sick in bed," said Cari. "He told me that Fritz had a tattoo of an X on his chest," said Cari. When he asked about it, Uncle Fritz told him it was the rune letter GEBO which represents "Partnership."

# CHAPTER 52: PARTNERS

"Let me get this straight," said Harry. "Both your uncle and this Helms fellow had a tattoo of a rune letter that represents partnership. So, we assume they considered themselves partners. The thing is, the robbery happened many years after Helms worked for your uncle. At the time of the robbery, Helms was working at a lumber mill."

"They must have stayed in touch. That is unusual, though. Uncle Fritz didn't really have any friends," said Pete. "I visited occasionally, even after my mother passed away, but Fritz wasn't very welcoming, so I never stayed too long. After a few years, he had given up on farming and let the place go to seed. He told me that he was getting too old to do any work and couldn't find anyone reliable to hire, so he just quit."

"Helms may have come to your uncle with his plans for the bank robbery. He needed a partner he could trust to help him. The bank was a small, local operation and didn't have very good security at the time. The police station is located a few miles away, so he had a bit of time to escape," said Harry.

"They may have been planning it for a while," said Wolf.

"Waiting for the right time - whatever that was," Cari added.

"There was a notation in the case file about the bank's security guard," Harry mentioned. "The regular guard had taken ill with food poisoning, and they called in the previous guard who had been retired. He was an older fellah, and was no longer very competent. He panicked when the robbery occurred. The police checked him out - there was no reason to suspect him. Their regular guard had been so sick he was nearly hospitalized. All the bank employees were cleared of any suspicion."

"Hmm...it appears that maybe the regular bank guard was given something to make him sick, so that the bank would be less protected," said Wolfgang. "Did the police investigate that aspect?"

"Yes, and the security guard went over everything he had eaten or drank for the days previous to the robbery. Nothing unusual. It seemed like an unhappy coincidence," explained Harry. "I don't believe it was. Somehow Helms or someone working with him got to that guard and poisoned him."

"I still have a hard time wrapping my head around this," said Pete. "Uncle Fritz connected to a bank robbery? He was not a nice man, but I would have never thought him to be a criminal."

"Maybe Helms threatened him somehow, so he had to help him. Fritz had no friends or family nearby, he was getting older and weaker. Helms may have forced him to get involved," Wolf said.

"Or what about this?" said Cari. "What if Uncle Fritz didn't realize what he was helping Helms with until it was too late. Once the robbery had taken place, he couldn't go to the police, or he would be considered an accomplice."

"You could be on to something there," said Harry. "If what you say about your uncle is true, Pete, he may have been roped into the robbery innocently, then Helms forced him, possibly at gunpoint, to assist with his escape."

"I know this is all speculation, but Uncle Fritz let it be known that he was being stalked by evil. All along I have assumed this was the troll, but what if it was Helms that he feared?" Pete said.

"If he had the money hidden, he knew when Helms got out of prison he would come straight to Fritz for the money," said Harry. "He hid the cash because he knew it would connect him to the robbery. Remember he said something to Patti at the diner about his treasure and enough time had gone by."

"Either way, we may never know what Uncle Fritz's involvement was, and Helms is surely looking to get the money, and figures it is hidden somewhere on this farm," said Cari. "It might not be easy to find, and Fritz is dead. Helms would need someone to help him look for it."

"Another partner?" asked Wolfgang.

"Talia?" said Cari. "He could have been the one that killed her."

"If she was his connection, with her gone, how is he going to get on the farm to look for the money?" Harry wondered.

"Good question. She could have found out who he was and what he was up to and threatened to alert the authorities," said Wolf. "I guess we won't know until the police figure out who killed her."

"Pete, I know you and Cari have seen this troll you speak of, but I think all the trouble here may very well be the work of Helms and another accomplice," said Harry. "It's all about the money."

"I somewhat agree with you Henry, but I know the troll exists," said Pete. The trouble may be coming from two different fronts."

"In that case, we have twice as much to be concerned about," said Cari.

While they speculated on Fritz and his involvement in the bank robber, another watched the house with his powerful binoculars. With his free hand he felt for the cord, it was still in his pocket. It was foolish to keep it, but he liked how it wrapped around his fingers. It felt good in his hand. Time to get rid of it now, though.

The memory was still fresh. He had quickly looped the cord around Talia's neck, got his foot wedged behind hers, and jerked hard, backward. He let her hang for a bit so that her own weight would strangle her. It was almost too easy, the stupid bitch never knew what was coming until the last moment. There was just one more to take care of and the treasure would soon be his.

# Chapter 53: Farm Fear

After their long speculative discussion with Pete and Cari, Wolf and Harry agreed that one of them would stay behind at the farm each evening. The possibility of danger lingered close by, and Pete was determined to remain at the farm, and Cari wouldn't leave him. Besides, she was injured

The farm had only one extra bedroom, so the one staying behind had to sleep on the sagging sofa. "I'll stay tonight," said Wolfgang. "You may want to check in with Chief Barkley tomorrow, Harry. He may have some news on the whereabouts of Fred Helms."

"Okay, that sounds like a plan," said Harry. "After I see Mike Barkley, I'll head back out here. Is there anything you all want me to pick up?"

"Nah, I think we should all meet in town for breakfast," said Pete. "I say we go to the diner.  Our favorite server, Patti, may be able to answer some questions about Uncle Fritz, or she may have some news about Talia Hovlund's murder. She seems to be a fountain of information."

"Good plan Pete," said Harry. "How about we meet around 9:30 tomorrow morning and then I'll give Mike a call and see if he has any news to share."

"After we return from town tomorrow, I say we should start looking for the money," said Cari. "If the money is found - then Helms has no reason to harm you Uncle Pete."

"He could have hidden that money just about anywhere," said Pete. "He did like to bury things, so that's a place to start. I have searched everywhere for a map of some sort when I was looking for the cash cans. I didn't find anything."

"Is there anything in Uncle Fritz's will that could give you a clue?" asked Cari.

"I don't think so, but I'll stop by his attorney's office tomorrow and get a copy. It's worth a try."

Pete announced that he was tired and tottered off to take a nap. Cari needed to rest her ankle, so she settled in with a book, keeping her foot elevated. Wolfgang and Harry walked to the car and had a serious discussion about the situation.

"I think I should leave my gun with you," said Harry. "Are you trained with firearms?"

"No, I am not really, so please don't," said Wolfgang.

"Helms could be dangerous."

"I realize that, but we don't have a clue where that money is, any more than he does."

"Yes, but he doesn't know that."

"I'll stay awake - my eyes and ears open all night," said Wolf. "I'm keeping my hotel room in town so I can catch a nap tomorrow. I don't expect to get any sleep on that lumpy sofa anyway."

"Okay, but if there's any trouble, you get them out of here," said Harry.

"No worries mate, I'm on it."

Harry knew from personal experience that Wolfgang would do whatever was necessary to protect his friends. He had literally saved Harry's life once, carrying a seriously injured Harry through a dangerous lightning storm to safety. Harry owed that man his life, and would never forget it.

The scenarios they had considered ran through Harry's brain as he drove into town. He felt fairly certain that somehow Talia Hovlund had become involved with Fred Helms, to her ultimate demise. He would ask Chief Barkley if he knew of any places that Helms frequented. It was possible that he may have been seen with Talia somewhere. It was a slight string to pull, but worth a try.

Helms had to be holed up somewhere. He would be difficult to find if he wasn't seen in public recently. If he had returned to his apartment, the police would grab him immediately; at least for questioning. There was more, Harry just knew it.

While Harry drove back to his hotel, the farmhouse was quiet. Wolfgang was scanning the perimeter of the farm while it was still light enough to see. The holes Pete had dug looking for cans of money pock-marked the backyard. Additional holes that Pete claimed were booby-traps dug by the troll dotted the area around the house. He walked around the farmhouse, then made his way to the barn.

The barn smelled like one. Dusty remnants of hay remained scattered around. The sun filtered through the cracks in the walls, revealing a shower of dust motes in the air. Wolf found an old broom and swept away some of the hay, looking for a trap door or opening of some sort in the floor. He did notice there were still blood stains where the young man had been injured by the falling farm implements.

Thinking about what had happened to Davey gave Wolfgang pause. Why would anyone want to injure him? He had nothing to do with the farm or Pete, other than as a clean-up guy. It may be that someone was watching the farm and saw what Davey was doing, and thought he was searching for the money.

By the same token, a person could have been observing the farm and noticed Pete digging around in the backyard. Assuming no one knew about Uncle Fritz's compulsion for burying small amounts of cash in old cans, it would seem as if Pete was searching for the robbery money - or as Fritz called it - treasure.

Pete had been quite certain his uncle wasn't involved directly in the bank job, but more of an unwilling partner to Helms. According to Pete, Fritz didn't trust people, so he must have had a good relationship with Helms while the man worked as his farmhand. A number of years had passed since Helms worked at the farm, perhaps they had stayed in touch and remained friends. Pete said Fritz had no friends, but possibly Helms earned his friendship and trust (as indicated by them both sporting rune tattoos representing partnership).

Now that Fritz was dead, there was no way to be sure what his involvement (if any) was in the robbery. If Helms got out of prison a few months ago, why didn't he go to the farm immediately to see Fritz and get the money? Easy answer: the police were watching him. He knew that if he was spotted anywhere near the farm, they would guess he was going after the money. Helms only had to bide his time, wait for the police to give up watching him and he could get the money from Fritz. As luck would have it - Fritz died before Helms could retrieve the cash.

On top of everything else, there was the possibility of an evil troll in the mix. Cari was sure she had spoken to the troll, and Pete claims to have seen it more than once himself. If the troll does exist; Pete's awakening it and breaking the curse is a grand coincidence. Talia Hovlund gets killed, her shoe (which she was not wearing when she was killed) is found by the silo, and the troll keeps playing nasty tricks, seemingly to get rid of Pete.

As Wolf speculated, he kicked around the dirt and dusty bits of hay in the old barn. He came up with a number of questions - but no real answers. Not yet. His foot kicked something small, he picked it up, turning it over in his hand. It was rune stone, made of black onyx. The symbol etched on it - he knew. It was a vertical line: ISA - representing "challenge, frustration and psychological blocks."

"Too true," thought Wolfgang, dropping the stone into his pocket.

# Chapter 54: More Questions

The morning arrived warm and bright. No incidents during the night, and everyone, with the exception of Wolfgang, had slept soundly. He deliberately stayed awake, periodically checking outdoors, and listening for any noises. Other than an owl hoot and some scrabbling of tiny creatures, it had been very quiet.

At daybreak, Pete wandered into the living room and told Wolfgang to take a nap on his bed.

"It's morning and light outside - ain't nobody comin' to kill us now, so you get a few hours of shut eye," he told Wolfgang. "I'll get you up about a half hour before we leave for town, so you can get ready."

"Are you sure?" he asked.

"Yup, I already made the bed, here's an extra quilt to wrap up in," said Pete, handing him some newer-looking bedding. Wolf happily fell on to the bed, and covered himself in the soft quilt. He was asleep in minutes.

An hour later, Cari joined her uncle in the kitchen, using only one crutch for support. She told Pete that while they were in town, she wanted to look for a cane, as her ankle was healing nicely, and she didn't need the crutches.

"Why are you up so early?" Pete asked.

"I smelled the coffee," she answered.

"What else?" he asked.

"I woke up and started to think about everything we talked over yesterday. You could be right about Uncle Fritz. I believe he got tricked into helping that Helms fellow and couldn't get out of it."

"The thing about them both having the partnership tattoos is kind of a puzzle," said Pete.

"You told us that Uncle Fritz had no friends. Maybe while he worked at the farm, Helms became his friend."

"The whole thing is pretty weird, but if you knew Uncle Fritz - he was weird. I guess I really didn't know him all that well. He never expressed any feelings toward me or your dad. I know my mother cared for him, so he must have had some good in him. Maybe he was just lonely and didn't know how to fix it."

"Quite sad, really," said Cari. "He kept people away, and ended up alone."

"Some people want to be left alone. He gave that impression. I still don't buy that he was a willing participant in stealing money from a bank. He didn't spend any money - he buried it in his yard. What would he do with more money?"

"We may never know the answers," said Cari.

After they finished their coffee and conversation, Pete and Cari spent some time walking around the farm, as Wolf had done the afternoon before. They also ended up in the barn and Pete noticed the floor had been swept. He figured it was Wolf, but made a mental note to ask him about it later. Pete pointed out the blood stains on the floor.

"This is where I found Davey. He was bleeding quite a bit, you know how a head wound does. I was pretty worried about him - he's a nice kid and a hard worker. I think I'll stop by and visit him today."

"That's a great idea, Uncle Pete. I'm sure he will appreciate it. Plus, you can ask him if he remembers anything else the night he was hurt."

"Sure, and you can come with me. He will certainly enjoy a visit from a pretty girl."

"Let's bring him something. Maybe some sweet rolls or even a pizza."

"Yep, we'll do that. After breakfast, we'll go see him and then I have to stop by the attorney's office and get a copy of Fritz's will. I also want to swing by the library. I have some books to return."

When they returned to the farmhouse, Wolfgang was in the kitchen, fixing himself a cup of coffee. "Good morning," he said. "A delivery came a few minutes ago from the hardware store. It's a metal detector."

"Good morning," Pete and Cari answered. "That must be the metal detector that Ned ordered. Took long enough. By the way, did you happen to sweep out in the barn yesterday?" asked Pete.

"Guilty. I was looking for a trap door or something like it on the floor. I didn't find a trap door, but I did find this," he said, holding up the ISA rune stone.

"Ha, ISA, that's interesting," said Cari. "We are facing a challenge and with it comes frustration. It's like that stone found you."

"Well, I guess that's better than being stalked by the Death Card," said Wolf. Pete looked confused and Cari just told him it was a long story from Wolf's visit to Colorado.

Once everyone was ready to go, they rode into town together. Wolf knew that Harry would be returning to the farm, and Wolf could catch a ride with him if Cari and Pete had other plans. He did want to go with them to visit Davey, as he was interested in what the young man had to tell them about his ordeal.

When they arrived at the diner, they found Harry had already gotten a table and was sipping coffee. He was having a conversation with Patti, who immediately greeted them and rushed off to get water and menus.

"So, how was your evening?" Harry asked.

"Uneventful," said Wolf.

"That's good," Harry replied.

"I slept like a rock," said Pete.

"Me too," said Cari. "My ankle isn't bothering me too much anymore, so I zonked out pretty good."

Patti returned with the menus and ice water, and told them she'd give them a few minutes to decide.

"I am so hungry," said Cari. "I'm getting eggs, bacon, pancakes, hash browns  and toast, if someone will share the toast with me."

"I'm in," said Wolfgang. "I'll get the same thing."

"Make that three," said Harry. "How about it Pete - split an order of toast with me?"

"Sure, as long as you're okay with sourdough, and I'm getting sausage instead of bacon."

When Patti returned, they gave her their breakfast order. Pete leaned over toward her and quietly asked if she had heard anything new on the killing of Talia Hovlund.

"Nothing that hasn't been on the news," she told them.

"Do you happen to know if she had been dating anyone?" asked Harry.

"Hmm...funny you should ask that," she said, tapping her pencil on the order pad. "The last time I talked to her she was on her way to get her hair and nails done. She said something about a date, but she didn't say who it was."

"Did you ever see her with a person that wasn't a client?"

"No, I don't think so. She did have business connections in town, though. I guess through her real estate job. She may have been dating one of them, but I'm not sure. She did talk a lot about her important business lunches and so forth, which would never take place here. She could have been bragging. Oh wait, I don't mean to speak ill of the dead. Oops, I'd better put in your breakfast order," she added, then hurried off.

"So, she could have been seeing someone, but not around town. It could have been Fred Helms," said Wolfgang.

"Dating or making plans to search for the cash?" asked Harry.

"She did spend time at the farm, even before she was hired as my realtor," Pete commented. "The question is, if she was seeing Helms, how did they get connected?"

"By accident or design?" Cari added.

"More questions," said Harry.

# CHAPTER 55: DAVEY'S MEMORY

After finishing their hearty breakfast, Pete and Cari were on their way to see Davey and Wolf asked to join them. Pete had called Davey, who was still at home and anxious for company. Harry was leaving for Alexandria. He called Chief Barkley and they agreed to meet at his office later that morning.

"Let's order some sweet rolls for Davey," said Pete. "I don't want to go there empty-handed." Patti packed a nice variety of treats for them to take along.

"Keep me posted if you hear anything new," said Patti as they were leaving. "And I'll do the same."

"Yeah, sure," Pete answered as they exited the diner.

"So, what information do you think we will glean from talking with Davey?" Wolfgang asked as they drove to Davey's house.

"I want him to go over what happened before the farm implements fell on him. He told Ned and Kyra that he was in the silo, and heard a noise, like hissing from the barn," said Pete. "I also want to find out when he can come back and finish the job."

"Remember, he said he saw a bull while he was loading the trailer, then the bull vanished," added Cari. "Legends claim that trolls shape-shift into eagles, bulls and dragons, like on Iceland's coat of arms."

"Those creatures are known as protectors," said Wolf. "If the troll shape-shifts, I wonder what he is protecting."

"His homeland or territory," said Cari.

"Protecting it from what?" asked Wolf.

"Humans," she answered stonily.

Wolf noted the suburban-style little neighborhood where Davey lived. He pictured the young man living in an apartment or condo, but it was very pleasant here.

When they pulled into the driveway, Davey waved at them from his front steps. He was using a cane as support, but the bandages were gone from his head.

"Hello Davey!" Pete shouted.

"Hey there Mr. Magnusson. How nice of you to stop by," Davey answered. "Please come in everyone," he added, when he noticed Cari and Wolf getting out of the vehicle.

They all entered the small living room, after Davey invited them in. Cari handed him the bakery bag of treats and the young man couldn't help but stare at her.

"Davey, this is my niece, Cari Magnusson and our friend Wolfgang Kilmer. Wolf and Cari, this is Davey Connor," said Pete gesturing to them.

"I'm pleased to meet you both," said Davey, who was holding on tight to the bakery bag and trying very hard not to keep staring at the lovely Cari. He got himself together and shook the hand she offered and turned to shake Wolf's hand as well.

"Please sit down everyone. Can I offer you anything? Coffee or tea?"

"No thanks, son, we just finished a big breakfast," said Pete. "You enjoy those sweet rolls."

"Thank you. I'll put them in the kitchen and be right with you," said Davey, who still seemed a bit shaken as he limped away.

When he returned to the living room, Pete asked Davey if he remembered anything else about the night he was injured at the farm. Davey repeated the story about hearing the hissing sound from the barn and then getting struck right afterward. He also mentioned seeing the bull in the field while he was loading the trailer.

"Can you remember any details about the bull?" Cari asked.

"Not especially. It was dark out and the bull was just standing there. It looked at me, then it snorted and pawed at the ground. It was a good sized bull, as far as I could tell. It was all black, at least what I could see of it," he answered.

"Did it make any other noise?" she asked.

"It just snorted, that's all. Then I went back to loading."

"So when you looked into the field again, it was gone?" she asked.

"Yep, it sort of disappeared into the darkness. Pretty quiet for a bull."

Clearly, there was no new information to be garnered from Davey, but it was a nice visit and confirmed everything that Ned and Kyra had told them. Pete asked Davey if he was willing to come back to work at the farm, and Davey gave him a resounding yes.

"I should be ready to finish up the job next week, Mr. Magnusson," said Davey. "I might not work as fast as before, but I'll get it done," he added.

"Thank you young man, and call me Pete. I'm grateful you're willing to come back after what happened."

"Hey, Mr. Pete, did you ever find out how all those farm tools fell at once? Was it rotten wood, or rusty fasteners?"

"Davey, I'll be honest with you, it seems like the fasteners had been loosened. It was vandalism of the worst kind. Are you still willing to come out and help me?"

"Sure, Mr. Pete. If I worried about vandals at job sites, I'd never get any work."

# Chapter 56: Helms

This time when Harry arrived at the police station, Chief Barkley was waiting for him. They shook hands, exchanged greetings and went directly to the chief's office.

The chief immediately explained that there was no sign of Helms anywhere, and they were keeping a close watch on his apartment. The police canvassed the neighbors, but no one had seen him recently.

Harry explained to Chief Barkley that Helms had been working as a farmhand at Fritz Kolbeck's farm many years ago, so there was a connection between the men. He also told him about the matching GEBO tattoo that Fritz had, and how that may have been a symbol of partnership with Helms.

"Pete is convinced his uncle was coerced, forced or tricked in some way to help Helms with the robbery," said Harry. "He doesn't have many good things to say about his uncle, but can't believe he's a criminal."

"What about the money?" asked Chief Barkley.

"One theory is that once Fritz found out what he was involved in, he agreed to hide the money, knowing his part in the crime would make him seem guilty, so he had to cover it up."

"That would explain why Helms never gave him up or admitted to stealing the money. He figured if Fritz didn't say anything about it - the money would still be there when he got out of prison. I bet he was surprised when he found out the old guy was dead."

"Yes, exactly. We think perhaps the realtor somehow found out about the stolen money and that's why she was at the farm before she got the listing. Helms may have been using her to get to the farm, but things went wrong and he killed her," said Harry.

"That is a lot of speculation, with no proof or evidence," said Chief Barkley.

"You're right about that Mike. It's all speculation. We're making assumptions about a dead old guy and a murdered realtor. Finding Helms would help to make the connection. He must be somewhere nearby, waiting to get his hands on the cash."

"He won't get too far without it. I talked with the local police and they're searching the surrounding farms, especially some of the old abandoned ones. He could be holed up in one of them. He may have someone else helping him. We checked back again at the timber mill where he worked. According to the manager, Helms didn't really have any friends there."

"Family?"

"None that we are aware of. His parents passed long ago. He has an older sister but she lives in North Dakota and hasn't been in touch with him since before he was incarcerated. Apparently they were far apart in age and not close."

"If he was the one who murdered Hovlund, she must have threatened him somehow. What would he have to gain by killing the one connection he had to the farm?" Harry wondered.

"Good point. Something must have happened to prompt the killing. We are assuming the killer was Helms, but we can't be sure. We really need to locate this guy."

"Yeah, you really do," Harry thought. "Pete's safety could depend on it."

Harry and Chief Barkley said goodbye and agreed to stay in touch while Harry was still in Minnesota. He told the chief that he would be wrapping up his stay quite soon, now that Pete was okayed to leave. Harry mulled everything over in his mind.

There were still so many unanswered questions. The crime itself, the robbery, was more than 15 years old. The perpetrator, Helms, was out of prison and had now disappeared. Was Pete's Uncle Fritz involved somehow? It was one theory, but since he was dead and there was really no solid proof, the old guy could be completely innocent and everything connected was purely coincidental.

The murder of Talia Hovlund was the current crime, the most disturbing. Was her death associated in some way to the robbery and the missing money? She was a successful realtor, which may explain her prodding Pete to sell the farm. It was in his best interest, of course, to sell it, since he had no desire to keep it.

All of these links - and the one he had the most difficulty believing was the troll. Pete and Cari were certain that the creature existed and was the main offender causing all the mayhem at the farm. Harry's logical side thrust the troll out of his thinking, but it troubled him a little. They both claimed to have seen the creature, and Cari said she spoke to it. She was an intelligent woman, why make up a story like that?

The past year had opened up Harry's imagination. Since meeting Wolfgang, he witnessed a wolf-like creature, a murderous witch and a shape shifting monster.

Never in all of his years as a detective had he encountered such bizarre anomalies, yet there they were.

"Okay, Harry admit it to yourself - the troll could exist." he said to himself.

"Now, let's prove it."

# Chapter 57: New Plan

It took nearly most of the afternoon, but Cari and Wolf searched the entire barn while Pete fired up the metal detector and buzzed around the yard and silo.

Harry arrived to find the three of them taking a lemonade break on the front porch.

"Henry, come and join us," said Pete. "Grab a glass and try this. It's Cari's homemade lemonade with a little vodka splashed in."

"That's the best offer I've had all day," said Harry, accepting an icy glass.

"Did you find out anything new from the Chief?" asked Wolfgang.

"Not really. Helms has disappeared and the police are searching far and wide for him. If he really is after the money, he won't be too far away. Did you all learn anything new from Davey?"

"Nope," said Pete. "Once he got over gawking at Cari, he pretty much just repeated what he told Ned and Kyra. He is coming back out here soon to finish the job cleaning up. That way I can see if there's anything worthwhile to auction off and get the hell out of here."

"What about our little troll friend?" Harry asked, sipping his lemonade.

"Haven't heard anything," said Cari. "Since I saw him the other night, nothing new has happened. No rocks thrown, no new holes dug. It's been quiet."

"I did find another can in the yard," said Pete. "I used the metal detector that Ned ordered and found it. It must have been one of the first ones he buried. The money was old currency and it was a bit moldy, even though it was in plastic. There was $27 wrapped up in an old bread bag, which had mostly disintegrated."

"So, that may have been the final coffee can, at least in the backyard," said Wolfgang. "The metal detector would probably have located any others."

"I suppose you're thinking about searching for that robbery money with the metal detector, hoping that it's buried in some sort of metal container," Harry concluded.

"If we do find the money, then the danger is over," said Cari. "At least from a human culprit."

Wolf told Harry that he and Cari had spent the afternoon searching the barn and came up with nothing but dust and dirt, but made another discovery.

"We noticed that some of the farm implements have gone missing," Wolf added.

"What?" asked Harry.

"A very large sickle and a pick ax," said Wolf. "And something Pete said is called a panga, which is a large knife."

"Oh, and don't forget the spade fork," Pete added. "It's like a pitch fork."

"Those sound like dangerous sorts of tools," said Harry.

"Exactly. The sickle and spade fork were here originally, but the panga and pick ax came later, I think. Remember I told you, some newer tools were showing up, before some of them fell on Davey," said Pete. "Now, they're missing."

"Whoever put them there, took them back," Cari said.

"Helms?" Wolf questioned.

"Could be," said Harry. "If he's holed up somewhere nearby, maybe he figures that he needs some weapons."

"You still got that gun in your car, Harry?" asked Wolf. "You should get it."

"I can certainly do that, and I will stay here tonight, unless everyone agrees to sleep at the hotel."

"I have an idea," said Wolfgang. "But you all have to agree."

"Let's hear it," said Pete.

"How about this? We all leave for the hotel, and the house looks empty. Harry and I sneak back here later and wait to see if Helms comes back to look for the money."

"That sounds dangerous," said Cari.

"We'll be careful, and Harry is armed. I think that if you and Pete are at the hotel and we all make a show of it in town, eat at the diner, and so on, we could draw him out."

"How would he know?" asked Pete.

"He may have a partner that's watching us in town, and if word got out that we're staying there, and the farm is vacant, that would be the perfect time to conduct a search. If it doesn't work - at least you two would get a good night's sleep in a comfy hotel room."

Harry was quiet while Wolf proposed his idea. He thought it was a good plan, but worried that the young man was putting himself in danger.

"What do you think, Harry?" asked Wolf.

"I'm concerned with your safety," said Harry.

"Me too," said Cari. "I'm concerned for both of you. He could be dangerous."

Pete agreed with Cari that leaving the place seemingly unoccupied could very well tempt the man to make a search, and put his friends in danger.

Finally, Wolf convinced them that it was a solid plan and he would take no unnecessary risks. "Besides, Harry will be here. He was a cop and has a gun."

They all departed, using all their vehicles, so the farm would appear completely vacated. When arriving, Pete and Cari checked in at the hotel and they all went to the diner to make sure they were seen.

Later, after dark, Wolf and Harry would drive to an area near the farm and go in on foot. It was a long shot, but they all agreed it was worth a try.

# CHAPTER 58: TROLL

Pete and Cari settled into their comfy hotel rooms, trying to get a night's rest, yet worried about their friends. Meanwhile, Wolf and Harry left in Harry's vehicle, which he had parked behind the hotel. They scouted an area on their way out that looked like a good place to leave the car, where it would be hard to spot.

"I hope this isn't for nothing," said Harry. "That seems like a long walk back to the farmhouse, and when you get close, the ground has lots of holes to trip in."

"We'll have to be careful, but I don't want to use the flashlight if we can help it," said Wolf.

When they got close to the area where the car would be left, Wolf turned off the headlights. He parked in a spot that was shielded by some droopy pine trees.

Quietly exiting the car, they walked silently toward the farm.

The walk was shorter and easier than anticipated. The moon was partially covered by clouds, but a little light showed the way, so the flashlight wasn't necessary. Wolf hoped the bit of moonlight didn't give them away.

When they got close to the farmhouse, Wolf grabbed Harry's arm and put a finger to his lips. He heard something nearby, so the two of them remained still.

After what seemed like hours, the noisemaker was revealed. A fat raccoon was waddling around looking for scraps.

Harry breathed a sigh of relief as they quietly entered the house from the back door, which had been left unlocked. They settled in, one watching from the windows in the front, the other in back. There was no sound but a loud ticking of a kitchen clock. The minutes ticked by - nothing happened.

Hours passed and it was getting more difficult to stay awake. Harry had a thermos of strong coffee that Pete left behind in the kitchen. Wolf was sipping on bottled tea that Cari had set out on a table in the living room. The caffeine was helping, but sitting for hours gazing out into the darkness was tough.

Suddenly, out of nowhere, something struck the side of the house. Then another strike. Harry hurried from the kitchen to join Wolfgang at the front window. What they saw was a shock. It appeared to be a small, stocky, bearded creature holding a brick and giggling hysterically. They remained silent, watching the thing, then it dropped the brick and completely disappeared. A moment later, an eagle flew very near the house and was gone.

"Troll," whispered Wolfgang.

"I'm afraid so," Harry whispered back.

Following a short discussion in hushed tones, they agreed to remain in the house. Either the troll would return, or it was done for the evening. Hopefully if Helms was anywhere around, it didn't scare him away.

Wolf found a plate of snacks that Cari had thoughtfully left for them. He offered Harry some cookies and crackers to help keep them awake.

More time passed, and the night returned to silence. The clock ticked away the minutes and once or twice an owl hooted. Otherwise it was soundless.

Wolf told Harry that he thought he should check around outside. "You stay here and watch, and I'll go out and scout around," said Wolf. "It's booby trapped with all those holes, so I think it's better if I go it alone. I'll shout if I need you."

Harry reluctantly agreed, and kept a close watch at the front of the house when Wolf tiptoed outside. He didn't like the idea, but he knew that Wolf had better footing out there in the dark than he did himself. They were getting nowhere sitting in the house.

It was darker than it had been when they arrived, and Wolf had a hard time seeing where he was going. He had the flashlight, but hesitated to use it. First he crept alongside the farmhouse, then worked his way over to the barn. There was no sound or indication anyone was around. Coming up to the silo, Wolf saw something, a big lump near one side of the old silo, the area where the grassy mounds were located. As he made his way toward the lump, he tripped over something. Holding himself back from yelling, he checked what had tripped him. It was a shovel, or maybe more accurately, a spade. A long handled garden spade.

He reached down to grab it, but then thought better of it. Fingerprints? He continued toward the lump on the ground, which grew larger as he approached.

He gasped when he realized what lay on the ground. Ack! It was a body. Wolf hurriedly approached, checking to see if the person needed help. He turned on the flashlight and discovered he didn't need to bother. The man was clearly dead, and he was covered in blood.

"Harry!" he shouted. "Come out here, now. I'm near the silo. You can use your flashlight."

"Are you okay?" Harry shouted back, hurrying toward the silo.

"Yeah, I'm okay, but I found something. Watch out for the shovel."

Harry came running up, out of breath, stopping suddenly when he saw what Wolf was standing over.

"Oh no," said Harry. "He looks dead."

"He's dead alright. I bet that's the murder weapon over there," said Wolf, pointing at a wicked looking large knife, resembling a machete. It was covered in blood. "That's probably the panga that Pete said was missing from the barn."

"I wonder who that is?" Harry asked, leaning toward the body.

"Take a look at the side of his neck."

Harry shone his flashlight on the dead man's neck and saw very clearly the large tattoo of an X on the side of his neck. It was slightly faded and had blood speckled on it, but it was the GEBO tattoo.

"Helms?"

"That would be my guess," said Wolf.

"We had better go and call the police right away. Be careful not to disturb anything, this is a crime scene," said Harry.

They returned to the house and Harry called the local police, explaining what they had discovered and that the man was most certainly dead. Right afterward, he called Chief Barkley, reaching him at home. He explained to the chief what they found and gave him the address of the farm. Barkley said he would be leaving shortly.

"I guess we were right about one thing," said Harry. "Helms must have had another partner. I'm guessing he was the one who did this."

"You know that Pete is going to say it was the troll. Especially after we tell him what we saw tonight. The troll that threw the brick and shifted into an eagle," said Wolfgang.

"I don't think the police will buy that. We can mention the bricks lobbed at the house, and the description of the...well um...small man," said Harry. " The eagle sighting won't be relevant."

Wolf and Harry stood waiting on the porch for the police to arrive, when they heard an odd noise coming from behind the house. Harry put a finger to his lips and they both slipped alongside the edge of the house toward the back. What they saw was yet another shock. Standing in the empty field beyond the backyard was a bull.

The bull stood still for a moment then looked straight at Harry and Wolf. It snorted, lowered its big head and pawed at the ground as if it was getting ready to charge. They kept perfectly still, not knowing exactly what to do. After a few moments the bull snorted loudly then turned away. It disappeared into the darkness.

When Harry found his voice again, he turned to Wolf and said, "Wolf, my friend, I can say this with absolute certainty. There is never a dull moment when you're around."

Wolf patted Harry's shoulder and said, "I could say the same about you. Let's go wait for the police."

# CHAPTER 59: MURDER

The first police cruiser arrived shortly after the bull disappeared. Wolf and Harry agreed not to mention the bull sighting either, going on the assumption that there must be a stray bull wandering around these parts. After all, it was possible, right?

The first officer arriving was Officer Anderson, who had been at the farm on two other occasions. He noticed Harry and Wolf waiting and immediately asked the whereabouts of Pete Magnusson, the current farm owner.

"He and his niece are staying at a hotel in town tonight," Wolf explained.

"Who are you again?" he asked Wolf.

"I'm Wolfgang Kilmer, I have been here visiting with Pete and his niece Cari.

This is Harry Chan, he is also a friend visiting Pete."

"I am a retired police detective from Chicago."

"Good for you, Mr. Chan. Were you the one who called about the dead man?"

"Yes, that was me. The man is located near the silo. He is covered in blood and there's a machete-like knife nearby with blood on it. We didn't touch anything."

The officer and his partner walked over to the silo with flashlights and returned a few minutes later. The second officer went to the police cruiser and got on the radio, probably to get more police on the scene.

Officer Anderson returned to the farmhouse and suggested they all go inside while his partner worked to secure the crime scene. Sitting at the kitchen table, the officer started right away asking questions.

"So what are you two doing here tonight?"

Harry tried to explain that they were trying to figure out who had been vandalizing the farm, and were waiting in the house to try and trap the person. The officer looked suspicious.

"Is that your vehicle parked about a quarter mile from here?" he asked.

"Yes, you see we didn't want the vandals to know we were here, so we walked in after dark."

"So, do you think the dead guy out there was vandalizing the property? Did you two decide to take care of him yourselves?" asked Officer Anderson.

"No, absolutely not. We don't know anything about what happened to him. I'm pretty sure who he is, but neither of us know him. We've never seen him before. If you wait until the Chief of Police from Alexandria gets here, he can explain more," said Harry.

"Chief Barkley called us and said he was on his way. Something to do with a man they've been looking for possibly connected with the Talia Hovlund murder case. What I don't understand is, how are you two connected in all this."

"We're not connected to anything," said Wolfgang.

"I suppose we'll have to figure that out. Walk me through this. While you two were in here waiting to catch a vandal, did you see or hear anything unusual?" the officer asked.

Wolf looked at Harry and said, "Someone was outside and threw a couple of bricks at the house. They should still be out there on the ground."

"Did you see the person? Was it the dead man?"

"No, it was a shorter, stocky person with a long beard. He disappeared after throwing the bricks."

"This short, bearded man, did you get a good look at him?"

"Not really. It was pretty dark outside," Wolf answered. "He was too far away to get a real good look."

"So then what happened?" asked the officer.

"We stayed in the house for, um, maybe another hour or so, then I went outside to look around," Wolf explained. "That's when I noticed a lump over by the silo, and decided to check it out. I saw the shovel, didn't touch it and then I noticed it was a person, and he looked past help. I shouted for Harry to come and look, then he called the authorities."

"While you were waiting around in the house, did you hear any disturbance outside?" questioned Officer Anderson

Both Wolf and Harry told him that they heard nothing unusual after the brick throwing incident.

"Mr. Chan, you stated that you're pretty sure who the dead man is, how do you know that?" Anderson asked.

"Again, the chief can explain this further when he arrives, but you'll notice the man has a tattoo of an X on his neck and we just happened to know that detail about him."

"Okay, I'll wait until Chief Barkley arrives before I ask you two any more questions. In the meantime, I suggest we contact Pete Magnusson as this is his property. By the way, do you know if Mr. Magnusson is acquainted with the dead man?"

"Um...actually he is, but he met him briefly, many years ago, probably at least thirty. The man may have been a farmhand for his Uncle Fritz," answered Harry.

"The coincidences keep piling up," said Anderson. "I am very anxious to speak to Mr. Magnusson."

# Chapter 60: Suspicion

Wolf called Pete and told him everything that happened. Needless to say, he was quite upset. "They're gonna think I killed that guy," said Pete. "I'm never gettin' outa' here."

"Calm down, Pete. First of all, you've been in town at the hotel all this time. When they determine when he was killed, which looked fairly recent, you're off the hook."

"But, you and Harry saw the troll and later on you found the dead guy. It must have been the troll, and I let it out," said Pete, sounding panicky.

"Please, when you talk to the police, don't say anything about the troll. Just forget all about the troll for now. If the troll did it, there's nothing you can do about it."

"You're right, they'll just think I'm nuts. This all just got me kinda shook up, that's all. I'll pull myself together, call Cari in her room and tell her what's going on, then we'll head back to the farm."

"Good plan. We'll see you when you get here," said Wolf breathing a sigh of relief.

While Wolf was on the phone with Pete, Chief Barkley arrived, as well as the wagon from the morgue and some more officers ready to process the crime scene. The entire driveway in front of the farmhouse was full of official vehicles.

Chief Barkley was in the kitchen speaking with Officer Anderson and his partner. Apparently, he explained that Harry had been working "unofficially" with his department, as they were looking for Frederick Helms. The officers discussed the search for Helms; their department had been on the lookout for him as well, due to a possible connection to Talia Hovlund's murder.

"My apologies for rudeness, Mr. Chan," said Officer Anderson. "We have to look at all possibilities, especially in the case of a murder."

"No apology necessary," said Harry. "Believe me, I understand that you're just doing what you have to - getting the job done.'

Wolf entered the kitchen and Anderson looked at him with slightly suspicious eyes. Not surprising, after all, Wolf was the one who discovered the body.

"We are spending a lot of time at this farm lately," said Anderson.

After his comment, both Harry and Chief Barkley further explained the possible connection between Talia Hovlund and the dead man (If he is definitely identified as Frederick Helms). In addition, they told of the association that Fritz Kolbeck had with Helms, as his employer years ago and the coincidental matching tattoos.

"So all this vandalism and mayhem happening out here could be related to the money that Helms stole and was never recovered," said Anderson. "Do you think it could be here somewhere?"

"It would explain what Helms was doing here, and why someone has been trying to scare Pete away. He was taking his time deciding when to sell the farm," said Harry trying not to yawn. It was very early in the morning following a long night.

At that moment, Pete and Cari arrived. They could hear Pete's booming voice even before he entered the house.

"We had to park in the North forty," Pete hollered. "I'm too old for that long of a walk. Hey, you guys got any cop cars left? Hope nobody commits a crime today," he added and burst into the kitchen.

Pete plopped himself heavily into a kitchen chair and Cari slipped in behind him, carrying a large bakery bag. She offered to make everyone some coffee, and said she brought donuts, muffins and pastries as well.

"Go ahead and ask your questions," said Pete. "May as well get this over with."

"We just want to know if you are acquainted with the dead man, who we presume is Frederick Helms," said Anderson.

"He was hired by my Uncle Fritz as a farmhand, many years ago. "I only met him once, when I visited here. I noticed the X tattoo, which I thought was odd. My uncle said it was the Viking rune symbol GEBO, which indicates a partnership, or contract, that sort of thing. I found out from my niece that my uncle had the same tattoo on his chest. My brother saw it one time when Uncle Fritz was sick."

"So you think they may have been partners?" asked Anderson.

"I don't know, but Fritz was hiding something. He had secrets, and in his old age started blabbing about treasure and somebody coming after him. Maybe his mind was slipping?"

Pete went on to explain about the coffee cans of cash buried in the yard, and that he had discovered some of them. The cans could be construed as his uncle's treasure.

"Did he leave any notes or messages about the 'treasure'?" asked Anderson.

"Not that I can find, and we've been looking. I started searching for a map or something like that the minute I got here," said Pete. "You see, I knew about the coffee cans and was hoping I wouldn't have to dig up the whole yard. My uncle used a compass and paced off the burial spots, but I ain't found anything that tells where. He coulda done the same with the robbery money if he had it."

"What about his will?" asked Barkley.

"I was gonna ask his lawyer for a copy of it, so I can take a better look. Once I found out I inherited the farm and everything on it, I didn't really read it over too closely. I was gonna go see the lawyer, Korhonen, today, but here I am back at the farm."

"You may want to do that as soon as possible," said Wolfgang. "Maybe your uncle left a message in the will that you didn't notice or pick up on. The sooner the money is found (if it is here) the better, and safer for you."

"Yep, people are gettin' killed, and I sure don't want it to be me, or any of my friends or relations," said Pete.

"We can have a cruiser stop in and check on the farm periodically," said Anderson. "In the meantime, you may want to continue staying at the hotel. There's a killer out there and they may think you know something about the money."

"Yes, and all the digging you have been doing out here may appear as if you were looking for the robbery money," said Harry.

"Shit, you're right about that. Nobody knew about Uncle Fritz's coffee can cash, so if somebody seen me digging, they could think I was searching for the stolen money," Pete exclaimed. "In fact Talia Hovlund commented about all the holes dug and I told her it was a groundhog."

"She may have shared that information with the wrong person, and it got her killed," said Harry.

The police finished their preliminary investigation, and said they would contact Pete when the scene was clear, most likely in a few days. In the meantime, Pete and the others were asked to keep away from the murder site, so they all agreed to stay at the hotel until which time they were okayed to return.

Pete locked up the farmhouse, gave Officer Anderson an extra key and they all departed for the hotel. Wolf and Harry were secretly glad to get back there and get a good night's sleep.

---

# CHAPTER 61: FRITZ'S WILL

---

After returning to the hotel, Pete and Cari saw Wolf and Harry in the lobby.

They decided to meet the next morning for coffee and went their separate ways. Pete made an appointment with Korhonen the following afternoon, to get a copy of his uncle's will. He spoke to a secretary. She relayed the message to Korhonen, who seemed surprised when he got on the phone with Pete.

"Is there a problem?" he asked.

"Not at all," said Pete. "I was in a hurry last time I was there and didn't get a good look at the will. I just want to take another glance at it."

"Certainly, Mr. Magnusson. You are the sole beneficiary, so you have the right. I'll see you tomorrow."

After too much coffee and a lighter breakfast at a chain restaurant, Pete said he was going to get a copy of the will in case there was something he didn't notice the first time, and Cari would go along. Harry and Wolfgang were going to catch up on some sleep.

"Let's meet up later and we can all take a look," said Pete. Everyone agreed and decided to order pizza, pick up some beer and convene in Pete's room, which was a large suite. Pete said he didn't like to stay in just a big bedroom, so he asked for a suite.

As soon as he and Cari entered the office of Korhonen and Associates, they felt as if they had been "talked about" before they arrived. The attorney's legal secretary handed Pete a copy of the will in a large, sealed envelope, with a sort of withering glance. Korhonen walked out of his office and after shaking Pete's hand looked at Cari questioningly.

"Oh, I'm sorry, this is my niece Cari Magnusson," said Pete. "Cari, this is the managing partner of the firm, Isaac Korhonen," he added, and Cari shook the lawyer's hand. He barely acknowledged her.

Another office door popped open and Korhonen's associate, Ollie Nilsen, stepped out and was introduced to Cari as Fritz Kolbeck's main attorney. Nilsen seemed to be briefly taken aback by Cari's looks, as were most people that first met her.

"Is there some sort of issue with your uncle's will?" asked Nilsen. "I worked on it with your uncle and it was fairly straightforward."

"Absolutely not," said Pete. I just simply wanted to take another look, in case he left me a message about something personal. In case I missed it."

"Personal? Your uncle?" asked Nilsen with a snort.

"I don't believe that's your concern," said Cari. Korhonen gave his partner a sharp look and told Pete that they would be at his disposal if he had any further questions. "Thank you for stopping by," he added in a dismissive tone, shook Pete's hand, turned on his heel and returned to his office.

"Nice to have met you," Nilsen mumbled to Cari, shook Pete's hand and hurriedly walked away.

On the way out, Cari and Pete both expressed surprise at both of the attorney's rudeness, appearing anxious to be rid of Pete and Cari. It was as if they were being accused of something. Made you wonder.

"I don't like either one of them, Uncle Pete."

"I agree. It should be the last time dealing with those guys."

Pete told his niece that he wasn't too hopeful that Fritz left behind any clues or secret message in his will, but it was certainly worth a second look, just in case.

His phone buzzed, it was the police telling him that the crime scene area investigation had been completed and the police tape removed. They could return to the farm. Since it was late in the day, and the rooms had already been paid for, they would stay the night and let Wolf and Harry know when they came for pizza.

"Since everything has been cleared, I'm gonna call Davey and ask when he can get back out there. We can get the rest of the junk cleared out and cleaned up."

Davey answered immediately and told Pete he would start the next day. He said he was fully recovered and ready to get back to work.

Cari ordered pizzas, breadsticks and salad for everyone while Pete went out to pick up some beer and a couple bottles of red wine.

The suite smelled delicious when Wolf and Harry arrived, minutes after the pizza delivery. While eating, they each took a close look at Fritz's will, but could find nothing unusual.

"It's straightforward, just like that Nilsen fellah told us," said Pete. "The only unusual thing I noticed is that it seems like someone had looked through it before we got it. I know this is a copy, so why does it feel like it has been handled?"

Cari was munching on a breadstick when she took a turn at a second glimpse at the will. "Hey, Uncle Pete, come here and look at the signature. It seems odd."

Fritz Kolbeck's signature did indeed seem off somehow. If one looked very carefully, there was something extra. Cari pointed out that there were very small symbols tucked in between the letters of his name. They studied it closer. Runes!

"Sowilo (S); Isa (I) Laguz (L) Othala (O)"

"He spelled out SILO," said Cari.

## Chapter 62: Return to the Farm

Davey was getting antsy just sitting around the house. The call from Mr. Pete was the best thing he heard all week. He decided not to wait until the next day, but to drive out there this afternoon and get started on cleaning up the silo.

After grabbing his jacket, a water bottle and some granola bars, he made a quick call to his cousin. "Hey, can I borrow your trailer again? I'm going back out to the Kolbeck farm to finish up that job."

"Of course, it's next to the garage. You should get your own trailer someday, you seem to be getting a lot of work."

"Yeah, you're right. After I finish up there, I'll check some out. Say, do you want to sell me your trailer?"

"Maybe, we'll see. You are welcome to borrow it anytime."

"Thanks."

Davey was full of energy when he picked up the trailer and hooked it up to his truck. He had been playing video games and watching movies so much lately, it felt as if he had been trapped in a cage. When he arrived at the farm, it was a bit surprising to see that no one was there. He figured that Mr. Pete had called from the farmhouse. "Oh well, I'm here so I may as well get started," he thought.

It was kind of creepy at first, especially since a pile of sharp farm tools had been dumped on him in the barn. Davey decided to stay out of the barn and just focus on cleaning up the silo. He put his headphones on and got right to work. While he was busy cleaning, Davey was unaware that someone watched him.

It seemed like he hauled ten tons of junk out of that old silo, but at least he was getting to the bottom of it. Stopping for a snack and a water, he noticed it was going to be dark soon. Something blew his way, some yellow paper? It was a piece of police crime scene tape. Hmm...interesting, he thought and tossed it in with the other trash.

Davey had been so busy with his video games and watching movies, that he was completely unaware of the recent incident that had occurred, and had no idea that a dead body had lain nearby very recently.

The next load was extra dirty and dusty. One old box was covered in something that looked like moss. Ew. He scraped at it a little with his thumbnail and saw there was a part of a symbol on it. Kind of like Thor's hammer. What was it called? Oh yeah, Mjolnir. That was a good movie, he thought as he tossed it in with the rest of the pile of crap into the trailer.

The trailer was nearly full, and it was getting dark; time to finish up for the evening. One more load, then the trailer could get emptied at the dump in the morning and he could start fresh.

While he loaded the last of the junk into the trailer, Davey felt like there was someone else nearby. "Mr. Pete, is that you?" he called into the darkness. There was no answer, and all was silent. The creepy feeling came back and he hurriedly finished up. Just as he was climbing into the truck, he heard giggling, but he couldn't see anyone. "That's it, I'm out of here," he said to himself. As he drove away, he saw something big moving in the field. It was that bull again, pawing at the ground. Jeez, what a weird night, he thought with a shiver.

Everyone was anxious to return to the farm and start searching the silo. They weren't too sure if it was a secret message from Fritz to Pete, but why else would he tuck tiny rune letters into his signature spelling out SILO. Fritz trusted no one but Pete, and knew that his nephew was well versed in Viking runes. A long shot for sure, but the best clue they found yet.

Wolf said he would pick up some groceries and clean up supplies. Harry wanted to stop in to see his friend, Mike Barkley. He would tell him what Cari discovered in the signature and that they were going to start an all-out search of the old silo.

Pete and Cari talked the whole way back to the farm about a search plan. He was expecting Davey to show up some time today and he would tell him they were searching for some important items that belonged to Uncle Fritz. The story about the stolen money and Uncle Fritz and Fred Helms would be left up to the police to tell.

Wolf arrived with the bags of groceries and after all had been unloaded, he along with Pete and Cari walked out to the silo. They were armed with work gloves, brooms, shovels and bug spray. Pete was worried about spiders.

"Someone's been here already," said Pete as he opened the creaky old door to the silo and cautiously stepped in. "A whole bunch of stuff is gone. Son of a bitch!"

"Are you sure?" asked Cari.

"Yes, I'm sure. I came out here shortly after Davey got hurt, to check if any of his belongings were in here. He had headphones, and a backpack and I thought he might have left them behind."

"It could have been Helms, before he got killed," said Wolfgang.

"You're right, I bet it was Helms," said Pete.

As they were debating who could have been in here, a vehicle pulled up. At first they thought it was Harry, but then heard a voice call, "Hey, Mr. Pete. Are you out here?" It was Davey.

The young man walked up to the silo, barely limping anymore. He said hello to everyone, then turned to Pete and asked, "So what do you think?"

Pete looked at him questioningly.

"Oh, I hope it's okay. I was anxious to get started, so I came out here yesterday afternoon and cleaned up a bunch of stuff. I probably should have told you, but I thought you would be here."

"So you're the one that cleaned up the stuff," said Pete. "That's fine, I just didn't realize it was you."

"I'm sorry Mr. Pete. Like I said, I thought you would be here. Once I got here with the trailer, it seemed a waste not to get to work. I have to say, this place sure is creepy when nobody is around. My imagination was working overtime, I started hearing things."

"Hearing things?" asked Cari.

Davey paused for a moment, gawking, then pulled it together and told them he felt like someone else was here. "I even called out to you Mr. Pete, and felt kinda silly about it. Then I heard giggling."

"Giggling?" Wolf asked.

"Yep, that's how I would describe it. Probably a bird or some animal. I got out of here pretty quick after that, then I saw the bull again. Somebody needs to get that bull corralled before he hurts himself or someone else."

Pete, Cari and Wolf all looked at each other, trying not to let on what they were thinking.

"Well, thanks for getting started Davey," Pete said quickly. "Here's the plan. My uncle might have left some things behind here, so we're all going to help you. I will still pay you the amount we agreed on, but the workload may be a little lighter."

"Um...sure. I hope none of that crap I hauled out already is anything good."

"No, no, don't worry about that. I'm sure it was all crap. We're mostly trying to get to the bottom of the silo, so we can check beneath the floor."

"You think your uncle put some stuff under the floor?" Davey asked.

"Yeah, he liked to bury things."

"Okay then, that's weird. Oops, I'm sorry, I didn't mean to say that about your uncle."

"No problem, he was weird. Let's get started."

When Harry pulled into the drive two hours later, he saw Wolf, Pete, Cari and a tall young redheaded man covered in dirt and carrying loads of junk and dropping it all into a trailer.

"The search begins," he said to himself.

Harry walked to the silo to see what the group had accomplished, which was very impressive. Pete introduced Harry to Davey, who gripped Harry's hand in his, which was covered in freckles and dirt. Nothing interesting had been discovered and they were starting to wrap things up as light was fading.

Since they were about done for the day, Harry headed back to the farmhouse and on the way was nearly hit by a large eagle flying by. He couldn't help himself, he had to say it...troll!

## CHAPTER 63: HULDRA

The feeling was mutual. Things were about to come to a head. Either the money would be unearthed, the killer of Helms found out, or the mystery of who actually murdered Talia Hovlund would be discovered. Did Helms kill her? Who killed Helms? Was it the troll?

Cari wanted to venture outside that evening to see if she could get a glimpse of the troll again. Her ankle was better and she was quite keen on seeing the troll again. "I can ask him if he killed a man. Maybe he'll answer me."

"I don't think that's safe," said Pete. "There's a killer out there somewhere. It could be the troll, and maybe he wants to kill you too."

"Or a human killer that quite possibly murdered both Talia Hovlund and Fred Helms," added Harry. "No, it's not safe out there for anyone."

"Alright, I won't go out there, don't worry about it," she told them, knowing it was a lie. The first chance she got, she was going to look for that troll again. It would have to be soon, there was a thunderstorm forecasted in a couple of days, and she knew the troll wouldn't come out if there was lightning.

Since there was nothing more to be done, and everyone but Harry was tired from the silo search, they all decided to turn in for the night. Harry and Wolf would return to the hotel, but come back early in the morning to begin exploring the silo once again. They reminded Pete and Cari that a police cruiser would be doing an occasional sweep of the area all evening.

Cari would wait again for her uncle to go to sleep, and would slip out in search of the troll. She had promised not to do it again, but she couldn't help herself. After Harry and Wolf left, she bid her Uncle Pete goodnight and quietly changed into dark clothing, tucked her platinum hair in an old black stocking cap she found and waited impatiently in her room.

While she was waiting to hear Pete's snoring, Cari relaxed her mind and focused her thoughts. She did a quiet rune casting to help guide her. The stones reflected, past: PERTHRO - mysteries, secrets; present: LAGUZ - dreams, fantasies and finally future: HAGALAZ - hail, wrath of nature, uncontrolled forces.

Cari reflected on the rune reading and knew in her heart it was accurate and she could no more stop what was happening then she could control nature. It was fate. The Norns, the Norse goddesses of fate, Urd, Verdandi and Skuld were spinning out the threads of life. The powers of good or evil, malevolent or benevolent? Soon they would know.  Cari was so intent on relaxing, it was as if she was in a dream state.

Finally the sound of Pete's snoring began. Cari very quietly crept through the kitchen and out the back door. She moved slowly and deliberately, making no sound. Staying close to the farmhouse at first, she crossed over to the silo. This was the danger zone. There were no trees or walls to conceal her, the silo stood alone near the old farm field. The night was still, no breeze and very little sound. Clouds were gathering, covering the moonlight, and hopefully she was concealed in the darkness. Reaching the silo, she plastered herself tightly against it and waited.

There was a hissing sound first, then a slight giggle. She knew he was close by, just as he realized she was hiding there as well. She pulled off the cap and shook out her long blonde hair. The hissing and giggling stopped and she heard a whisper, "Huldra."

"Ja," she replied. "Hva vil du?" (what do you want?) she asked it.

"hefnd, pa frior," (revenge, then peace), he answered.

"Ja, endir," (Yes, the end), she answered.

"taak," (thank you)

Cari could barely see the troll, he was in the darkness and shadows. Their brief conversation in Old Norse was spotty at best, so she hoped she could make him understand her in English and then she translated into Norwegian.

"If you can understand me, hear this. I realize you were harmed by humans. I know there have been more evil humans coming here. We are not evil and do not intend to harm you. I think you wish to be reunited with your family who are here with you now. I will do my best to help you. There is an evil human trying to harm us as well."

"taak, Huldra," he replied, then was gone.

A moment later, Cari heard a snort and looked toward the field. There stood a large bull, pawing the ground. She could have sworn the bull bowed its head. In a blink of an eye, it was gone.

The next morning, when Cari awoke, the recollection of her conversation with the troll was blurred and fuzzy. Was it a dream? Recalling the rune stone LAGAZ which indicated dreams and fantasies made her wonder.

After getting dressed, Cari picked up her shoes, which had dirt on them and then she noticed her dark clothing piled up in a chair. Nope, not a dream, she thought.

# Chapter 64: Finders Keepers

The search of the old silo continued the next morning. Wolf and Harry showed up early, and after coffee, fruit and bagels began the hauling and cleaning. There seemed to be more than a lifetime of junk in the building and Harry wondered if it ever actually functioned as a silo should.

After a while, Pete toddled out of the farmhouse to the silo and looked through the junk they had stacked outside. Shortly afterward, Davey showed up with his empty trailer and then the real work began. The young man loaded the things on the ground into the trailer, after checking with Pete that it was truly all just trash.

"I'm sure there's nothing of value in that pile," said Pete. "Toss it in."

Cari showed up a few minutes later, and Davey stopped for a second to stare at her, then continued with his work. "You're distracting him," said Wolfgang walking over to her with a grin on his face.

"He'll get over it," she answered. "You did. In the meantime, I'll clean up some space in the barn for the stuff that's going to be auctioned."

Harry came out of the silo next, dusting off his hands and announced he was taking a break. "You know, we should probably spray something in there. I saw a couple of big spider nests," he said.

"That does it for me," said Pete. "I ain't goin' in there, I'll look over the stuff out here in the fresh air."

"No problem, Mr. Pete, I can take over," said Davey.

After a few hours and several loads of junk, along with some items of indeterminate value that could possibly be sold, Davey announced they had found the bottom of the pile. His trailer was full, so Pete suggested he get it to the dump before it got too late. The items they found that looked worthy for an auction were all hauled into the barn, which had been swept and tidied up quite nicely by Cari.

When Davey had driven away, everyone went into the silo to work on prying up the old floorboards. Pete lingered in the doorway, still worried about spiders. Wolf had found a pry bar in the barn and started with the most rotten of the boards.

"Here's something," he announced, reaching into the space beneath the floor. He pulled out an old green metal box, about the size of a shoe box. It took a bit of an effort to get it open and they were surprised to find it full of moldy postcards.

"Hoo, that's a smell," said Wolf and carried the box full of postcards outside.

Pete thumbed through the cards, which were from all over the United States and were falling apart in his hands. "He must have collected these, there's no writing on them. Kind of sad," commented Pete, unaware that someone was watching him through powerful binoculars as he looked through the old box.

Wolf and the others returned to the silo to pry up some more floorboards. A tea can, similar to the one Pete found buried in the yard, was under one of the boards. The can contained all the Viking rune letters, except for ALGIZ the protection stone that was the stone Pete found buried in another tea can.

More floorboards lifted yielded more unusual findings. Assorted metal containers gone rusty that contained playing cards, agates, and arrowheads that were probably found in the field, according to Pete. One box had a figurine of a hula dancer that wiggled when you turned the crank.

It was as if Fritz put things under the floor to fool someone. Fake items to distract or mislead the searchers. He was a strange man that Fritz.

"I don't think there's anything else here," said Wolf. "We have pulled up just about every floorboard and searched all around. There's no money in this silo."

"Yes, you're right," said Pete. "Either someone got here before us, or the symbols weaved into Fritz's signature were a bad joke on his part. He was an old son of a bitch, so that wouldn't surprise me. I bet he never had that money at all, and the treasure he talked about was his coffee can money."

"So the mystery of the stolen bank money may have died with Fred Helms," said Harry. "Unless he got here first, found the money and was killed for it."

"That makes sense. In which case, we're off the hook and don't have to be concerned about a killer looking for the cash. He's already got it.," said Pete.

"I hope you're right," said Wolfgang. "I suppose we should put these boards back on the floor, you have to try to sell this place, Pete."

Wolf gathered up the boards and nails and began putting everything back in place with Cari's help. They told Pete and Harry that they'd finish up, so the two men could return to the farmhouse.

"I didn't want to say anything in front of Uncle Pete, but last night I sneaked out and had a visit with the troll. At least I think I did. It's entirely possible it was a dream all along," said Cari, handing him the final rotting board.

"I won't mention it to your uncle, but it could have been dangerous, you know," said Wolf as he nailed the last board to the floor.

"Yeah, yeah, I know, but I couldn't help myself. I did a rune casting and sort of went into myself and then snuck outside. The details are a bit fuzzy, that's why it could have been a dream."

"Well, we're out here now, walk me through it," said Wolf.

"Okay, well I came out the back door, dressed in dark clothing and a cap. I crept alongside the house, then crossed over to the silo, hoping not to be seen. I hid by the silo near those grass mounds, then I heard hissing and giggling. I took off my dark cap, shook out my hair and heard a scratchy voice say, "Huldra." I replied Ja (yes) in old Norse and we had a brief conversation.""

"Conversing with a troll, this just gets better and better," said Wolf.

"I asked it what it wanted and it answered 'revenge and peace'. I told it I would end it and it thanked me. At this point, the old Norse was getting difficult, so I spoke in English and Norwegian. I said we were not evil, and would help it return to its family, but there were other evil humans trying to harm us all. It replied thank you Huldra, then disappeared."

"Wow," said Wolf.

"A few minutes later I saw the bull in the field pawing at the ground. Just like Davey had seen, over there," she said pointing toward the empty farm field.

"Let's take a walk over there," said Wolf pointing at the empty field of dirt. "The bull seems to always appear in the same place."

Wolf and Cari walked to the area where she estimated the bull had been standing. They looked around and did see some dirt disturbed by what could have been the hoof of a bull.

"What's this?" said Wolf, pointing at a rock sticking out of the ground. He squatted down and brushed away the dirt, pulling at the rock, which was bigger than he thought and mostly buried. "I'm gonna go get a shovel," he told Cari and ran toward the barn.

Cari stooped to look at the rock's pointy end, brushed at the dirt and saw something that made her gasp.

Wolf came running up, out of breath, and began carefully digging around the pointy rock. Cari helped by pushing off the dirt and eventually they pulled out the stone, which was jagged on one side and about the size of a small loaf of bread. The stone had runic writing etched upon it.

Sitting in the dirt with the stone in front of her, Cari kept brushing off the dirt, trying to read it. "It's the same curse, only this releases the troll from this realm. It can return to its family. Basically it kills him off - and I'm quite sure that's what he's asking for. He shifts to the bull and paws at the ground, trying to dig up this stone. We've found a way out for all of us," she said with a sigh of relief.

A clap of thunder startled both of them out of their reverie. A storm was coming; dark ominous clouds gathered. Wolf picked up the stone and he and Cari hurried to the farmhouse.

# Chapter 65: The Storm

Wolf and Cari just made it inside before the rain started. Lightning streaked through the sky and thunder claps shook the old house. The rain came down in torrential buckets.

"Uncle Pete, wait until you see this," Cari shouted as soon as they entered the house.

Wolf dropped the stone on the kitchen table and the minute Pete saw it, he said, "Well, I'll be damned."

Harry walked in close behind him, and looked at the stone. "Did you find another rune stone?" he asked.

"We found a piece of the other stone," said Cari. "It's the rest of the original stone, which must have broken off and got plowed into the field. The Viking seeress must have added this to the stone - to put a final end to the troll."

While Cari was explaining, Pete leaned over the piece of rock and was quietly reading the runic writing to himself. "Now this makes sense," said Pete.

"The runes mention frelsi (free), utlagur (banish) and myrkr (darkness) The trolls were all killed but one. The seeress must have realized she had to curse it, to sleep or death. This added piece frees the troll, banished to join the others in darkness," explained Pete.

"So basically it will be dead," commented Harry.

"You see, that's what the troll wants, to join its family. They are buried in the mounds outside the silo. He was too, but not dead, in a dormant sort of state. That's why it hates humans and says they're evil. Trolls want to be with their family above all else, and the curse took that away," Cari explained.

"How did you figure this out?" asked Harry.

"I'm sorry Uncle Pete, but I snuck out last night and saw the troll again. It thinks I am Huldra and can be trusted. I told it we would help and we're not evil. The troll shifted to a bull and pawed at the ground in the field. That's where Wolf and I found the piece of the rune stone."

"I guess you had the right to do what you did, you are an adult after all. I suppose that it's a good thing. Now we can put the stones together, read the whole curse all the way through and be rid of that damn troll," said Pete.

"We have to wait for the storm to pass," said Cari. "If there's lightning, the troll won't come out."

"I thought for a second there that you two found the money," said Harry. "I guess the rune stone is a great treasure to find as well."

"Oh shit," said Cari reaching into her pocket. "I don't have my phone. I must have left it in the silo. I better go and get it, I promised my assistant Sara that I'd call her by the end of the week."

"It's raining pretty hard, you should wait," said Pete.

"A little rain won't hurt,"she said. "I'll be right back."

"I'll go with you," said Wolf. "I wanted to make sure I got all the boards nailed down. I meant to go back to check, but then we found that stone and I forgot."

"Take an umbrella," said Pete. "There's one by the front door."

Wolf and Cari grabbed the umbrella and made their way to the silo. The rain was really coming down and making a lot of noise. When they arrived at the silo, they noticed the door was ajar.

"Good thing we came out, I must have forgotten to shut the door," said Wolf.

They entered the silo and realized they weren't alone. A man was kneeling on the floor pulling at the boards. He jumped up, startled when he saw them.

"Who are you?" Wolf asked.

"It doesn't matter who I am," the man said. "What matters is this," he added, lifting an arm and pointing a gun at them.

"Well, shit," said Cari.  "I know exactly who he is. I suppose you're looking for the money."

"Very smart, pretty girl."

"Wolfgang, this is one of my great Uncle Fritz's lawyers. His name is Ollie Nilsen."

"Right again, young lady. I saw Fritz Kolbeck's will and figured out the rune symbols in his signature. You're not the only one who can read runes you know."

"Yeah, the internet is full of that stuff," said Cari. "You can dig all you want, the money isn't here. We looked everywhere."

"I've been watching you all through my binoculars. I saw your uncle looking in boxes. Then I saw you two running in the house carrying something. I suppose that was just junk."

"It was a rune stone, asshole, not a box of money," Cari answered.

"Well, we'll soon find out. I can see nothing is left out here, so my guess is that you found the money and it's in the farmhouse with your uncle and that other fellah. Sorry, but we're going to have to go and get it."

"Then I suppose you'll kill us all," said Wolf.

"No use worrying about that yet, pretty boy, let's get that money first."

"Answer some questions for me before we go in. I'm curious. How did you know about the money and why did you figure it was hidden out here?"

"Fred Helms. I knew him from years back. When he went to prison and didn't tell anyone where the money was, it was just a matter of waiting until he got out. He wasn't able to go for the money right away, the cops were watching him. He figured Fritz had it, since he was the driver in the robbery. Fritz was scared that he was in trouble, so he wouldn't touch that money, so he hid it. Fred was sure of it."

"Then when Fred got out, he waited, right?" asked Wolf.

"Yeah, he waited too long, the old guy died. Now how was he gonna find that money?" said Nilsen. "He got the bright idea of kissing up to Talia Hovlund, since she was a realtor and could get on the property without raising suspicion."

"How did you find all this out?" asked Cari.

"From Fred. He confessed it to me when I saw him one night drinking with Talia. I figured it was all connected to the money and the cops were watching him. I offered my help."

"Did you kill Talia?" asked Wolfgang.

"Nope, that was Fred. She was getting greedy."

"So you killed Fred," said Cari. "Why?"

"Now why would I tell you that?" he asked. "Oh, I know. It won't matter, cuz you are gonna be dead soon. Another couple murders at the farm. First of all, I need that money. If you don't get it for me, I'll kill your uncle and his friend."

"Please don't. We'll get you the money," said Cari. "They're going to come out looking for us soon."

"Here's an idea. Pretty boy, you go in and get that cash. I'll stay here with the sexy lady, pointing my nice big gun at her. If anything seems off, boom. If you play nice, maybe I'll just tie you all up and leave you here. Nobody will find you for days, so I'll have plenty of time to get away. Remember, if I kill her, I'll have to kill all of you."

"Understood," said Wolf. "I'll get the money and bring it back out here. I can tell Pete and Harry that you are still looking for your phone."

"Oh yeah, gimme your phones, both of you," said Nilsen. "Don't even think about calling the cops. If I have to shoot my way out of here, it won't be nice."

# CHAPTER 66: THE BULL

Harry started to wonder what was taking them so long in the silo. At first he thought it was two young people, attracted to each other needing a little privacy. The silo seemed an unlikely spot for a liaison. It was dirty and full of spiders.

"Hey Pete I'm gonna go and check on Cari and Wolf. They're taking a long time."

"Yeah, I think she would have found her phone by now. I suppose they're waiting for the rain to let up. It's coming down in buckets."

"Maybe, but I'll go check anyway," said Harry, the hackles on the back of his neck were up. Something seemed off. His gun was in the lockbox in his car, so he'd stop and get it - just in case.

As Harry was putting on his jacket, Wolf showed up at the door, soaking wet.

"Where's Cari?" he asked.

"She's in the silo. Listen, a guy named Ollie Nilsen is in there holding a gun on her. He is here for the money that we didn't find. I told him I would get it for him from the house. He's got that gun pointed at her head," said Wolf in a panicky voice.

"Ollie Nilsen? The lawyer?" said Pete as he entered the room. "That son of a bitch. We gotta go help her."

"My gun is in the car in the lockbox. Give me a little time and I'll get it. Wolf, you are going to have to stall him. Pete, do you have a box or bag in here that looks like it was holding money?"

"Ah, I have my old suitcase, maybe that would work," said Pete, as he hurried to retrieve it.

"Does the suitcase have a lock?" asked Harry.

"Yep," answered Pete, his hands shaking as he held it.

"Throw some stuff in it and lock it. That'll buy some time. Hurry!"

Pete was trying not to panic as he tossed some paperback books and clothing into the bag. He locked it and shakily handed it to Wolfgang. "Don't let him hurt her, Varg."

"No worries, she's going to be okay, I promise."

Wolf left with the suitcase and Harry went out the back door, carefully making his way to his vehicle. The rain had let up a little and the lightning show was over.

It was hard to remain unseen, the farm was mostly barren and the trees were thin and scrubby. No place to conceal himself.

Wolf got back to the silo with the suitcase, and glanced at Cari, who had somehow managed to remain calm. He held the case in front of him.

"It's in here, all the money. I grabbed it when they weren't looking. I told them that Cari was in here trying to get a signal on her phone. It's locked but I couldn't ask Pete for a key without arousing suspicion," lied Wolf.

"Good boy," said Nilsen. "Now you open it for me."

Wolf pretended to struggle with the locks on the old case.

"Just pry it open."

"I can't," said Wolf.

"Here, lemme find something," he said looking around. "Use this," said Nilsen, handing him the pry bar that had been left behind. No funny business with that bar either. I've got my gun pointed at Miss America here."

As Wolf pretended to work at the suitcase with the pry bar, they heard a vehicle pull up next to the silo.

"Go see who that is and get rid of them," said Nilsen, gesturing with his gun.

The door opened and there stood Davey.

"Hey there, Ms. Cari, Mr. Wolf," said Davey with a big smile, followed by a questioning look. "Cousin Ollie, what are you doing here? Did you need your trailer back? It's at my house. Wait, is that a gun?"

"Well, shit," said Nilsen.

The distraction of having Davey standing in the doorway, gave Wolf and Cari the break they needed. They both ran for the door without looking back, trying to pull poor, confused Davey along with them. He went back to the silo doorway and stood looking at his cousin. "What's going on?" he asked, frowning.

Nilsen pushed past Davey and ran after Wolf and Cari, leading with the gun. He was close behind them, as Harry was retrieving his gun from the lockbox.

Suddenly a very loud noise came from the field. It was the bull and it was angry and charging. Cari saw the bull and yelled to it in old Norse: "duga" "duga" (help,help). The bull charged directly at Nilsen before he knew what was happening. The bull hit Nilsen from the side and knocked him down, hard. He got up quickly, a little shaken. He lifted an arm, pointing his gun directly at Wolf and Cari, getting ready to fire. Time seemed to stand still for a moment, then a shot rang out. Nilsen dropped to the ground, for good this time.

Harry ran toward the silo, still holding his gun. The bull had disappeared. Pete was in front of the house, watching the whole scene. Cari and Wolf saw Davey, still in the silo doorway, looking shocked and confused at what he had just witnessed.

Before the police arrived, Cari sat down with Davey to explain to him what had happened. "I'm sorry about your cousin, but he was not a good man," said Cari.

"I actually didn't know him very well. He is my second cousin on my mother's side. I needed a trailer for my business and he let me borrow his. Wow, this is all so weird."

"Why were you coming out here today, Davey?" asked Pete.

"Um...I wanted to give you this old box I found in the silo. It was in the first load of junk I took the other day, and it had moss, or something gross growing all over it. At first I was gonna throw it away, but after I scraped some of the stuff off it, I noticed a sort of a symbol on it that looked kinda like Thor's hammer, you know, Mjolnir. I learned all about that in the Avengers movie."

"Okay," replied Pete.

"Anyway, like I said, I was gonna throw it out, but I decided to scrape off all the moss, and see if it was something good that you could put in your auction sale. It took me a long time, but I got most of it off."

"Well, thank you Davey, that was so nice, but it could have waited," said Pete.

"Um...you don't understand, Mr. Pete. After I cleaned it off, I tried to get the box open. I could tell it wasn't empty. Something had to be inside. It wasn't easy to get unlocked, because I didn't want to damage the box, so I took my time. Finally I got it to open and you'll never believe what was in the box."

At this point Davey paused with a very excited expression. He shifted in his chair, clearly excited about what he was ready to disclose. They all waited.

"A bunch of money! I'm pretty sure it's real. Can you believe it? That's why I'm here, I wanted to bring it out to you right away."

"The bank robbery money," said Harry.

"Bank robbery?" asked Davey.

"It's a long story, and we will tell you everything. That's why your cousin was here with a gun. He was after the money," said Cari

"He was a bank robber too?" asked Davey.

"No, like I said, we will explain everything, it's a long story," said Cari.

The police sirens sounded loud in the quiet after the rain storm. It was going to be a long night.

# Chapter 67: Sordid Story

When the police cruisers pulled into the driveway, the whole bleak farm was lit up like a Christmas tree. The box with the robbery money inside sat on the kitchen table. In it was nearly a million dollars in cash. There was so much to tell the police, they brought in one extra officer to make notes and recordings.

Cari had the most to tell. After Wolf had gone to retrieve the supposed 'money', Ollie Nilsen told her everything that had happened. He assumed he would be killing her anyway, so what was the harm?

As it turned out, he did kill Talia Hovlund the last night she had been in the bar with Helms. Nilsen said he knew they were up to something and would probably squeeze him out of the money when it was found. He waited outside and then strangled her with a cord. He drove her car out to Bagley Road, dumped her body in the pond and walked back to town. He found her broken shoe in the back seat of her car and threw it in the dirt near the silo. All this to make Pete look guilty.

Nilsen was the phantom potential 'buyer' of the farm property. The plan was that he would buy the farm and they could search to their heart's content until they discovered where Fritz had concealed the cash. Getting rid of Talia just meant another realtor would take over and he could still buy the Kolbeck farm, and not have to share the money with her.

Helms had been spying on the farm from a distance, using powerful binoculars and saw Pete digging in the yard. He assumed that Pete had found something in the house telling of the money's location. The plan was to scare Pete off, if not then he would have had a terrible fatal accident. The arrival of Pete's family and friends threw a wrench in the plans. There were too many people around to get rid of Pete.

Helms was the one that loosened the hooks holding farm tools that fell on Davey. It was meant for Pete, but the young man got in the way. Ollie had lent his trailer to Davey, so the kid could work cleaning up at the farm and he could keep tabs on anything that was found. Davey had no clue what his cousin was up to. Nilsen was angry when Davey got hurt, not because he was his cousin, but since he was injured, he could no longer work at the farm. Ollie Nilsen was cold and calculating.

Once Nilsen had killed Talia Hovlund, Helms was getting worried. He wasn't sure he was safe anymore, and the cops were watching his apartment. He could be the one suspected. He was a bank robber, not a killer. Helms disappeared and hid out at an old abandoned farm nearby. Nilsen lured him to the Kolbeck farm by telling him he found the money. He killed Helms with the panga knife that he found in the barn, leaving the body behind, hoping the police would blame Pete. Nilsen knew the money hadn't been located yet, news like that would have gotten out right away once it was found. Nilsen was a regular at the diner and kept his eyes and ears open for updates from the gossip mill.

When Pete requested to look at a copy of Fritz's will, Nilsen wondered why. He figured it had something to do with the search for the money. He looked over the will carefully and noticed the rune letters hidden in the signature. Now he knew that Fritz Kolbeck had hidden that money somewhere in the silo, leaving the cryptic message for his nephew Pete.

Nilsen watched from a distance as Wolf, Cari, Harry, Pete and Davey tore apart the silo. After they finished he went in to see if anything was left.

The floorboards had been replaced by Wolf, so Nilsen started to pull them up, when he was surprised by Cari and Wolf.

At that point, the 'cat was out of the bag', so to speak, so he threatened them with the gun, forcing Wolf to get the money, not believing that they actually hadn't found it.

Nilsen was dead; shot by Harry, just before he would have shot Cari and Wolf. The man would never know that the money was actually in the possession of his young cousin.

Chief Barkley showed up and was amazed at how the story had unfolded. Harry Chan had been right all along. Helms' partner in the robbery had actually been Fritz Kolbeck. According to what Helms told Ollie Nilsen and Talia Hovlund, old Fritz had indeed been an unwilling accomplice. For some reason, he trusted Fred Helms and agreed to give him a ride. When Helms ran out of the bank with the money, telling Fritz to drive away quickly, the old man still had no clue.

Once they had reached the farm, Helms told Fritz that he had stolen the money and that Fritz had to hide it for him. They argued, and Helms said no one would believe Fritz, and he would be sent to jail if he told. Fritz was scared and hid the money. Helms got caught and went to jail. When Helms got out years later, he was being watched by the police so he waited. It was too risky to be anywhere near Fritz or his farm. While Helms was biding his time, Fritz Kolbeck died.

At this point, Helms had to find a way to get on the farm. He got drunk one night and spilled his secret to Talia Hovlund. She wanted in on the plan and a share of the cash. She enlisted the help of her old friend Ollie Nilsen. He would buy the crummy old farm from the heir (Pete) and they would all be able to conduct an all out search for the hidden cash.

The plan to scare Pete off actually backfired. They thought he was searching for the hidden robbery money, when he was just digging for some old coffee cans holding a few hundred dollars. Greed had been the end of all three of them.

# Chapter 68: Finishing Up

It took a couple of weeks, but finally the farm was cleared of police and crime scene investigators. The inevitable crime scene tape came down and everything went back to normal. Once the police had completed their work and basically closed the case, rumors spread through the small town like wildfire.

First, there were numerous news stories regarding the 15 year old bank robbery, involving Helms. Then came the tale of the ultimate participation of Talia Hovlund and Ollie Nilsen, two of the town's upstanding citizens in recovering the stolen cash. It resulted in the death of all three. Unfortunately, Fritz Kolbeck's complicity was revealed with the caveat that he was an unwilling partner. Pete didn't think his uncle would care. He was dead after all, and most people here didn't know him anyway.

Nilsen's law partner, Isaac Korhonen was cleared of any wrongdoing. He had no idea what his associate had been up to. He was completely horrified and offered Pete a genuine apology, and hired a new associate immediately.

Davey Connor was cleared of any complicity as well. He was an innocent bystander, who just happened to be related to a killer. He actually received a reward for the recovery of the robbery cash. Davey used it to buy a trailer.

Everyone marveled at how close he came to throwing the box full of money in the dump.

Harry left for home, bidding goodbye to everyone and told them they would meet again soon, probably in Trygghaven Bay. It was a nice place to vacation and he loved the people there. He had no immediate plans, being that he was retired, but he was anxious to sleep in his own bed. Pete shook his hand and went in for a Scandinavian hug, (one sided with a back pat). "Thanks for all your help, Harry. I don't know what would have happened if you wouldn't have been here."

"Glad to do it, Pete. You take care and we'll see you soon, and please get rid of this farm."

"I'm planning on it, Harvey. Safe travels now," said Pete, giving him a wink.

Harry felt light, but a bit sad as he drove away. So many unusual incidents and some real odd coincidences occurred in his short time here. He wondered about the troll. The bull charging at Nilsen actually saved Wolf and Cari. Since meeting Wolfgang, who he now considered a good friend, Harry had encountered some very strange things. It was weird and exciting at the same time. He had always expected that being retired would be boring. It was anything but that. So far it has been more like an adventure.

Pete finally was able to have his auction, and got rid of all the scary farm implements. He wasn't sure if some of them didn't actually belong here, but no one said anything. There was no way to know what belonged and what didn't. He had assumed it was the troll, but it could have been Helms, hanging dangerous farm implements up to hurt Pete. The irony was, one of the tools, the panga knife, was the weapon used to kill Helms. "Like my old man used to say, what goes around comes around."

Some valuable items, jugs, old pottery, metal signs and a few antiques had been unearthed and sold. The items that had been stored in the barn after the silo had been cleaned up netted a few hundred dollars.

Shortly after the auction, Pete received a fair offer on the farm. It wasn't nearly as much as Talia Hovlund said he could get, but then she had a hidden agenda.

"We still have one more thing to do before we can leave Uncle Pete," said Cari after the auction was finished and the farm under contract. "Now that everyone is gone, we have to free the troll, I promised to," she added, but had a questioning look on her face when she said it.

# CHAPTER 69: BYE TROLL

After Harry's departure, Pete wandered off for a nap. Cari and Wolf were getting things packed up and talking about what was next in their future.

"I kind of like the way things are, for now," said Cari. "I think we should keep things casual. I am enjoying myself. How about you?"

"I totally agree. I travel a lot for my job and sometimes for my cryptozoology hobby. My next assignment is coming up and I'll be on the East coast for a while. I'll be working in collaboration with a study being conducted regarding the added presence of sea life, specifically sharks nearer the shoreline. I may be doing a bit of diving, which I am pretty excited about."

"That sounds interesting," said Cari. "Be careful out there with the sharks."

"It couldn't be much more dangerous than hanging around an old farm," he added with a grin. "What about you?"

"Since I have been here, I have decided to delve further into rune casting. I want to offer it more to my clients and educate them regarding Viking runes. I do love my tarot reading, but like I said, rune reading is important to me, and I want to clarify that it should be taken seriously."

"Are you anxious to get home?" he asked her.

"Yes, I am. I love my home in Lake Geneva and have been away from my shop for far too long. I'm sure Sara has done a fine job, but I need to get back there. I have vowed to spend more time with my Uncle Pete, as well as my parents. I'm hoping to get them to the Upper Peninsula and have a proper family visit."

"Well, you know the Kilmer family homestead is there, as well as Ned's summer place. We all like to vacation up there. In the meantime, I would love to continue to visit you in Lake Geneva. Ron and Lelani are there as well. So I will be there often."

"I expect I will see you soon, either in Lake Geneva or in the Upper Peninsula."

"You can visit me in Chicago," said Wolf. "I live in the suburbs and you haven't been to my house yet."

"Okay, it's a deal. I'll come and see you next. How about when you get back from your East coast assignment."

"Sure, that's a plan."

"Remember, Wolf, before we can leave, we should release the troll. I have the rune stone put together and ready to read. Uncle Pete and I will take care of it tonight. I hope it works."

"We haven't seen or heard anything since all the stuff happened with Ollie Nilsen and the sighting of the bull. That bull saved our lives. Nilsen was ready to shoot and Harry was still trying to get to his gun," said Wolf.

"I suppose if we owe that troll, we have to do our best to release it from the curse," Cari added. "Although, according to the rune stone, he was a killer," she thought to herself.

"You know, at first everything was getting blamed on the troll. I figure that he was behind the rocks and bricks thrown, the holes dug, rock piles and other tricks, but I don't think anything he did was particularly evil. It was the humans that did that," said Wolf. Cari looked pensive after Wolf made the comment about evil in the humans.

The dark of the evening arrived and Cari did a rune casting. The three runes: Past: THURISAZ: reactive force, defense, conflict; Present: JERA: Peace, prosperity; Future: PERTHRO: Mysteries, Secrets, Occult abilities.

The last rune cast PERTHRO confused Cari. She started to think more about the troll and hoped she was wrong.

The house was quiet, the clock ticking the only sound. Wolf stayed in the background letting Cari and her Uncle Pete complete their task.

Pete read the rune stone - all the way through to include the new piece they found. He read it again and then again, out loud.

Cari stood in front of the house and saw the troll. He bowed to her once more and disappeared. They all heard a rumbling noise and then all was silent again.

The next day Pete, Cari and Wolf walked out to the silo and looked at the grassy mounds. All were now covered. The mound that had been disturbed was now covered in green grass and yellow flowers. The flowers also now grew on the other mounds as well.

"Safe journey to you troll," said Cari. "I hope you are with your family now."

"So it's done then," said Wolfgang.

"I hope so," said Cari. "But something is worrying me. We may have made a mistake. I'm quite sure that I'm wrong, but a part of me is doubtful. Maybe the troll didn't actually think I was Huldra, but used me for its own purposes."

Pete and Wolfgang brought the two pieces of rune stone out to the backyard. They dug a very deep hole and buried the pieces. Cari tossed the ALGIZ rune stone (the one Pete had found in the tea can - the stone to ward off evil) on top of the two big rune stone pieces, but when she dropped it, the small ALGIZ rune stone disintegrated. "That's not good," whispered Cari. Wolf heard her whisper and noticed she was very distracted afterward.

When they finished covering the stones, Pete went into the house to rest. Wolf pulled Cari aside and asked her what was wrong.

"What if we had this all backwards, and the troll was behind all of this from the beginning," she said. "The situation with Talia Hovlund and Ollie Nilsen happened after Uncle Pete read the first piece of the stone and the troll was awakened. Both Hovlund and Nilsen had spent time here at the farm."

"How could the troll do anything like steal money, or strangle someone in town?" questioned Wolf.

"It didn't have to do anything but force the hand of the humans. Think about it. The troll has been here for thousands of years. Trolls all want to be with their families. The Norse men had the witch put a curse on the troll. I thought he wanted to return to his family, but what if he wanted the family returned to him?"

"Okay, but how did it force the hand of the humans? Connect to them, kind of like a demon?"

"Exactly. If he encountered a human with a weakness - he could prey on the weakness. He could have started years ago with Fred Helms and Fritz."

"So you think Fritz could have read the stone and released it, then it preyed on Helms and Fritz. Made them do evil things."

"Precisely. Remember trolls have magic and are shape shifters, even to human form."

"So how did it end up cursed again?"

"Uncle Fritz must have used the stone. He had found it in one piece, read the curse, and goodbye troll. That's what he was babbling about. Bad moon rising, evil one after him, burying the ALGIZ stone," explained Cari. Fritz must have broken the stone into two pieces and buried them separately."

"Why didn't it work when Pete tried to curse it again?"

"He didn't have the whole stone. He read the first piece, which released the troll, but couldn't curse it back to sleep. Finding the rest of the stone and reading the curse again with the second piece was what the troll was waiting for someone to do. By shifting to the bull and pawing at the ground, it led us right to the missing piece of the stone."

"So what you're saying is - by reading the stone in pieces, then as a whole, you...."

"Unleashed the other trolls."

"It all sounds quite fantastic," said Wolf. "You don't actually believe that's what happened."

"No, not really. It's just pure speculation," Cari answered with a sigh. "Let's finish packing and forget all about what I said."

Pete was finally able to leave the farm and return to his beloved home and Lake Superior. He teared up a bit as he said goodbye to Cari and Wolfgang. The three of them parted ways, promising to stay in touch, and see each other soon.

In an old, dead tree nearby, five large eagles sat on a branch, watching them and giggling hysterically.


*the end.*

Ned had just gotten off the phone. He had been talking to Wolfgang, who told him all about his latest work on the Maine coastline. He hadn't spoken to Wolf in months, since he called to tell him what had ultimately happened at the farm in Minnesota. Ned had been glad of the time spent there with Kyra and Wolfgang as well as Cari and Pete Magnusson. Most especially his time with Kyra. She was still on assignment, but would be done soon. He was hoping she would come to Chicago for a visit soon. If not, he would go to see her.

It was getting late and Ned was tired. Things had been busy at his law office lately and he put in extra time to catch up. When his phone buzzed, he thought for a quick second that it was Kyra, since she was on his mind. Nope. It was his sister Signe calling. He hadn't talked to her in a long time. Why would she call so late?

"Ned, oh I'm so happy you answered. I'm so worried and I don't know what to do. She has gone missing. We haven't heard from her in nearly two days."

"Calm down Signe. What happened? Who's missing?"

"It's Birgitta. She went on an assignment for the news station and no one has seen or heard from her since. I talked to the police, and Grant has been out searching. Oh, what if something has happened to her Ned. I couldn't, I just couldn't handle it... I don't know what to do."

"Signe, please calm yourself. I'll come out there right away," Ned told his sister.

"I'll get packed and get the next flight out of O'Hare. I can fly into Raleigh and hopefully get a connection to Wilmington. I'll rent a car and drive to your house. No need to pick me up.  It will be okay, sis."

"Oh, thank you Ned, I need you here. Thank you."

"I'll make my plane reservations and pack. You stay in touch, okay?"

"Yes, I will. Please hurry," said Signe and she hung up.

Signe Ferris Davis was Ned's older sister. She was married to a real estate mogul, Grant Davis and had two daughters, Brigitta and Anika. Birgitta was in college doing an internship at a news station. She had been interested in TV journalism since she was a young teen. Signe owned a successful catering business. Anika was still in high school. They were a typical up and coming family living in coastal North Carolina.

The last time Ned had visited them was more than two years ago. It had been for Birgitta's graduation. Ned loved his nieces, they had re-connected years ago, when Ned's father had been killed. Nearly every summer the girls would come to visit Ned at his summer place in Upper Michigan. It was a relief from the hot summer in North Carolina and the girls always had a good time with their uncle.

Ned hurriedly packed after making plane reservations. He was fortunate enough to get a seat, and in first-class to boot, (the only seat available on short notice). His flight was leaving the next morning at 10:00 am. He called his law partner Matt, explained the situation and apologized for being gone once again.

Matt was more than understanding and told him not to worry, he would take care of anything that came up.

Ned spoke to his sister once again before boarding and then to his brother in law. Surprisingly enough, Grant sounded as panicky as Signe and thanked Ned for taking the time to travel to North Carolina. Grant was usually cold and very business-like. He must be extremely worried.

The plane trip was uneventful, got his connecting flight and his rental car was ready and waiting for him. The drive to his sister's house took about a half hour, and he was on the phone most of the time with his sister, who was still beside herself with worry.

When he arrived at his sister's house, she came running out the door, her eyes filled with fear and sadness. "They haven't found her, Ned. She went to cover a news story about some new additions to the Aquarium in Kure Beach. It was her first assignment as a reporter, she was so excited about it," Signe said, brushing the tears from her cheeks, before continuing.

"She must have gotten into an accident. We called her many times and her phone went directly to voicemail. We've all sent texts and there's been no answer. Grant went to the news station where Birgitta is doing her internship to get more details."

They went inside to wait, along with Signe's younger daughter Anika, who was glad to see her uncle. About forty minutes later, Grant returned from his visit with the news station and filled them in on what he knew.

"According to the news station, Birgitta never got to the Aquarium. They talked to the Aquarium manager. He said the cameraman, Cliff, was waiting for her to arrive, and got a phone call. Cliff told them that the reporter had gotten lost and her car was stuck. He was going to go get her and they would both return shortly to do the story. Neither one of them came back."

***

Debra (Kimar) Oas, a journalist and author, has written four "Cryptid Mysteries"
(*Sinister Bay, Whitewater Witch, Mountain Walker and The Rune Stone Curse*) as well as four children's books, "*The Dachsie Adventure Series.*"

Originally from the Upper Peninsula of Michigan, she currently resides in Southeastern Wisconsin.